D0454870

"Say, kid, how do you do it?" Briar asked, his curiosity getting the better of him. "Make their magic light up like that?"

The girl spun to face him, as wary as a wild animal. She was a foot shorter than Briar's five feet seven inches, and she looked to be nine or ten. A skinny waif, she had the bronze-colored skin and almond-shaped brown eyes of a Yanjing native. Wisps of black hair stuck out from under the dirty scarf wrapped around her head. She wore a long tunic and trousers of unguessable color, aged and speckled with holes. Even though it was autumn, she was barefoot.

"It's all right," Briar assured her cheerfully. "I'm a mage myself. Are you calling to magic already in them, or are you just laying a charm on them?"

The girl put down her basket and cloth. She smiled just as cheerfully as Briar had — and ran.

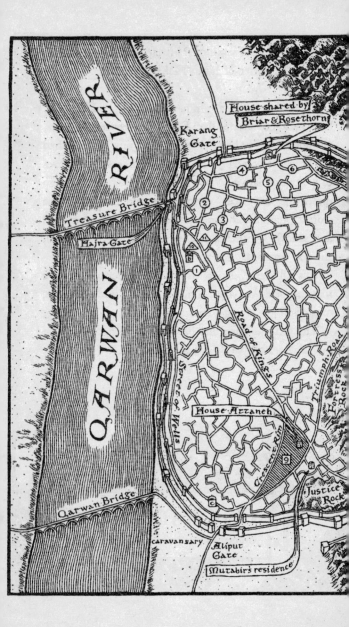

QARWAN RIVER

Karang Gate

House shared by
Briar & Rosethorn

Treasure Bridge

Hajra Gate

Street of Wells

House Attaneh

Road of Kings

Crescent Rim

Triumph Road

Fortress Road

Qarwan Bridge

caravansary

Aliput Gate

Justice Rock

Mutabir's residence

Princes' Heights

Evvy's Squat

Street of Victories

...ell-diggers' Island

Heartbeat Heights

Eagles' Gate

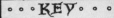

KEY

1. Oleander Way
2. Karang Road
3. Street of Tentmakers
4. Street of Hares
5. Cedar Lane
6. Street of Wrens
7. Ibex Walk
8. Palace Road

9. Jeweled Crescent

△ Golden House
△ Grand Bazaar
△ The Market of the Lost

▣ Earth Temple
▣ Water Temple
▣ Fire Temple
▣ Air Temple
▣ Shaihun's Temple
▣ Mohun's Temple

© MM · IAN · SCHOENHERR · MMM ®

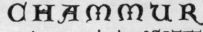

CHAMMUR
on the eastern border of SOTAT

POINT

TAMORA PIERCE
The Circle Opens

Street Magic

POINT

SCHOLASTIC INC.

New York Toronto London Auckland Sydney
Mexico City New Delhi Hong Kong Buenos Aires

To Gwen Weber
So eager to get to this world of great books
that she showed up early, and to her loving parents,
Heather Mars and Eric Weber,
who will ensure she gets plenty to read!

ISBN-13: 978-0-590-39643-1
ISBN-10: 0-590-39643-9

12 11 10 9 8 7 6 5 4 3 2 1   7 8 9 10 11 12/0

Printed in the U.S.A.   01

First Scholastic Trade paperback printing, January 2002

Map art copyright © by 2001 Ian Schoenherr

The text type was set in Adobe Caslon.
Book design by Elizabeth Parisi

1

In the city of Chammur, on the eastern border of Sotat:

For centuries it had been called "fabled Chammur," "Chammur of the Flaming Heights," and "Mighty Chammur." For twelve hundred years the city on what was now the easternmost border of Sotat had straddled the trade routes from Capchen to Yanjing. Chammur was guarded on the west by the Qarwan River. In the north and east were riddled mazes of the flame-colored stone that provided the oldest part of the city with a sanctuary from bandits and warlords alike.

For Dedicate Rosethorn of Winding Circle temple in Emelan and her fourteen-year-old student Briar Moss, Chammur was a stop on a journey to distant Yanjing. Briar had only ever heard the name of the city and little more. Rosethorn, though, had been fascinated since she'd first read of it, and she was able to tell him something of its history on their way east. Her knowledge came from books:

this trip with Briar was her first chance to actually see the place that she had studied for so many years.

The original town, Rosethorn said, had been built first on, then in, the spur of stone called Heartbeat Heights. Then it spread to the cliffs on either side. The shepherds, goatherds, and miners who originally settled the area had kept to the rocky mazes that stretched out for miles. It was easy to hide from any force that tried to prey on them in thousands of wind- and water-carved heights and canyons.

As trade prospered between east and west, the value of Chammur's site and its nearness to the river drew merchants and farmers, who took advantage of the security of the stone apartments. As the city grew crowded, the wealthiest and most powerful moved their homes to the flat, open ground between the heights and the river, where they could surround themselves with elaborate houses and gardens. They also promoted themselves to the nobility: the cousins of the present *amir*, or ruler, were among them. Although Chammur belonged to Sotat on any map, and its people bowed to the king in Hajra in the west, the truth was that the Chammuri *amirs* were kings in everything but name, and had been so for centuries.

Rosethorn and Briar's journey was a kind of working study program for Briar. No matter where they went, people could always find work for green mages, skilled with plants and medicines. Chammur was no different. Within days of their arrival, before they had completed their sight-seeing, they had gotten so many requests for magical aid that Rosethorn knew they had to stay for a while. She moved herself and Briar out of the Chammuri Earth temple's guest quarters and into a house next door on the Street of Hares. Once settled, she began to work with Chammur's farmers, Briar with the local Water temple and its stores of medicines and herbs.

Six weeks after their arrival, Briar at least had finished his work. The Water temple now had a store of powerful medicines and herbal ingredients that would hold them for a year, two if they were careful. After weeks of intense magical labor, Briar decided he owed himself a treat.

He approached the giant, enclosed arcades that held the *souks*, or markets, of Golden House and the Grand Bazaar with his hands in his pockets, whistling. He looked like many local males in his linen shirt, baggy trousers made from lightweight wool, and boots. His golden brown skin was vivid against the cream-colored linen. He wore no turban or hat as the Chammuri men and boys did, but left his black, coarse-cut hair uncovered. His thin-bladed nose might have come from any family native to the area. Even his gray-green eyes could have come of a match between a local and a passing merchant: races mingled here every bit as freely as they did in Briar's former homes of Hajra and Summersea.

His destination was Golden House. He'd been in and out of the Grand Bazaar for weeks, buying oils, dried imported herbs, cloth for bags and jars, all for his work at the Water temple. Shopping there had given him the chance to look over the big and lesser specialty markets of the Bazaar. It wasn't until he'd tried to arrange for a day and a booth from which to sell his miniature trees that he learned of Golden House. That was the place for him, the men who sold booth spaces had explained. In Golden House buyers found mages and magical supplies, precious metals, rare woods like ebony and sandalwood, jewelry, and precious and semiprecious stones. Briar's miniature trees, which were not only works of art but were also shaped to draw particular magical influences to a home, belonged in Golden House.

By the time Briar had made arrangements for a stall there, he'd had to rush to be home for supper. Today he wanted a good look at Chammur's wealthiest marketplace.

As he approached the two muscular guards at the door, he smiled impishly at them. They stirred, wary. He knew he looked like a student, perhaps, or even a merchant's son, in clothes that were very well made by his friends in Summersea. He was even wearing boots. The guards had no real reason to bar him from entering, no matter how loudly their instincts might shout that he had the air of a thief.

"Hands," one of them said when Briar would have strolled by.

He held them out, palm-down, and sighed. The guard who had spoken looked for jailhouse tattoos, and saw a riot of leafy vines that went from under Briar's nails up to his wrists. The guard blinked, looked into Briar's eyes, looked at his hands again, and nudged his partner. The other man looked at Briar's hands, blinked, met the boy's eyes, then stared at those vines again.

Briar was used to it. At one time he had indeed had prison tattoos, a black ink X etched into the web of skin between the thumb and forefinger of each hand. In most countries, they marked two arrests and convictions for theft. When Briar turned thirteen, he'd gotten tired of being turned away from places or followed in them. Without consulting Rosethorn, he'd brewed some vegetable dyes and borrowed his friend Sandry's best needles. His plan had been to create a flowering vine tattoo to blot out the telltale Xs. He had not realized that vegetable dyes, exposed to his green magic, might not stay under his control. The final, colorful result blotted out the jailhouse tattoos as surely as if those crude black Xs had never existed. The new designs also made Briar's hands into miniature, often-changing gardens that were far more conspicuous than his old tattoos.

"Hey, they moved — and they're moving under the fingernails," one guard exclaimed, pointing. He looked at Briar. "Don't that hurt?"

"No," Briar said patiently, used to the reaction and the comment. "But my arms do when I have to keep holding them out like this."

Both guards scowled and waved him into the *souk*. Briar tucked his gaudy hands in his pockets and wandered into the main aisle. He avoided the stalls that peddled precious woods and gums. There was enough living power in those things still to hurt, especially when a touch would show him the original tree in all its splendor. He walked by the gold and copper aisles with only a glance. His friend Daja, a metal mage, would have plunged in here. One day he would explore and write her about it, but not today.

He turned down Pearl Alley, going from stall to stall, examining bowls of pearls with an expert's eye. Every color and size imaginable was here, from tiny white seeds destined as trimming to black orbs the size of his thumbnail, for use as ornaments or ingredients for magic. The neighboring aisle brought him to sapphires of every color. Rubies came next, then emeralds, then opals.

At no point did Briar take his memorable hands from his pockets. Every stall was supervised by an alert shopkeeper and by one or two guards. They had reason to be wary. Briar guessed that one in five shoppers might be a thief, working alone, with a partner or two, or even with the better class of gang here in Chammur Newtown. He couldn't have said what told him someone was not on the straight, but he trusted his instincts.

He particularly suspected those young men and women who were his age or just a bit older. A number of them sported a small yellow metal nose ring from which hung a roughly shaped garnet the size of a pomegranate seed. Still others wore a distinctive costume, white tunic over black breeches or skirts. The jewelry was high-priced for a gang mark — Briar's old gang had just wound a strip of blue cloth around their biceps — but the nose ring and pendant looked like a gang mark all the same, and the black and white clothes had to be gang colors. He wasn't surprised to find more than one gang here — *souks* were traditionally grounds where gangs roamed under truce.

He came to a long aisle where those who peddled semi-precious stones sold their wares. Here the crowd was thicker: more people could afford carnelian and amethysts than pearls. That was particularly true of the local mages, hedgewitches, and healers. Only rich mages could afford to use pearls and rubies in their work, but even students could find moonstones or mother-of-pearl discs that would be acceptable substitutes in their spells.

Briar was looking at a basket of malachite pieces, wondering if they might anchor the magic in his miniature trees, when a flicker of light caught his eye. He turned, scanning the aisle. This time the light came as a dart of silver in a stall across from him. Briar knew that particular fire well. Few mages could actually see magic as he did; no one who was not a mage would even notice it. Curious, he sauntered over for a look.

Now, here's something, he thought as he drew near. The stall's owner, a barrel-chested man, perched on a stool among his baskets and bowls of stones. Beside him a scruffy-looking girl picked through a bowl of tiger-eye pieces, polishing selected ones with a cloth and setting them aside in a round basket. As she rubbed, silver light flowered, then faded to ember-strength, in the pieces she handled. Briar also saw that the guard who stood watch between this stall and its neighbor kept his eyes on the traffic, not on the girl, though the owner never took his eyes off her. She was known, then, or she wouldn't have been allowed to stop for half a breath within reaching distance of the stall.

This man sold a bit of everything. Briar identified jade, amber, moonstone, onyx, lapis lazuli, jet, malachite, and carnelian before his knowledge of stones ran out. Now that he was looking closely at the wares, he could see a row of small baskets like the one in which the girl put her polished stones on a shelf beside the stall's owner. Those stones all showed a seed of silver to Briar's magical vision.

"Say, kid, how do you do it?" Briar asked, his curiosity getting the better of him. "Make their magic light up like that?"

The girl spun to face him, as wary as a wild animal. She was a foot shorter than Briar's five feet seven inches, and she looked to be nine or ten. A skinny waif, she had the bronze-colored skin and almond-shaped brown eyes of a Yanjing native. Wisps of black hair stuck out from under the dirty scarf wrapped around her head. She wore a long tunic and trousers of unguessable color, aged and speckled with holes. Even though it was autumn, she was barefoot.

"It's all right," Briar assured her cheerfully. "I'm a mage myself. Are you calling to magic already in them, or are you just laying a charm on them?"

The girl put down her basket and cloth. She smiled just as cheerfully as Briar had — and ran.

He stared after her, baffled. "What did I say?" he asked the stall's guard. The man ignored him still, watching passersby in the aisle.

The stall's owner left his stool to walk over to Briar. He was short, his body powerfully muscled under his rich silk tunic and draped satin trousers. His skin was a little darker than Briar's, his hair and eyes black. Briar figured him for a westerner, since he didn't wear the turban preferred by eastern men. "What did you run her off for?" the man demanded sharply. "Evvy's no thief."

"I never said she was," Briar protested.

"You said *something*," argued the stall's owner. "Now look. She'd barely started."

"What's she do here?" Briar asked, curious. "What's her name? 'Evvy,' you said?"

The owner shrugged, not quite meeting Briar's eyes. "She's just a street kid," he replied. The word for baby goat was slang for a child in Briar's native Imperial as well as in Chammuri. "She polishes some of my pieces, and I throw her a few coppers."

"Then he triples the price and sells them to the mage trade," the shopkeeper across the aisle called, his voice waspish. He was seated at a bench as he worked on jewelry. "Just because he realized the ones she handles sell quicker."

"I'd pay her more," protested the muscular stall owner, glaring at his neighbor. "But she won't handle all the rocks. And what does she do, anyway? She polishes them with a rag, cleans them up a bit."

"*He* spoke of magic, Nahim Zineer," the sharp-voiced man retorted, pointing at Briar. The boy glanced at the awning overhead: gold embroidered letters read NAHIM ZINEER: CRYSTALS, PRECIOUS, AND SEMIPRECIOUS STONES.

"If she's a mage, what's she doing living in some Oldtown cave like an animal?" Nahim demanded, glaring at the jeweler. "She's just got a hand with cleaning stones, that's all." To Briar he said, "And I'd appreciate it if you wouldn't frighten her off again."

"At least not until she's done all the baskets," quipped his neighbor.

Briar wandered off, shaking his head. It was possible the girl might not know of her gift. Some magic hid in most things, waiting for a mage with the right power to call it forth. That had been the case with Briar and the three girls who had shared a house with him at Winding Circle temple in Summersea. None of the four had shown the traditional signs of magical power, but all their lives they had been fascinated by particular ordinary things, things they later discovered were magically bound to them. In Briar's case his magic had drawn him to plants. Only at Winding Circle, under the supervision of four extraordinary mage-teachers, had he and the girls learned about their unusual magics, and the ways they could be used. What if there was no one like Niklaren Goldeye, the mage who had seen Briar's magic and taken him to Winding Circle, in Chammur? This girl might never be trained in the use of her power. Worse, if it broke away from her — as magic often did when its bearer could not control it — she would find herself in real trouble.

Briar was so lost in thought that he didn't realize he had attracted companions until two youths slid up on either side of him. Two more oozed out of the crowds ahead to block his advance. If Briar had cared to gamble he would have bet there were two more behind him. All of the ones he could see wore the yellow metal nose ring and garnet drop; all moved together without discussion. They nudged him to one side, trying to direct him down a dimly lit aisle. Briar stopped. There was no telling what they'd do in some dark niche. He had no intention of finding out. He saw no weapons, but that meant nothing: he carried nine. Theirs were probably tucked in the same places that his were. They were barefoot or in sandals, so at least they had no boot knives, and he did.

The ties that kept his wrist knives in their sheaths were twisted hemp. They came undone at his command, letting the hilts slip down into his palms. "You kids run along and play," he told the youths in heavily accented Chammuri. "I'm just minding my own business."

One of them, a short black youth, crossed his arms over his chest. "You're on Viper ground, *eknub*" — foreigner.

"You got me wrong." Briar met the speaker's eyes. "I'm not in your business." His tongue fumbled with the unfamiliar Chammuri words. He hoped they meant the same things they did in the west. "I'm just shopping. Besides, *souks* are free zones. You can't claim them for territory."

The youth beside the first speaker raised an eyebrow. He was tall, lean, brown-skinned, sixteen or seventeen years old. His eyes were like stones. "If it barks like a dog, eats like a dog, walks like a dog — it's a dog," he said lazily. "You look like competition to us, *eknub*. And outside these doors, you're on Viper territory."

Briar scratched his head. A rude answer, even if it made him feel better, would only dig him into more trouble, not less. "The competition's all in your minds, boys," he informed them. "I'm just passing through."

The black youth met Briar's eyes. "You better be telling the truth," he cautioned. "We don't like poachers."

"Not at all," the taller boy added.

The Vipers faded into the crowd with the ease of long practice.

Briar slid his wrist knives back into their sheaths, and

ordered the hemp ties to lock them in place again. So the nose ring and pendant meant Viper. He wondered who the black-and-white gang was, and if they knew the Vipers had claimed the streets around Golden House.

Not my headache, he realized, turning down the aisle where charms were sold. *I've said my good-bye to gangs.*

It lacked an hour to sunset when he left Golden House and turned his face toward the home he and Rosethorn had rented on the Street of Hares. Traffic was heavy now as people came inside the walls, their workday at an end. Briar dodged camels, mules, and people, briefly touching each plant that reached for him from the ground and from the windows of different houses, giving them some affection before he ordered them back to their pots or trellises. He was still thinking of that street girl.

His last stop was the small *souk* near home, to purchase what he needed for supper that night. He'd learned to cook in the four years he'd lived with Rosethorn, her friend Lark, and the three girls, and it was a very good thing. When Rosethorn finished her day's work here, she could barely think, let alone cook. Briar had taken over the chore completely without comment.

Once most of his other purchases were made, he stopped at his favorite cookhouse for meat. Trying to choose between roasted chicken or braised mutton, he also decided to do something about the Viper who had followed him from Golden House. He'd already considered losing the other boy — had they no girls at all? — but it was too much like work. Worse, in all likelihood *he* would be the one to get lost in the mazes of Chammur's streets.

He picked the mutton. As the shopkeeper wrapped it, Briar watched the Viper from the corner of his eye. This made no sense. How could the Vipers be so eager to rid themselves of a stranger while the black-and-white-clothed gang strolled through Golden House as if they owned it? For that matter, why hadn't the black-and-white gang run the Vipers off? Briar had seen at least twice as many of them as there were Vipers. Moreover, his shadow was now on the territory of yet another gang, the Camelguts. Did he think the Camelguts would ignore him?

Briar knew gangs. Until Niko had transported him to Winding Circle, Briar had lived, bled, and nearly died for his gang. The Vipers weren't acting according to the rules that governed any gang's life. To Briar, it was as if the sun had risen in the north. The only reasonable explanation for their behavior was that they might be new as a gang, and looking for victories. The black-and-white gang was too big for them, but a lone foreigner was easy prey.

The shopkeeper exchanged the wrapped mutton for Briar's coins, and thanked him for his business. Briar returned the thanks, then strolled out of the neighborhood *souk*. Should he let the Viper tail him all the way to the house? No — he'd told them to leave him alone. Besides, these Vipers had to learn respect for other gangs.

He turned back onto the Street of Hares. Up ahead Briar could see three green-sashed Camelgut youths. They were hunkered in front of the Earth temple, pitching coppers against the wall and keeping an eye on their street. As Briar approached, one of them looked up and grinned. It was a boy he knew, Hammit.

"Hey, *pahan*," Hammit called, using the Chammuri word for "mage" or "teacher." "You do good work." He pointed to a cheek that was more pink than brown, the last trace of a fearsome burn he'd gotten a week ago. Briar had treated it with healing salve. "You should sell that stuff you gave me, not give it away."

Briar crouched beside Hammit, watching the game. "I do sell it," he replied absently. "I charge rich folk three times my normal price so I can give it to anyone I've a mind to. Say, you lot know anything about a gang called Vipers?"

One of the other Camelgut boys snorted. "They're no gang," he said, his voice thick with scorn. "They're some *takameri*'s play toy." It took Briar a moment to identify the word: it was the feminine form of the Chammuri for "money person," or rich person.

"So they go where they want?" Briar asked, all innocence.

"They needn't respect Camelgut territory? Because one followed me from the *souk*. He's back by Cedar Lane."

Three pairs of eyes flicked in that direction: the Viper had stopped by the Cedar Lane fountain and was splashing water on his face, pretending to ignore Briar. Camelgut hands collected their coppers and tucked them into green sashes. Without another word the three rose and trotted down to Cedar Lane. The Viper was still pretending he wasn't interested in Briar. The Camelguts were on him before he realized who they were.

Briar smiled grimly and straightened. He'd given his salve to Hammit because he'd known that burn would rot without care. In doing so, it seemed he'd bought himself a bit of insurance as well. Whistling, he walked past the Earth temple gate and turned into the house next door.

Overhead, Evumeimei Dingzai, useless daughter and runaway slave, watched as the jade-eyed boy she had followed from Golden House went home. She was interested to see he knew three Camelguts well enough to call on them to rid him of his Viper shadow. Still, he couldn't be that clever. He's never once looked up at the rooftops, or he might have seen that she, too, followed him.

That, more than even his accent, said he was an *eknub*, a foreigner. Everyone in Chammur knew there were two sets of streets, one on the ground, one over the flat roofs where many houses and buildings were snugged against each other. On these streets, ladders were set to reach higher rooftops, and the bridges jumped streets on the ground. Anyone who was not clearly a thief or an outsider could use the roof paths and did: no nasty-tempered camels and mules up here, no chair-bearers and lords on horseback.

Evvy knew the higher streets like she knew the cliff warrens where she lived, in Chammur Oldtown. She was accepted here, rags and all, as long as she kept moving and took nothing. Dogs might watch until she was gone, women might keep an eye on her as they worked their tiny gardens or hung up their washing, but they were used to all kinds of people up here.

She crouched, staring at the small house beside the foreign temple. Who was the jade-eyed boy? Why did he ask about magic? If she'd had any, her parents would not have sold her to a Chammuran innkeeper before continuing west. If she were a mage, she wouldn't have to live in Princes' Heights as a street rat who scraped to feed herself and her cats.

Her cats! Evvy sighed. Without coppers from Nahim today, she couldn't buy dried fish for them as she'd planned. She'd better get back to Oldtown. If she had enough time before dark, she might be able to catch some lizards on the rocks atop the Heights. That would satisfy the cats at least, and she could eat bread she'd hidden away.

Below her the Camelguts were pounding the lone Viper. The jade-eyed boy had a mean streak, it seemed, setting them against the Viper like that. Crazy *eknub*, Evvy thought. Don't go pawing at my life! Straightening, she trotted down the rooftop road.

In the cool hours of the evening, Lady Zenadia doa Attaneh reclined on the sofa that was placed for her comfort in her garden. She was the picture of a Chammuran noblewoman in wide skirts, head veil, and draped sari, all made of expensive maroon silk embroidered in gold at the hems. Her short gold blouse, baring a midriff as lean and supple in her fifties as it had been when she was a girl, was hemmed with teardrop-shaped pearls, its neckline and sleeves with tiny seed pearls. Obedient to custom, she wore a silk veil before her male guests, but the gold fabric was so sheer that her gold nose ring and the fine gold chain that hung between it and her earring were visible, as was her crimson lip paint. The veil only covered her nose and the lower part of her face, leaving her large, dark eyes with their strong black brows bare. Between her eyes glimmered the unfaceted emerald that marked her status as a widow.

As if they had been placed to form the rudest possible contrast to her elegance, the Vipers who had talked to Briar in the *souk* knelt three feet from her couch, palms and foreheads pressed to the blue patio tiles. The rough shirts and breeches that she had bought for them were clean — no one went dirty into her presence — but cloth and make were no better than what she gave to her lowliest servants.

Only brass nose rings, with a garnet drop hanging from them, set them apart from rag peddlers and camel drovers. The boys had told her about the foreign lad who had marked a street girl as a mage, then turned into trouble for the youth who had followed him. Now they awaited the lady's verdict.

"I have no interest in *eknub pahans*," she commented at last, staring into the distance. Her voice was deep and musical, almost hypnotic in its effect on her guests. "They are troublesome, and they are not of Chammur. They are beneath my attention. But he told this girl she might have stone magic?"

The tallest Viper, the lean, brown-skinned youth who was their *tesku*, or leader, looked up from the tiles. He was the one who had told Briar that he looked and moved like a thief. His eyes were fixed on the lady, as if she were his sun. "He asked her how her magic made the stones light up, Lady," he repeated. "He wanted to know if she called on the power in the stones, or if she just put a charm on them."

The lady turned her large eyes on him and smiled. "You may approach me, Ikrum Fazhal," she said. The thin *tesku* crawled forward until she placed a gentle hand on his dark hair. "You were wise to report this to me. A Chammuran *pahan* is always useful, but a street child from Oldtown, new to her power, and that power with stones — such a *pahan* has, umm," she hummed, "*unique* possibilities. She would be grateful to those who took her in, would she not?

You need not answer," she added when Ikrum opened his mouth. "Tell my Vipers to watch for this child, and to bring her to me when she is found."

She lifted her hand from Ikrum's head; he promptly crawled back to join the other two. It had taken painful training, but now all the Vipers who were permitted into her presence knew exactly what her unspoken signals meant, and obeyed them.

"As for these others, the ones who assaulted our Sajiv —" The lady flipped her fingers at the third Viper, a lean, brown youth with tightly curled black hair.

"Camelguts," he muttered. His nose bled sluggishly: they had torn out his ring and garnet drop.

"Dreadful word," the lady said with disgust. "What is their strength?"

"Twenty-six boys and girls," Ikrum said promptly.

The lady inspected the patterns that had been drawn in henna on her palms. "Fewer than the Gate Lords," she murmured, naming the gang who controlled the streets between the Hajra Gate and Golden House, the ones whose colors were black and white. "Fewer, and poorer." She looked up at her guests. "They must learn respect for my Vipers. I have obtained enough weapons for you at last. Armsmaster Ubayid —" She raised a finger. An older man standing in the shadows by the gallery approached and bowed to her. "You will present my Vipers with weapons, those, those blackjacks. Instruct them in their proper use." Ubayid bowed to her again. To the boys the lady said, "Once you have taught the other Vipers the use of blackjacks, you will enter Camelgut" — she wrinkled her nose — "territory by stealth. Separate these upstarts from their gang one or two at a time. Take them coming and going from their homes, when they will not be with a group. Deal with them harshly, and leave them where they will be found. Try not to be seen. The less people know, the more they will fear. Am I understood?"

The Vipers nodded vigorously.

The lady smiled at them. "When you judge the Camelguts to be on the brink of collapse, offer to admit them to the Vipers." The kneeling youths stirred, on the verge of protest. She touched her forefinger to her lips over the veil. "You have said the Gate Lords possess the advantage of numbers. Here is a way to increase yours. Of course, the newcomers must prove their loyalty before they can be fully accepted into your ranks." She looked them over. "You will have to trust me. I understand these things as you do not. Now. Ubayid, before you give them weapons or lessons, feed my hardworking boys," she ordered. "Not too much, of course. Information is precious, but not as precious as victories." She dismissed them and her armsmaster with a flick of the hand.

Once they were gone, the lady considered her next move. Until now she hadn't known how to give her pet gang confidence: the Gate Lords, who controlled the territory she

2

The house where Briar and Rosethorn currently lived was clean and bright, with potted plants everywhere. They set up a welcoming chorus to Briar, reaching for him. As always when he came in, he made the circuit of the first floor, greeting each in the front room, dining room, kitchen, and rear courtyard. If he forgot any one of them, the plants would droop until reassured of his affection.

Once they were calm, Briar sent his power through the house. Rosethorn wasn't on the second floor, where their workroom and bedrooms were. All he felt there was the magic embedded in the tools, plants, and medicines in the workroom, and the varying blazes that marked his miniature trees. Briar quested past that and found the banked, steady fire that was Rosethorn on the roof.

Like most Chammuri houses, this one had a staircase that led to the roof from the second floor. The other houses Briar had visited in Chammur were the same: it was as if the roofs were as much a part of the house as the kitchen, something he found odd. He climbed up and out into the waning afternoon light with the voiceless song of happy plants vibrating in his skull.

Their roof was almost solid green: tubs and pots filled with the plants Rosethorn thought would help local farms covered every inch of space. All were in different stages of growth regardless of the season, magically encouraged to sprout, flower, and fade over a matter of days while Rosethorn harvested seed for the locals to use.

Rosethorn herself sat on a bench, carefully writing on a slate. She was a broad-shouldered woman in a long-sleeved dark green habit, the emblem of her dedication to the earth and its gods. Her large brown eyes were fixed on her slate. Briar saw she had already been to the Earth temple baths: her chestnut hair, worn mannishly short, was dark against her skull, the strict part white against her wet hair. Her creamy skin bore just a trace of gilt from a summer's work and travel — she was vain of her ivory complexion, employing hats and various lotions to keep it from going to leather as farmers' skin did. Though she was now two inches shorter than he was, Briar always thought of her as towering over him. She still did, in learning and power.

"Tell these weeds to calm down, why don't you?" Briar asked Rosethorn in their native language, Imperial, rubbing his ears. "You think they'd be used to us by now."

"They can't help it," Rosethorn informed him absently

in the same language, reviewing her notes. Her speech was a little slurred, one result of her illness four years before. She had died of it, but Briar and his foster-sisters had called her back to life. The precious minutes she had been dead left their mark: a clumsy tongue, and a slight tremor in her hands. "And when we pump them up to rush them through their growing, it makes them talk more." Nevertheless she sent out her magic like a calming bath, soothing the greenery around them until it quieted.

"How were those western farms?" Briar wanted to know as he sat on the waist-high wall that fenced the roof. "Weren't you going out there today?" Word that a famed green mage had come to Chammur had spread like wildfire in the days after their arrival, bringing group after group of farmers to see Rosethorn. They needed serious help: their harvests had been shrinking every year. Rosethorn had gone out every day to inspect different fields.

"Desperate," she told Briar now, her red mouth twisted wryly. "As desperate as the eastern and southern ones. Everyone says I needn't bother with the northerners — they've been growing rocks for three generations." She rubbed a note out with her sleeve and carefully chalked something else in its place. "How was the Water temple?"

"Finished. Stocked up for a year at least, with plenty extra. All their medicines are at more than full strength. I told you I could do it in a month. Say, Rosethorn —"

"What?"

"Stone mages are common, right?" Briar asked, stroking the fleshy leaves of an aloe vera plant beside him. "You know, ones that magic crystals and jewels and things."

"Stone magic is common, yes," she replied. "Most mages deal with spells for stones at some point. Are you asking if there are stone mages like we're plant mages?"

Briar nodded.

Rosethorn considered. "Yes, there are more whose power comes from stones than there are other kinds of ambient mage."

Briar scratched his head. He knew that word "ambient." "Oh, right — mages that work with the magic that's already in things."

Rosethorn looked up at him, her large, dark brown eyes sharp, her mouth curled with wry amusement. "Don't go playing the country bumpkin, my buck. You know very well what 'ambient' means."

How could he explain he'd been thinking like a street rat, after talking to the Vipers and Camelguts? Even now, after four years of regular meals, affection, and education, he sometimes felt as if his head were split in two. Magic and the Living Circle temples didn't exactly mesh with a life in which meals were stolen and mistakes were paid for with maiming and death.

"And academics?" he asked. There was no sense in talking about gangs to Rosethorn. She had no interest in that life, having never lived it, and she worried when he ventured too close to his old ways. "They do spells with rocks?"

Rosethorn tapped her slate with her chalk. "Like the spells I taught you for use with jade and malachite. Stones are the best objects to hold and store power. Are you wondering about someone who can work magic over a stone, or use what's in the stone?"

Briar shrugged and wrestled his boots off. Once he'd peeled away both footgear and stockings, he told her about the girl Evvy and what he'd seen.

Rosethorn put her slate aside. "You'd better hope there *is* an ambient stone mage in Chammur," she remarked when he was done. "I know one lives in the *amir*'s palace. Well, they'd have to have at least one, wouldn't they?"

Briar frowned. "I don't understand."

"Over half the city lives in those cliffs." Rosethorn waved a hand toward the orange stone heights of Oldtown. "Most of their walls are on stone as well as made of it. Their cisterns are dug into stone. If you don't keep a stone mage around to tell you when a stack of apartments is about to collapse, you're just asking for trouble."

Briar sat cross-legged, grimacing as tight muscles stretched. "But howcome *I* have to hope there's a stone mage here? It's no skin off my neb."

"Why, not howcome, and off my nose," she corrected absently. "We never explained the rules to you four, did we? About new mages?"

"What rules?" he demanded sharply. This was starting to sound too much like chores for his liking.

Rosethorn sighed. "If there is no mage about whose magic is on the same order as that of a newly found mage — that's your friend Evvy —"

"I don't even know her," objected Briar.

Rosethorn continued, ignoring him. "— if there's no mage of her craft available to instruct her, then it is the obligation of the mage who discovers her to teach her the basics. The sooner the better. If her magic hasn't broken away from her before, just the fact that you saw it means it's expanding outside whatever unconscious control she's had until now. Sooner or later it will really break out. If she's a stone mage, I can think of all kinds of things that can go wrong, right here."

"I'm a *kid*," Briar objected. "Fourteen isn't old enough to marry, let alone teach!"

Rosethorn shook her head. "Doesn't matter. You're a mage and you found her. If there isn't a local who understands her magic, you have to teach her to meditate, to control her magic, and some of the most basic spells. Academics, too. She'll need to learn different kinds of rocks and their magical applications, astronomy, reading, writing, mathematics —"

"Not from me she won't," said Briar. "I couldn't even teach our dog to walk on a leash, remember? You need some unexcitable person to be a teacher."

"Wrong again. You either teach her or hand her over to another stone mage." Rosethorn reached over and held Briar's wrist. "Trust me, you do *not* want to know the penalties for leaving an untaught mage to shift for herself."

"Who's gonna work those penalties on me?" Briar demanded crossly. "They'd best bring their supper to do it. They'll be working a while."

Rosethorn let him go. "That would be the closest member of Winding Circle's Initiate Council or the Mage-council of the University at Lightsbridge. They set and enforce the laws for mages from the Endless Ocean in the west to the Heaven Mountains in Yanjing."

"Then I'll go. They can come find me," Briar snapped. "I ain't their errand boy."

"The nearest member of both of those councils is me."

Horrified, Briar met Rosethorn's eyes. The affection she always had for him was there, but it mingled with iron purpose. He didn't ask if she were exaggerating to make a point. He knew her. She would land on him with both feet if he didn't listen. And she could. Four people in the world had the ability to make him sorry he had crossed them. She was at the top of that short list — his foster-sisters were the others, and they were inside his mind when the four of them were together. Rosethorn didn't have to be. He'd known for three years that she was what their world called a great mage, but even before learning that, he'd felt the breadth and depth of her power. He also knew there were times he could tease her, and times he could not. This time, he could not.

Seeing that he understood her very well, Rosethorn picked up her slate again. "You'd better track down the *amir*'s stone mage," she said mildly. "Sooner, rather than later. When do we eat?"

Briar sighed and padded downstairs to start supper. Afterward, while Rosethorn cleaned up, he'd go over to the Earth temple. One of their dedicates would know if there were stone mages who lived closer to the Street of Hares than the one in the *amir*'s palace. He'd also have to find a way to talk to the girl Evvy. She was a wary street rat, just as he'd been. She'd go back to Nahim Zineer's — she'd never walk away from the few coppers he paid.

She'll think since I saw her in the afternoon, I'll come back in the afternoon, he reasoned as he set out food. *So she'll go there in the morning. Which means if I'm to talk to her, I'd best get there before she does. I'll have to hide, or she'll run off as soon as she sees me.*

And he'd wait to approach until after the stone-merchant paid her, this time. He didn't want to cost a fellow street rat any more meals.

Evvy rose with the dawn, not because she wanted to, but because Mystery was perched on her collarbone, kneading busily, her thin, needlelike claws hooking into Evvy's skin. Once Mystery had been petted, the other six cats wanted affection, too. At least they were not hungry this morning. Evvy had been digging in the garbage heap of one of the Ibex Walk inns just as a cookmaid tossed out a bowl full of meat scraps. Heibei the Lucky smiled on Evvy twice, because no one else was scrounging there at the same time. She'd gotten it all, plus some half-rotted vegetables. The meat went to her seven companions. She'd picked the rot from the vegetables and added a three-day-old round of bread for a feast of her own.

Since she was awake, Evvy decided to visit Golden House as soon as it opened. If that crazy boy thought to find her there, he'd probably come in the afternoon. She could work her way through Nahim's baskets and be gone by then, if Nahim let her. She couldn't think why he wouldn't, but no one had ever accused her of magic before.

If Nahim remembered that, he said nothing when Evvy arrived. Instead he produced the polishing cloths and returned to working on his accounts. She sighed inwardly in relief and picked up the first stone to catch her eye, one in a basket of turquoises. She couldn't have said why this stone called to her and not another, only that it would like polishing. Once she finished it, she placed it in the bowl Nahim gave her for the stones she'd handled, and searched through the turquoise basket for more such pieces.

She was tired by the time the Golden House clock struck twelve. Sadly she put down a basket of peach-colored moonstones. It was time to stop: anything she handled once her bones started to ache would turn gray and lifeless in her hands, its value and beauty gone. She folded her cloths and draped them over the bowl of finished stones, looking sidelong at Nahim.

He was picking through the contents of his belt-purse. He stopped and frowned, then smiled at Evvy. She blinked. Should she run? He'd never smiled that way before, as if his teeth hurt. Still, she'd promised the cats dried fish two days ago, and she hated to disappoint them. Gingerly she held out one hand, ready to bolt if he did anything odd.

He dropped not one copper *dav* or two, but — three, four, *five* copper *davs* into her palm! Evvy closed her fingers on the money, in case he changed his mind.

"You earn it, girl," Nahim said, his eyes still squinched up, as if something important ached ferociously. "I don't know what you do, but those stones you polish are the ones I sell first."

"He means if you become a mage he doesn't want you thinking he cheated you," his neighbor called from across the aisle. As long as Evvy had been coming here, almost a year now, the two men had needled each other constantly. "He wants to keep you working for him."

Evvy shook her head and slid the coins into a small pocket on the inside of her ragged tunic. Usually she just took the money and left, but five whole *davs* seemed to call for some kind of response. She gave Nahim a smile only a hair less odd than his own, then left before he tried to take his money back. So confused was she that she didn't see yesterday's stranger emerge from behind a tapestry drape across the aisle. She did hear a guard shout "Hey," but thought nothing of it.

Only when she turned down a side corridor did she look back. The jade-eyed boy was following her. Where he'd come from she didn't know, but if he thought he could track her, he was mistaken. She'd been followed in Golden House before, by people who wanted to know how she got in and out without the door guards turning her away.

Quick as a mink she darted into a deep-end gap between two empty stalls. The only things back here were two giant rolls of carpet stacked against the wall. She headed for them at a dead run, turned to pop through the gap between them, and vanished.

When she started to run, Briar tossed out a vine of his power, letting it wrap around her. She might be out of view, but he could now follow her as he liked, without spooking her. Squinting in the dim light of the back passages in Golden House, he found his vine and tracked it. It slid between two very large rolls of carpet. Only when he was right in front of them did Briar see they covered an opening in the wall of the *souk*, one barely visible in the shadows.

Briar shouldered through the gap and into the street outside. Looking for his vine, he found the girl. She was three blocks away, turning down a narrow side street.

Briar followed, picking up speed in the less crowded road. She led him a proper chase, around one turn and another, down the twisting ways that threaded through the city. She almost shook him near the large *hammam*, or bathhouse, on the Street of Tentmakers. She had vanished and Briar was squinting to see his magic in the sun's glare when the sound of a pot shattering made him look up. She climbed a building using the iron grates over the windows as hand and foot holds, to reach the roof.

Briar followed, embarrassed that he was not as quick to climb as she, and relieved to be above the streets. Too often those narrow ways with their small windows, seamless front walls, and twists and turns made him feel trapped.

The roofs gave him an entirely different set of problems. Evvy had a good lead. Trotting along nimbly, she dodged flowerpots, drying laundry, baskets, children, women, and dogs. She leaped the short walls that divided one house from another easily, drawing farther away from Briar.

Neither realized others followed. Two male Vipers kept pace in the street below; a female Viper pursued them on the rooftops, careful to stay two houses behind Briar.

The women and children might curse Evvy for her rush across the rooftops, but they reserved their fists and attempts at capture for Briar, realizing there was something alien about him. He shook off children and dogs and ducked the women's fists, sticks, and baskets. Even if he had walked slowly and greeted everyone, he knew they would have tried to stop him.

Evvy jumped the narrow gaps that were the streets below easily, rarely using the plank-and-rope bridges to cross. Briar gritted his teeth and did the jumps where necessary, but he wasn't happy, and he meant to discuss his unhappiness with her at length. When he caught her.

He lost track of where they were. Working his way through a stand of grapevines, trying to talk the vines out of hanging onto him from sheer affection, Briar looked up and swore. Some way ahead loomed the orange-and-brown stone heights of Chammur Oldtown. His girl was making a beeline for the tunnels, holes, and honeycombs of dwellings in the rock cliffs within the city's walls. She had been headed for them all along.

Oh, no, Briar thought wearily as he braced his hands on his knees and fought to catch his breath. Not Oldtown. I won't follow her there. The arcades, halls, and tunnels that led to the apartments in the orange stone were lit by torches if they were lit at all. The smell was indescribable. The Earth dedicate who had given Briar and Rosethorn a complete tour of the city had said that parts of the heights had been inhabited for nearly twelve hundred years. As far as Briar was concerned, they smelled like it.

The thought of following a native there gave him the crawls. He ought to track down a stone mage first. He could catch the girl the next time she left Oldtown. His —

"Thief!" A basket filled with laundry slammed into his back. The grape vines fluttered with dismay. They recognized the woman who tended them and gave them water. Why was she pounding their new friend? "Murderer! Thief!" the woman cried.

"I am *not*!" Briar protested.

"*Eknub*!" shrieked the woman. She thumped him with her basket even harder. "*Eknub, eknub*!"

She acts as if that's worse than murder and theft, Briar thought crossly, shielding his head. And my accent must be awful. "Look," he said, being more careful with his Chammuri, "I just want to get to the street! I'll go, just show me —"

She gave him a final whack and marched to the edge of the roof. Gathering a rope ladder heaped in a corner, she hurled it over the wall as if she meant to do the same to Briar. "If you loiter I'll call the Watch!" she scolded as he tested the ladder's anchors. "See if I don't, spawn of Shaihun, *eknub* parasite!"

"The next one who asks me if folk here are friendly, I'll send 'em to you for a blessing!" he retorted as he swung his leg over. "The gods' sweet day to you for your charity!"

He was a foot down when she yelled: "Whoever taught you Chammuri had the accent of a hen!"

"I'd love to travel, Rosethorn," Briar growled as he clambered past small, grate-covered windows. "I'll learn new languages and be insulted in them. I can ask civil questions and people will run off. Travel would be just the thing!"

The moment he set foot on the street, the woman yanked the ladder from his hold and pulled it up. Briar stuck his tongue out at her and turned to survey his location. The street looked just like every other sun-bleached residential street in Newtown.

Well, think, idiot, he told himself. The cliffs were visible over buildings to his right. If he kept them there, and started walking, he would run into the north wall.

A thock of wood overhead gave him the smallest of warnings. Reflexes he hadn't needed in years made him leap sideways. A stream of dirty wash-water poured down where he'd just been, soaking his left arm. When he looked up, the woman he had offended gestured rudely, and walked away from the roof's edge. For a moment Briar considered asking her grape vines to grip her and keep her prisoner until dark, but then he shook his head. There was no sense in getting the vines in trouble, too. With a sigh he searched for a street that led north as he wrung out his sleeve.

Evvy saw it all from a roof across the street, hands clapped over her mouth to hush her giggles. The jade-eyed boy had looked so much like a cat as he climbed down and as the angry woman had dumped water on him. Evvy half-expected him to shake himself off, then sit to wash himself angrily. Instead he had stalked away down the street. He didn't even look for Evvy.

After chasing her all this way, he was just going to give up? He'd done well for an *eknub* on the roofs — surely he wouldn't let an angry Chammuran and a bucket of water drive him away!

And yet it seemed he would. Evvy crept along the roofs, trailing him. He wasn't even looking up. Why follow her all this way, just to quit?

She knew she had five *davs* and could perhaps get more by begging, but that wasn't as interesting as the boy. She trailed him, trying to work out who and what he was. He'd said he was a mage. She wasn't sure if she believed that. All the mages she'd ever known — magic-workers, healers, and hedgewitches — were adults in their mid-twenties or older, very full of themselves and whatever scraps of magic they could use. People who were younger rarely claimed the title, but he said it as casually as if it were his name.

And now that she looked him over, keeping a house behind as he walked through the streets, she could tell that his clothes were better than even Nahim's. She sometimes made a *dav* or two picking rags: she knew quality tailoring when she saw it. The boy's clothes fit as if made for him and no one else. Interestingly, the cloth didn't wrinkle like normal clothes did. His sleeve was wet, but apart from that his garments looked as clean as if they'd just been washed. Evvy had acquired another layer of dirt on her clothes in that rooftop run, but he was still fresh. His boots were sturdy and well made. They at least carried a layer of dust from the street.

She had followed him three blocks when she saw a green-and-yellow ribbon drop onto him from a second-story window: it landed across his shoulders and curled around his neck. Evvy swallowed a gasp, thinking a serpent had dropped onto the boy from the iron-grated window. He stopped and wrapped both hands carefully around the thing, lifting it over his head.

Then Evvy got a better look and almost wished it had been a snake. The thing was a *vine*, the kind Chammurans called "Traveler's Joy"; the yellow spots were its whiskered flower petals. It hung from a box under a window grate on which it grew. Unlike any plant Evvy had seen in her life, this one moved, twining and wrapping around the jade-eyed boy's head and arms, making her think of hungry cats who know when a human has a treat for them.

She couldn't hear what he said, but his lips moved. Finally he raised his arms toward the window-box. Slowly, chagrin in its drooping leaves and blossoms, the vine retreated to wrap around its grate once more.

Evvy rocked back on her heels. It *reached* for him, she thought, her mind spinning. Like it was alive. Like it had feelings!

She peered down at the street again, just as the boy turned the corner. In a flash she was up and running, following in earnest. As she did she saw rosebushes in pots lean toward him. Grapes, vines, and bean plants threw runners down from rooftops. His progress slowed; if he could not reach a plant to touch it, he stood beneath it for a moment, until it returned to its proper home. Flowers turned their faces as he passed, and grass sprouted from cracks in the street in his wake.

Always he made his way north, until he turned west on the Street of Hares. He stopped briefly to talk to a cluster of boys and girls wearing the Camelgut green sash. Whatever they said, it had to be funny, because everyone laughed. Eventually the boy walked into the house she had seen him enter the day before. Just before he went in he turned and inspected first the street, then the roofs. Evvy jerked back and down; when she looked again, he was closing the door behind him.

Evvy perched on the roof of a warehouse across the street from the *eknub* temple and wrapped her arms around her knees. He really was a *pahan*, a mage. It was the only explanation for what she had seen, though she had never heard of magic that made plants act like animals. Where had he come from, this jade-plant boy? What could he possibly want from her?

"If we grab her here, we'll reap trouble," argued Orlana, on a rooftop a street away. The Vipers who had followed

40

Evvy in the street had joined her there when it became clear that the girl was settled for the time being. From their position they could see Evvy clearly. She sat without moving, her gaze intent on something below. "This quarter is full of Camelguts," Orlana continued. "If we make a noise they'll be on us, probably worse than they were on Sajiv yesterday."

"We need to teach them respect," growled Sajiv, touching his nose. The lady's healer had fixed the damage the Camelguts had done in tearing out his gang ring, but it would be a moon before his flesh was strong enough to get another, and his nose still hurt.

The third member of their group, the black-skinned boy who had spoken first to Briar the day before, laughed contemptuously. "Why should they respect us? A year ago we were just a bunch of messengers in the Grand Bazaar, and all Chammur knows it."

"That's changing, Yoru," the girl Orlana told him in a hot-voiced whisper. "The lady's going to get us respect."

"What a good little lapdog you are, Orlana," replied Yoru with a sneer. "So we go from message runners to pets without never once standing on our own hind legs!"

Sajiv punched his shoulder. "If it's so bad, why did you come today?" he wanted to know. "Maybe you're wasting your time here, too."

"I ain't a fool, Sajiv," retorted Yoru. "If it's stones, if that kid can make the stones talk? You know how the *takamers* hide money stuff to keep it safe." He pointed to Evvy, who'd removed her scarf to scratch her head. "She'll know where they're hid. *That's* real power for Vipers."

Orlana and Sajiv traded looks of dawning wonder. Without further debate they settled down to wait Evvy out.

Briar had sensed that he had company just as the Traveler's Joy vine got emotional enough to drop on him. The poor thing was suffering with a kind of fungus infection. Briar sent his power through every vein the Joy plant had, scorching through every hair on its roots, cooking the fungus to a fine white dust. Normally Briar had nothing against fungi, but when they preyed on other plants, he always sided with the victims.

The sense that he was followed continued after he left the vine. Peeks back down the street as he walked north showed him nothing, until he remembered the roads over the city's roofs. He couldn't look up without giving himself away, so he waited until he was at his own door before checking the skyline. There: quick movement back from the edge, a head scarf the nameless color of dirt, across the street. Feeling for the magic vine he'd attached to her, he found it was short and fairly thick. It was Evvy.

Well, well, Briar thought, opening his door. I made kitty curious. He considered ways to deal with her that wouldn't scare her into running away.

A door across the street opened. One of his young

neighbors knelt to place a saucer heaped with chopped meat on the ground. A gray-and-black spotted cat separated itself from the shadows at the base of the wall and trotted over to devour the food. Smiling, the girl petted the cat as it ate.

Briar grinned.

3

Rosethorn had set the table for midday when Briar came in. She watched, startled, as he took food out of the pantry and set it on a tray: a cooked sausage, several thick slices of cheese, hardboiled eggs, cold slices of fried eggplant, and flatbread. Glancing at the table, he saw she'd been to the *souk* that morning. Lamb dumplings steamed in a bowl next to mutton-and-barley stew. "Can I have these?" he asked, hooking three dumplings onto his tray, then blowing on his scorched fingers. "I won't eat any."

Rosethorn propped her fists on her hips as he grabbed oranges from a bowl. "Boy, what in Mila's name are you doing?" she demanded.

"Start without me," Briar said, ignoring her question. "I'll be right back." He put a clean drying cloth over his shoulder and carried his tray to the roof.

He glanced at the loomhouse. Again there was a quick flutter on its higher roof, as if someone had just ducked below the rim. Briar grinned again and set tray and cloth on the bench in plain view. The many plants around him craned in, trying to see if there was anything on the tray they would like.

"Stop it," Briar chided. "That's people food. Or cat food. You get more than enough food of your own. I need one of you to go back inside with me. I want to know if anyone comes to take this."

If there was a discussion — he was never sure if the plants talked among themselves — the Yanjing jasmine won. It extended a creeper that grew longer and longer to keep up as he went back inside. It followed him all the way to the table, and busied itself twining between his chair and Rosethorn's, as if they formed a trellis.

Briar dished up a bowl of stew for himself. "Whatever you feed them to move them along, it sure makes them active," he commented. "I hope they're worth all the fuss you're making over them."

"Yes." Rosethorn cleaned her bowl with a piece of bread. Putting so much of her power into so many plants, bringing them through a year's growing cycle in days, made her eat well at every meal without gaining a pound. "Who else are we feeding, anyway?"

Briar told her about his morning's adventure as he ate. After they finished, he washed the dishes with no alarm from the jasmine. Rosethorn went to run errands while Briar got the vine to follow him into their workroom.

Rosethorn had said nothing one way or another, but

Briar knew she hoped to leave Chammur before the autumn rains began, if that was at all possible. Now seemed to be as good a time as any to start making the protection balls that he and Rosethorn liked to carry, for use in case they were robbed or kidnapped on the road.

As the Yanjing jasmine laid a stem across his shoulders like a friendly arm, Briar took down the jars of seeds he required and began to mix their contents. The original idea for the balls had come during a pirate attack on Winding Circle nearly four years before. To protect the side of the temple city vulnerable to landing parties in the cove, they had put together seed mixes made entirely of thorny plants, and used their magic to make the contents grow explosively, with dreadful results to anyone standing on them.

Since then Briar and Rosethorn had refined the mixture, making variations for people who had no magic, and creating mixtures that would perform different tasks. Some of the balls that Briar put together now simply produced ropes to tie up those close to where they grew. Some grew the kinds of vine that over time destroyed the mortar that held stone and brick together. Others, the deadliest, included the seeds of plants that Rosethorn and Briar had cultivated specially to produce long, viciously sharp thorns.

Laying out squares of cloth already prepared for magical formulas, Briar heaped his seed mixtures at their centers: crimson for the killer thorns, gray for the wall-destroying ivys, and yellow for the rope vines. To each he added a touch of the tonic he and Rosethorn used to speed up a plant's growth, then tied each ball shut with silk thread. He split the finished balls in half, stowing his in the outer pockets of his mage kit, and leaving Rosethorn's on her worktable, partly as a hint. He didn't think he wanted to be stuck in Chammur over the winter either.

Once that was done, Briar turned to his own work. The miniature trees needed attention: his stall at Golden House would be open for him in a few days, and he wanted them to look their best. He and Rosethorn lived on the money they brought in.

One of the miniature figs had become difficult. Briar finally gave it a choice: either it could change the shape of its left-side branches to fit the design he showed it, or he would force them to take the shape by wrapping them with wire. The fig was still arguing when the jasmine vine tapped Briar's arm urgently. It seemed his stray cat had come to the rooftop to feed.

"You need that bend to draw fertility to the house. One way or another, you're going to be shaped," he told the fig. "We can do it my way or your way, but we *are* going to do it." He climbed to the roof in silence. His clothes didn't even rustle: his foster-sister Sandry, who had woven and sewn them for him, had included that in the cloth as a joke about his former life as a thief.

*   *   *

Evvy had watched the food, and watched and watched it, sure there was a trap laid somewhere. She left her post once to make water; as soon as she finished she hurried back. The Karang Gate clock rang the hour twice. No one else came to the roof of the house, and that bounty just sat there, surrounded by plants. What if the jade-eyed boy had left while Evvy had tended to her business in a private corner? He could have, easily. The woman had left before the clock even struck once.

Sausage was better for cats than salted fish. She was very partial to sausage herself. Asa and Monster loved cheese.

Finally Evvy retreated to a bridge that crossed to the far side of the street. Working her way cautiously along the roofs, she reached the closest house to the boy's. From there it was a piddling two-foot drop to her destination.

No one was in sight among the horde of plants that grew here. Some looked quite strange, but then, she knew nothing of plants. One vine even trailed through the open door to the house. Evvy shook her head, thinking that green things around the jade-eyed boy were much too lively. Then she crouched beside the tray. She opened the folded cloth that lay beside it and began to load it with food to take home.

Like most Chammurans, Evvy thought eggplant was the queen of vegetables. She stuffed a slice into her mouth, savoring the taste. Eating only needed one hand: she grabbed another slice and took a huge bite while she continued to put food onto her cloth.

She didn't hear the boy come onto the roof. She saw him, though: he raised his hands in the air, holding them palm-out to show he came peacefully. Evvy nearly choked on her eggplant. She dropped the rest of the slice and scrabbled for the corners of the cloth, bundling her food.

"I won't come a step closer," he said in calm Chammuri. "I just want to talk." He knelt beside the entrance to the house and lowered his hands. The plants around him leaned in, forming a green roof over his head.

She eyed him for a moment more. He seemed to be settled. No matter how fast he was, by the time he could actually lunge forward and grab her, she would be gone.

She opened the cloth and dumped the rest of the tray's contents onto it. One eye on the boy, she retrieved her dropped slice of eggplant, wiped off the rooftop dirt, and stuffed it into her mouth.

"You have to know about your magic," he went on. "Maybe you can't see it — most mages can't. But you must feel something, when you handle stones."

Evvy hesitated. So the stones that morning — all right, every day at Nahim's — felt warm in her hands, nice-warm, like kittens, so what? And her den in Princes' Heights, with all the stones she liked pressed into the rock of the entrance way, had never been invaded, unlike every other squat she knew of. What of it?

He's a mage. Wouldn't he *know?* argued half of her. Mages know things!

He's a boy, not a man, so he's a student, not a mage, her street-self replied. Students mess up all the time.

He's awfully sure, replied her good-girl self.

So are students, the street girl snapped. Right before they mess up.

Quickly Evvy tied up her bundle. She wasn't about to leave all this food behind. If the boy wanted it for himself, he shouldn't have left it out here.

"You can't go on as you have," the mage-boy continued. "You have to learn how to control your magic, or you'll get into trouble. Once people know you're a mage —"

Evvy tucked her bundle into the front of her tunic. Gripping the edge of the next door roof, she swung herself up and over.

"If you come tomorrow, I'll have more food," the mage-boy called as she fled.

"Do you think she listened?" asked a quiet voice in Imperial. Briar looked down, into the house. Rosethorn had come back: she stood on the floor below.

"Dunno," he said in the same language. "She ate. That's something. She'll probably perch close by all night to see if I put more food up and lay a trap for her."

Rosethorn shook her head. "She's even more feral than you were," she remarked. "At least you had that gang."

"Oh, she's got to be ganged up," protested Briar. "How else do you survive here?"

The look she gave him was half-vexed, half-amused. "There are plenty of people in Chammur who don't belong to gangs," she pointed out.

Briar gently removed the jasmine from his arm. "Not if you're a kid from Oldtown, I bet," he replied. "Only way to be safe is with a gang. When people fool with you, they know they're fooling with your mates, too." He thanked the vine and sent it to its trellis.

"You manage without a gang now," argued Rosethorn.

"I'm a mage now," he pointed out. "Besides, I have a gang. If the girls aren't my mates, who is? And you and Lark and Niko, Frostpine, Crane — that's my gang," he explained, naming the adults who had taught him and his foster-sisters at Winding Circle.

"So what symbol — no," Rosethorn said, cutting herself off. "I am not going to encourage you in thinking like that. What's your next move with the girl?"

Briar sighed. "Earth Dedicates say the only stone mage in town is this Jebilu Stoneslicer, up at the palace. I guess I better talk to him about teaching her."

"Good idea." Rosethorn reached into the pocket of her habit and produced a metal token. "It'll take you forever to walk there and back. You remember where we stabled our horses? Get one of them."

Briar nodded, and accepted the token to show the

stablemen. "Thanks, Rosethorn." He walked by her, then stopped. Not sure why he did so, he turned back and kissed her lightly on the cheek.

"Oh, stop that!" she said irritably, as he'd known she would. "People will start to think I like you if you pull that kind of nonsense!"

Briar grinned. "They already know you do," he said reasonably. "I'm still alive after years in your company." He walked away before she could think of a cutting reply.

The Newtown roofs stopped well short of the rocky skirts of Princes' Heights, where Evvy made her home. She climbed down from the last of them and looked around warily. Then she crossed the Street of Victories, where clusters of ragtag and furtive stalls housed the Market of the Lost. Behind every facade of respectable merchandise — rags, spices, cheap food and liquor, secondhand clothes, used pottery, and furnishings — lay much less respectable items. Drugs and weapons could be bought, as could ill wishes, outright curses, poisons, and healing services for those who dared not go to, or could not afford, more respectable healers.

Evvy scanned the stalls. If soldiers of the Watch were about, long-timers would vanish, warning locals that the law was around. If they hadn't been in their usual spots, Evvy would have lingered in Newtown a while longer. The

Watch wasn't always precise in who they hauled to Justice Rock's prisons when they conducted a sweep in Oldtown.

Everyone who should be there was. Feeling safe, Evvy trotted through the mazes of stalls until she reached the tumble of gravel, dirt, and loose rock at the foot of the heights. The stone cliff towered above her, riddled with paths, streets, windows, doors, and the arches that led to the tunnels. Evvy smiled at those orange-flame heights. She was almost home.

Three Vipers encircled her, putting the treacherous gravel pile at Evvy's back. She scrambled a few steps up onto it anyway, feeling the loose tumble of dirt and stone slide under her feet. She pinwheeled her arms to remain standing.

"Hello, kid," the girl Viper said with a smile on her face. "We're your mates. We'd like to buy you supper." As she talked, the two boy Vipers closed in.

"All real friendly," said the light-brown boy with a painful-looking red weal on one nostril. He was the only one of the three who wore no nose ring. "Nobody gets hurt."

It was the third, a black-skinned boy, who grabbed for her. The other two came on as Evvy scrabbled up and back two more steps. She stumbled and sat down hard as the ground slid under her. Panicked, she seized two fistfuls of gravel and hurled them at her attackers, crying to the rocks in her hands, "*Do* something!"

The stones flared with light and heat as they struck the Vipers' faces. Both Evvy and the Vipers were blaze-blinded; the brown-skinned boy screamed. All three Vipers clapped their hands to their faces. Staggering, they lost their footing and rolled to the foot of the slope. Their clothes smoldered in a handful of places, as if Evvy had thrown burning embers on them. Their faces were speckled with small, red burns.

Evvy pushed herself up the slope on her backside, her heart galloping. The Vipers started at the noise she made and struggled to their feet. Bobbing and weaving, hanging onto each other, they fled into the marketplace.

Evvy rubbed her eyes: light-spots still danced through her vision, half-blinding her. The Market of the Lost and Oldtown were not places where it was wise to let others see her handicapped in any way. She was in no condition to find her way among the maze of trails between here and home, and the locals would be after her in a moment. She needed a hiding place until she could see clearly again. Lurching to her feet, Evvy walked-skidded down the slope and found her way to the back of Sulya's herb and charm stall. Sulya kept the large baskets she used to tote her wares tied to a post there. Evvy groped her way between them and settled, whispering "It's Evvy, Sulya," through the cracked wood of the stall's back.

"Don't break nothin', strangers' child," Sulya warned.

She had the sharp ears of a desert fox, and a large cudgel that she used on those who touched her property.

"Not me," Evvy assured her. She rested her head on her knees, praying to Kanzan, goddess of healing, for her sight to return. What had she done?

Briar had been riding east on Triumph Road, winding around pedestrians, riders, flocks, and camels, when he felt a surge of fright come down the magic-vine that connected him to Evvy. He couldn't sense thoughts through it, unless the tie was to another plant mage or his foster-sisters, but feelings came easily. He was about to ride on — Evvy wouldn't be as old as she was if she couldn't take care of herself — but the next big surge of fright slammed him. He felt her magic flare, wildly out of control.

Briar wheeled his mount and rode back the way he had come, ignoring the people who dodged out of his way. The closer he came to the intersection of the Street of Victories and Triumph Road, the steadier his connection to Evvy felt. Her fright was there but under control. What could have happened?

She was nearby. He slowed his mount, looking around the part of the Market of the Lost at the base of Princes' Heights, hoping to spot her. Someone blundered into his horse. Briar, shaken from his concentration, yelled, "Watch where you're going, bleater!" in Imperial.

A girl wearing the nose ring and garnet of a Viper braced herself against his mount. Her face and clothes were marked with small burns; she peered at him as if she were nearly blind. Two youths swayed beside her, speckled with burns just as she was. They pulled her away.

"Mind your manners, *eknub* scum!" snarled the black youth in Chammuri. He was one of the Vipers who'd stopped Briar in Golden House. The trio stumbled on down the street, cursing.

Briar watched them with a frown. What were they doing halfway across the city?

He shook his head and picked up the invisible vine of his magic, following it behind a cluster of stalls. In the shadows his power gleamed as it threaded through a heap of large baskets.

Briar dismounted and walked over to them, the horse's reins in one hand. He pushed two aside, uncovering Evvy. She stared up at him, her eyes watering, terror in her face and in the magic between them. Then she whipped around and clawed at the baskets behind her, trying to escape.

Briar was in no mood to be kind. He called to the reeds woven into the baskets, waking them from their dead slumber, sparking them into new growth. He also called to the madder seeds that lay in the ground under Evvy. The madder surged gleefully in his magic, tough stems erupting from the ground; reeds unwove themselves to wind around the madder stems and grow with them. Together the combined plants wrapped around the girl's limbs and waist, binding her tight. Evvy shuddered and went still, closing teary eyes.

"It's just me," Briar said, remembering to speak in Chammuri this time. "What did you do, Evvy? You used your magic, didn't you?"

Her eyes flew open: she gave him her best glare. The bundle of food she'd stashed in her tunic leaked, painting grease stains in the cloth across her chest and belly.

"I won't hurt you," Briar continued patiently. "I'm trying to help."

"Then let me go," she snapped.

"So you can scramble off again?" he asked, not unreasonably, in his mind. "I don't feel like teasing you out any more today, thanks all the same. Why are you blinking?"

"Let me *go*," she insisted.

"No," he said, his voice flat. He waited.

At last Evvy growled, "I threw rocks at them and told the magic to do something." She wiggled, trying to break free. The ropes only tightened their grip. "It made some rocks light up and go hot enough to burn, and now I'm seeing spots, and it's all your fault for telling me about the magic, so there. I hate you. You ruined my life."

"No, *magic* ruined it," Briar pointed out sympathetically. "It ruined mine, too, for a while. You'll survive." He went to his horse and drew his mage's kit from a saddlebag. Like his clothes, the cloth of his kit had been woven, sewn, and treated by his foster-sister Sandry, which meant that when he touched the knot that closed it, the knot came undone. The kit unfolded itself. Briar looked through it until he found the small jar labeled EYEBRIGHT. "Did your magic touch *you* at all?" he asked.

She squinted, trying to see him through the bright, dancing globes that covered her vision. "*No,*" she said, unhappy with the situation and his question. "I threw it at *them,* not at me. I'm fire-blind, is all. And tangled up in *your* magic." She tugged at her bonds, but the reeds and madder had used the time they'd been talking to wrap still more stems around her. "My nose itches."

"That's nice." Briar opened the eyebright jar and dabbed the tip of his index finger in the salve. "So who were *they?* How many were there? Hold still and close your eyes."

Evvy jerked her head as far back from him as her bonds would let her. "You're going to do something awful."

Briar growled, exasperated. "Now, look, youngster, I'm just going to help you see. It won't hurt. I happen to be pretty good at this, so stop arguing and close them. If you're good, I'll let you loose."

Evvy flinched as he dabbed salve first on one eyelid, then the other. "It's cold," she complained.

"No, it's an aromatic, or some of it is," he retorted. "It just feels cold. Stop fussing and open your eyes."

Evvy obeyed. "The spots are gone!"

"Told you I knew what I was doing." Briar wiped the extra salve into the jar and closed it, then did up his kit again. "So who did you throw magicked stones at?"

Evvy shrugged. "Vipers. Three of them. They were trying to grab me!" she cried, misreading his frown. "I had to protect myself!"

"Of course you did," Briar replied absently. "Two boys and a girl, right? But this isn't Viper ground, is it?"

"Market of the Lost is open ground, same as any other *souk*. Anybody can come here," explained his captive. "But they followed me through Camelgut and Snake Sniffer territory." She frowned, trying to remember her route from the Street of Hares. "Rockhead, too. That's bat-dung crazy, that is. Rockhead's are too stupid to know they're killed, so they never lay down."

"I don't know anyone like that," Briar said drily. "Now, what do I do with you?" It wasn't really a question. He already knew her well enough to expect that anything she suggested would not help him.

"You said you'd let me go," Evvy pointed out.

Briar looked at her, checked the angle of the sun, and eyed her again. Had they enough time to go to the *amir*'s palace together?

"I can't pay for lessons, you know," she added after a moment. "I haven't two *davs* to my name. And I want to go home. My cats are hungry."

Briar raised his eyebrows. "Cats, is it? Why am I not surprised? One, you don't pay your magic teacher except with chores. That's to help you learn the tools and some discipline. Two, I won't be your teacher. You need a stone mage. I'm a plant mage." They would never reach the *amir*'s palace before dark. Even if they could, the guards wouldn't admit a ragamuffin like Evvy. "If I let you go, you have to swear on your honor and your soul you'll come to my house by the time the clocks ring the third hour after dawn," he told her sternly.

"*Thukdaks* have no honor, everybody knows that," she retorted.

"What a *thukdak*?"

"Me. I'm a *thukdak*. Those beggars over there, they're *thukdaks*. Don't you know anything?" Evvy shook her head at Briar's ignorance.

"Ah," he said, enlightened. "Back home we're called 'street rats.'" He gave the name first in Imperial, then translated it awkwardly into Chammuri.

"*Belbun's* good eating," Evvy said, using the Chammuri word for rat. "Nobody wastes a *belbun* meal on *thukdaks*."

Briar opened his mouth to ask if she *always* thought and talked of food, then closed it. How could he have forgotten what it was like, to always have an empty belly? What else had he ever thought of, besides just staying alive, until his arrival at Winding Circle?

"Do *you* think you have no honor?" he asked Evvy. "You'd better find something to swear by, because I won't let you go till you do."

Evvy rolled her eyes. "I swear by my cats and by Kanzan the Merciful, Lady of Healing, goddess of Yanjing," she told him, face and voice overly patient. "I'd spit on it, too, but it would just go all over my face."

Briar looked at her for a moment, trying to see if she meant to trick him. It occurred to him, suddenly, how nearly impossible it was to tell if someone lied or not by looking into the person's eyes. He would have to trust his instincts after all.

He released his hold on the reeds and madder plants. The reeds unwound from the madder stems, then wove themselves into their basket frames, the leaves and stems they had grown dropping away. Most were grateful to return to their former, unliving state. They had forgotten how much effort sprouting things and sinking roots took. The madder plants, firmly rooted and determined to stay that way, drew away from Evvy.

She sat up, rubbing circulation back into her arms and legs. "Third hour after dawn," she told Briar wearily, and spat on the ground next to her to seal the promise. The madders instantly drew her wet spittle into their roots, buying more green time above the ground, even in the market shadows.

"Here." Grubbing in his pocket, Briar found a silver *dav* coin, worth three of the copper ones. "Find a *hammam* and clean up," he ordered, holding the coin out. Evvy grabbed it, but Briar didn't let go. "Hair, ears, neck, you name it, it gets washed between now and tomorrow morning. Understand?" Evvy nodded, and Briar gave her the coin. "Have you any other clothes?"

There again was that too-patient, don't-you-know-*anything*? expression on her face. "This is my best thing," she replied, and looked at the front of her tunic. It was covered with grease from the food she carried. "Maybe I can wash it at the *hammam*."

"Don't bother," said Briar. He hadn't lived with Sandry for years without gaining some knowledge of cloth and grease stains. "I'll find something." All the Living Circle temples kept clothing for the poor. If the Earth temple wouldn't give him any, Briar would find a secondhand clothes dealer. Until he could hand the girl off to Jebilu Stoneslicer, he stood in the place of her teacher, which meant he was responsible for her needs. At least, that was how Rosethorn and the girls' teachers had always acted.

"It would be nice to have something good," Evvy remarked wistfully.

"All right. My house, tomorrow, third hour of the morning. And Evvy," he said as she turned to go. She looked back at him. "I found you today. I can find you whenever I want. Don't go thinking you can disappear and keep that coin. If I have to track you, you won't like what comes of it."

Evvy spat on the ground, to remind him that she'd already promised, and trotted up the path to Princes' Heights. A hundred yards away she turned around. Cupping her hand around her mouth she yelled, "Who *are* you, anyway?"

Briar grinned. "Briar Moss," he called back.

"Tomorrow, Briar Moss," the girl yelled. She raced on up the path.

4

Briar was just two blocks from home, the Earth temple and his house in plain sight, when someone whistled shrilly, making the narrow street ring. He looked for the source and saw a stocky girl in a Camelgut green sash trotting toward him.

"*Pahan*, we need help," she said when she reached him. "It's Hammit, that you gave the medicine for." Briar remembered the boy whose facial burn he had treated and nodded. "We can't wake him up," the girl continued, her brown eyes worried. "Looks like he was jumped and hit on the head, but nobody saw who done it. This way." She led him down the Street of Wrens.

When she turned into a dark gap between the houses, Briar halted. "I can't take my horse down there, and I must look plain silly if you think I'll leave him out here."

The girl undid her green sash and used it to tie the horse to a nearly dry fountain. She opened a cock in the stone over the spout, filling the basin with enough water for the animal to drink before she closed it. "Nobody will dare touch him, tied up with my sash," she assured Briar.

He dismounted, using his motion to hide the fact that he was checking the placement of his knives. Then he took his mage's kit from his saddlebag. "After you, Duchess," he said with a gallant bow. Girls usually giggled and blushed when he teased them, but not this one. She gave him a half-smile, her mind clearly elsewhere, and led him down the narrow passageway, into a small alley, and down a stair into a basement.

From the weapons on the walls and the bedrolls around the room, Briar guessed that this was that gang's main den. Either they trusted him or they were desperate. When the cluster of Camelguts near one wall gave way, revealing his patient, Briar knew he'd been called in desperation. Hammit's face was swollen and black with bruises.

"Light," Briar said, dropping to his knees next to Hammit's mattress. Someone passed over a lamp that filled the air with the scent of burning fat.

Some healing was the lot of every plant mage, since they not only grew many ingredients for medicines, but they made up the medicines themselves. In the last three years, Briar had acquired a great deal of medical knowledge. First he pried open each of Hammit's eyes to look at his pupils. Both were completely dilated and remained that way as Briar moved the lamp to and fro. Normal pupils would have grown or shrunk depending on how much light fell on them.

Briar turned Hammit's head. One side of his face drooped, as if he'd had apoplexy. Gently he felt through the fallen boy's hair, ignoring the bugs — lice or fleas — that ran over his hands as he checked the skull. There was a dent behind Hammit's ear. The other boy had been panting when Briar started; now his breathing slowed. Briar checked the pulse in his throat: it, too, was slow. With both pupils opened up all the way, he knew they'd waited much too late to call for help.

He sat back on his heels, slow fury heating his belly. "What happened?"

"Found 'im in the fountain at Cedar Lane and Street o' Hares near dawn." The speaker was a boy who had been pitching coppers with Hammit the day before. "He left to visit his ma last night, and never come back. He come around a bit near midday. Said he never saw who got 'im."

Briar tried to think of a way to tell them what was coming, without saying that if they'd gotten him to a healer right away, he might have lived. With the bleeding in his skull so gradual that it had only begun to kill him now, even the slowest Water temple healer might have fixed things if the Camelguts had taken Hammit in right away.

He was still trying to control his anger and helplessness when Hammit's mouth opened impossibly wide, revealing shattered teeth and bloody gums. His body stiffened; his arms went straight as his palms turned out from his body.

The Camelguts shrank away. As tough as they were in the streets and in battle, this was unknown, alien.

"You're a *pahan* — fix him!" cried the girl who had fetched Briar.

He clenched trembling hands. He'd seen this often enough to know it for what it was. Hammit collapsed. The air blew from his lungs in a last escape, bubbling through his nose and bloody mouth, until his lungs were empty. The Camelguts drew close as Briar checked the pulse in Hammit's big neck vein. There was none.

"He was dead hours ago," Briar said softly. "His heart and lungs kept going for a while, that's all. That's why one side of his face was all funny. His head was bleeding inside somewhere." He closed Hammit's staring eyes. Before they could pop open again, he drew two copper *davs* from his purse and placed them on the eyelids to keep them shut. He'd wanted to use silver — he'd liked Hammit — but that would have been asking too much of the Camelguts. This gang didn't have enough money that they could afford to bury silver with their dead.

For the thousandth time Briar wished he'd been a healer rather than a green mage. Medicines only did so much. Sometimes it took a magically gifted healer to turn the tide. Briar was there too often when such times came around, and the only mage in sight was him. It was Lakik the Trick-ster's favorite joke on him.

Two more Camelguts, a boy and a girl, lurched through the door. The girl's face was bruised, the eye on that side puffed completely shut. To Briar it looked as if she had been clipped hard on the cheekbone.

"Vipers," wheezed the boy, helping the girl to sit. "They was on her when I got there."

"Will you *try* to help this time?" demanded the girl who had summoned Briar.

"He's a *pahan*, Mai, not a god." Briar's defender was the one who'd said where Hammit had been found. "You do medicines, but you can't heal, am I right?"

Briar nodded and went over to the injured girl. At least he could do something for her. With the balms in his kit Briar lowered the swelling and eased the pain of a shattered cheekbone. That was something, and it was more than the Camelguts would get from any local healers. Only the Living Circle Water temples offered free medical care to the poor, but Chammurans mistrusted foreign temples as well as foreigners.

No sooner had Briar finished with the girl than a third victim lurched into the room, one broken arm dangling. He, too, identified his attackers as Vipers. He'd also seen the weapons they had used, small, rounded batons that were far heavier than they looked. "Sounds like blackjacks," Briar commented as he examined the newcomer's arm.

"Since when could they afford those?" demanded the fiery Mai. "This is more of that *takameri*'s doing, I bet!"

"They won't have hands to hold their new toys when we're done with them," snarled another member of the gang. They clustered together to lay battle plans as Briar finished his examination of the newest victim. His request for two long, straight pieces of wood for splints only distracted one Camelgut from the conference. As soon as he gave them to Briar, he went back to planning.

When the splint was secure, Briar told his patient and the girl with the broken cheekbone, "Look, I know the Living Circle Water temple is an *eknub* place, but the healers work for free and I've done all their medicines. You won't have to pay so much as a copper *dav*. They'll have someone who can do broken bones. It's on the Street of Wells — let them know you talked to Briar Moss."

He knew they wouldn't go right away. By dawn, though, the painkilling balm he'd put on their hurts would wear off. They might decide even a visit to an *eknub* who was mad-brained enough to work free of charge was better than the ache of broken bones.

It was nearly midnight when the Viper *tesku* Ikrum and the three who had tried to capture Evvy made their reports to Lady Zenadia, who had returned late from a family supper. She heard them out in silence, though she smiled briefly when Ikrum described the first attacks on the Camelguts. Of the four Vipers, he was the only one unmarked by the day. Orlana's, Sajiv's, and Yoru's faces glistened

with burn salve. They still wore the clothes that Evvy ha
decorated with burn holes.

"An exciting day," remarked the lady when Ikrum fir
ished. "I hope that my other Vipers continue to harry th
Camelguts."

Ikrum bobbed his head. "Just as my lady ordered, cu
ting them out of the pack and giving them glory wit
these." He stroked the blackjack thrust into his sash. "W
haven't talked to them yet about joining, though."

"You must judge when the time is right to make an of
fer," the lady replied. "With only a few down, they are mo
likely of a mind to fight. They will have to take more casu
alties before they will see where their best interests li
Now, these two." She pointed to Orlana and Yoru. "Yo
will find the girl-child Evvy again. Follow her — do not tr
to take her now. In due time, we shall find a way to mak
her eager to join us. You two and Ikrum have my leave t
go. Sajiv, I desire a private word."

Ikrum, getting up, glared jealously at the still-kneelin
Sajiv. His mouth worked briefly as he considered a protes
Something in the lady's face, a trace of iron in her dark eye
made him change his mind. Instead he bowed and followe
Orlana and Yoru out.

Once they were gone, the lady sat up on her couch, rest
ing her sandaled feet on the courtyard tiles. "Sajiv," sh
murmured, her voice soft and musical. "How you have dis

appointed me! Two errors in as many days — am I supposed to accept this?"

His forehead still pressed to the tiles, Sajiv muttered, "Not my fault."

"But surely you can see that it is hard to assign blame elsewhere," she said reasonably. "First you allow your nose ring, which I gave to you, to be taken by three mere *thukdaks*. Then you and two others who have never disappointed me fail to capture a girl I wish to meet. Do you see where I might be forced to wonder at your contribution?"

Sajiv forgot himself and glared up at her. "The astrologer said this week was not a good one for me."

The lady clenched her hands. "Do not talk to me of astrologers!" she said sharply. "Only dirt-people who will be useless all their lives heed their babble. It serves as an excuse to avoid trying to better oneself, and I have no patience with it!"

Sajiv sat up on his knees, pale with rage. "Toss you and toss your patience!" he snarled. "You with your airs and jewels, telling us how to be a gang when you was never bound in your life!" He thrust out his right arm, pointing to a pair of deep puncture scars through the back of his hand and his palm. "I paid in blood to be a Viper — you *never* paid, you never will! We're your festering toy whilst your own kids chase gold and power for themselves! You got Ikrum believing you'll make us kings of Chammur, but you don't fool me, and you don't fool some of the others!"

The lady folded her hands in her lap, listening as closely as a student might listen to a favorite teacher. When Sajiv stopped for breath, panting, she undid the veil over the lower half of her face. The smile on her lips was thin and icy. "I see the inner truth of what you fumble to say," she told Sajiv. "You present me with a situation I must remedy, and carefully. A generous person would give you a fresh chance, to err a new." She raised her hand. "Or perhaps it is only a weak person who would do so."

Sajiv had no sense that someone had come up behind him until the silk cord dropped over his head and around his neck. He barely had the chance to gasp before the tall, hairless, fat man at his back yanked it tight. Thick muscles flexed under dark brown skin as the eunuch applied his strength; the cord bit deep, closing off the youth's windpipe. Sajiv weakened slowly, his burn-marked face passing from scarlet to blue to purple. His bowels let go at the end, filling the air with stench as their contents dripped through his trousers.

Through it all the lady sat gravely, unveiled, her eyes solemn. She did not even wrinkle her nose at the smell. When the eunuch let the boy's corpse drop to the tiles, she stood. "Dispose of that," she ordered. "Have these tiles taken up and new ones laid down. A different color would be nice — red, I think."

The man bowed to her. The traders who had made him a eunuch had also cut out his tongue, to get a higher price from wealthy people with secrets.

The lady patted his shoulder as if he were a dog. "You did well. Wash yourself before you enter my presence again." She walked into the house.

Evvy surprised Briar when she arrived in the morning. Not only was she clean from top to toe, but she had found another garment somewhere. It looked as if it had once been a well made linen shift: it had no sleeves, and there were tiny holes where thread would have held lace on the garment. It may have been white at one time, before too many washings in hard water with bad or no soap had turned it gray.

"Better?" Evvy demanded, glaring up into his face. She was bareheaded, her clean black hair sticking out at all angles. Briar suspected that she cut it herself, with a knife and no mirror.

"It's a start," he said, and drew her into the house. He pointed to the dining room table. Despite having only four hours' sleep after his late return from the Camelgut lair — two more victims had come as he'd been about to leave — Briar rose an hour after dawn. He'd gone to the local *souk* for secondhand clothes. They lay neatly folded on the table, beside a pair of sandals he'd guessed would fit her. "Go try that stuff on." He indicated the little pantry. "If you hurry, you can eat when you come out."

Evvy, about to protest, noticed a steaming teapot as well as figs, dates, bread, cheese, and honey on the sideboard. She snatched up the clothes and dashed into the pantry, closing the door behind her.

"Don't eat anything in there!" Briar called. Perhaps he should have asked her to change in a room where there were no jellies, preserved fruits and vegetables, onions, loaves of bread, and cheeses on the shelves.

"I'm not!" she yelled back.

She was back shortly, dressed in a clean, faded, pink cotton tunic that fit her perfectly, and beige leggings that were a bit too large. Briar blessed Sandry, Daja, and Tris, who had taught him about female clothing whether he wanted the lessons or not. When he saw that Evvy struggled to tie the pink and lavender headscarf properly, Briar took over, making sure her dreadful haircut was covered before he twisted the sides and tied the scarf in a proper Janaal knot in back. The scarf, being cotton, understood what he wanted. It settled easily into a snug grip on the girl's head.

The minute he finished, Evvy grabbed some food. "Sit," Briar ordered her. Evvy obeyed, figs in one hand, a piece of cheese in the other, and a slice of bread half in her mouth. Briar sighed. "We use plates," he informed her, putting one in front of her. "And cups, and knives."

He filled her cup with tea. He set out a knife for the

bread and a spoon for the honey, then moved the remaining food to the table. When she put the fruit, cheese, and the remainder of her bread on the plate, Briar looked at that neat layer of pink cloth over her bony chest and realized he'd forgotten something important. Before she could protest, he had a linen napkin tucked firmly into the tunic.

"You'll spill," he said firmly when she squeaked. "I'd as soon you didn't do it on clean clothes, if it's all the same."

A stifled noise from the hall made him turn. Rosethorn, leaving for her next farmers' meeting, leaned against the door's frame. Her face was crimson from the effort it took to hold in sounds; she had stuffed her arm into her mouth to smother them. When he glared at her, she uncorked her mouth and straightened her sleeve.

"What's so funny?" Briar demanded crossly.

"You," Rosethorn said, snorting. "Teaching table manners. *You!*" She gasped and said, "Please — don't let me interrupt! I'll see you tonight!" Cackling, she left the house.

"Who was that?" Evvy asked through a bite of fig.

"Don't talk with your mouth full," Briar ordered as he picked up a sandal. "Left foot."

She thrust out the required bare foot, already coated with grime from the street. Briar dusted it with his handkerchief, making her giggle. He then slid the sandal on and tightened the laces to see if it fit. It was large, but he'd chosen ones that would stay on if tightly laced. He did that briskly, then commanded, "Right foot."

Evvy dropped her newly shod foot and let Briar take the bare one. "Where are we going?" she asked as he dusted the worst of the street dirt away. "Why I have to be shop-keeper-neat when I'm no shopkeeper's get? Why are *you* all prettied up?"

Briar glanced at his own clothes. Knowing servants and nobles judged people by their looks, he'd worn a clean white cotton shirt, full-legged brown linen trousers tied with a golden brown sash, and a green silk overrobe with an em-broidered design of colorful autumn leaves. The robe was his favorite of the things Sandry had made him. He'd even polished his boots. "Because the only other stone mage in the city lives in the *amir*'s palace," he explained as he se-cured her right sandal. "They won't let us through the gates if we look like we did yesterday." They would have admitted him — he'd worn good clothes for the trip that had ended at the Market of the Lost — but he included himself to spare her feelings.

Evvy had been enjoying the sight of this elegantly clad young man waiting on the likes of her almost as much as she did the food she was stuffing into her face. Now she jerked her foot out of his hold. "Palace?"

Briar sighed. "The mage who is to teach you is Jebilu Stoneslicer. He lives in the *amir*'s palace. We'd never see him if we dressed like street people."

Had he been bitten by a foam-mouthed rat last night, to

come up with such a skewy idea? She folded her arms over her chest. This had to be stepped on fast. "No."

Briar frowned up at her. "What do you mean, 'no'?"

"I won't go there and you can't make me."

Briar scowled. "You have to be taught," he told her. "Even you know that now."

Evvy shook her head, her chin thrust forward stubbornly. She might not know much, but she knew this: palaces and the people in them were a cobra's kiss for any *thukdak*. Yes, all right, she had to be schooled, but not by some palace *takamer*. "Why can't *you* teach me?" she demanded. "You're a *pahan*."

"Absolutely not!" snapped Briar. "I'm a plant mage, not a stone mage. You need to learn from a *stone* mage."

"Not one that lives in a palace," she replied flatly. "I —"

"*Pahan* Briar! *Pahan!*" Someone pounded on the door.

Briar scowled at Evvy once more and went to see who had come. The visitor, a small, monkey-faced girl of fifteen years or so, wore the green sash of the Camelguts. This one, Douna, had assisted him late the night before. "What do you want, Douna?" asked Briar.

"*Pahan* Briar, you have to come," the older girl said, bracing her hands on her knees as she caught her breath. "They got five more with their blackjacks — we didn't even find 'em till this morning. They're a mess."

"Can't you get a *real* healer?" Briar demanded, feeling

pulled in two by Evvy and the Camelguts. "I just make medicines!"

The look in Douna's small brown eyes made him ashamed that he'd asked. What could a poor gang offer a healer to make it worth the risk to visit them? Even if they had enough coin for one of the locals, what kind of healing could they get? Up until he reached Winding Circle, Briar himself would have found the idea of getting a healer for his gang's wounds hilarious. Street kids, whether they were called rats or *thukdaks*, learned to fend for themselves.

"Sit," he ordered Douna, pushing her toward the table. He pulled off his overrobe and folded it neatly, putting it on the sideboard. "Have some tea and something to eat. I'll need to get some things. Evvy, grab that basket and come with me." They'd have to argue about her schooling later. Right now he would use the healer's trick of putting every idle pair of hands to work.

Evvy stuffed the rest of a large slice of cheese into her mouth and grabbed the basket he'd pointed to. He led her upstairs to the workroom. It wasn't as elaborate as the one at home at Winding Circle, but there were still plenty of lotions, balms, teas, and syrups, some of them his, some Rosethorn's. He'd replenished his kit the night before out of habit, but he would need as much extra as he and Evvy could carry. He fully subscribed to Rosethorn's belief: sometimes thinking ahead was just as good as magic.

Quickly Briar filled small jars from the large ones, wrote

down contents on the corks that stopped the jars, and tucked them into Evvy's basket. Next he stopped at the linen chest and cushioned the jars with pads which could be made into bandages. From the roof he fetched a number of thin, flat boards used for gardening: they made good splints. Another length of bandage was converted into a sling for the boards, which he hung on his own back.

"What's all this for? And why are you letting some Camelgut order you around?" Evvy wanted to know.

"Because I can help and they won't get anyone who can help better," retorted Briar, trying to think if he'd missed anything. Suddenly he noticed a flaw in his plan to put Evvy to use. "What gang are you with?" he asked. Some gangs had treaties, allowing members to cross territories. If her gang had a treaty with the Camelguts . . .

She interrupted his thoughts with her abrupt reply. "I'm not in a gang."

Briar made a face. "Evvy, this is serious."

"So am I," she insisted. "I didn't belong, I don't belong, and I'll never belong."

"Because if the Camelguts are at war with your gang," he began.

"Is 'I'm not in a gang' just too big an idea for you?" she cried.

Briar shook his head. He'd get the truth out of her later. Right now he needed an extra pair of hands. Not only had Evvy shown she was inclined to obey him — within

5

The Camelgut den was in chaos. Gang members lay on pallets as others tended them. Apparently there had been fights throughout the night. Very few Camelguts sported no bruises at all, and there were eight fresh victims, not five.

Briar took a deep breath. For some reason he remembered a talk he'd had during one of Summersea's medical crises, one of the many times he'd been pressed into work with the sick. "Why do they obey you?" he'd asked the woman as those who were well enough to work carried out her orders.

"It's no mystery," she'd said then. "I act as if they should. And they're frightened enough to turn instinctively even to those who only know a bit more than they do."

Act as if they should obey, Briar thought now. And they did send for me again, after all. They must trust me *some*. He turned to Douna. "Get that pot filled with water and put it on to boil," he ordered. "Evvy, stick close to me."

"Oh, I will," she muttered, watching the Camelgut from the corners of her eyes.

Briar unslung the staves from his back and leaned then against the wall. Then he scratched his head and consid ered the room. Since his arrival at Winding Circle, he ha worked in sickrooms in three epidemics and a border wa but he'd always been under the guidance of Rosethorn an experienced healers. What would they do?

First straighten out the mess, Rosethorn's voice said is his mind. *You won't be able to find your ankles with both hands and a lamp otherwise.*

"Here's how we start," he called loudly. All conversa tions stopped. Even those who were moaning fell silent *Urda save me*, Briar thought, *they are actually* listening! He didn't try to savor the moment, but rattled off instructions He'd already found with Evvy that if he didn't give her time to argue, she wouldn't. He put that knowledge to use with the Camelguts, ordering some to move the pallets into rows and others to clear away the mess of jars, rags, crates, and barrels that littered the floor.

"Why are the doors and windows covered?" he asked one of the Camelguts.

The boy, who was about Briar's age, shrugged. "We got tired of local kids peeking at us all the time."

"But it's not that this is a secret place?" Briar wanted to know. The Camelgut shook his head. "Then uncover them," Briar ordered. "Let's get some light and air in here."

The Camelgut pulled aside the rags that covered the windows and doors and secured them: now some light and fresh air entered the room. A group of three was sent with jars and handfuls of sand to fountains, where they had orders to scour the jars with sand, fill them with water, and bring them back. The fire was built up and trash taken outside. Even with the windows uncovered, the den was still shadowy. Two Camelgut boys made rough torches and thrust them into holders on the walls.

As the gang members cleaned up, Briar inspected each victim. Those whose bruises and cuts didn't look serious were ordered to clean up or sit on a bench against the wall. Dealing with the less seriously hurt was easy for Briar — growing up in the slums of Hajra, he'd learned about all kinds of injuries and wounds, including the ones that might eventually kill someone. In Summersea's epidemics he had seen how the healers sorted groups of the sick, treating the worst off first. He found those now, and got to work.

Briar could do little for the boy whose forehead was visibly dented, except make him comfortable. Sometimes people recovered from such injuries; sometimes they didn't. He moved on to another boy, squinting as he tried to see the extent of his injuries. The nearest torch burned poorly, dumping smoke into the air. Briar's eyes stung. It was hard to tell if he was looking at a mammoth bruise or dirt on his patient's shin. His hands told him it was a bruise, but it would have been nice to *see* the difference.

That gave him an idea. "Evvy," he said.

"Yep." The girl crouched beside him, careful not to jar the contents of the basket she carried.

"Put that down." She obeyed as Briar grubbed in his breeches pocket. He found his worry stone, a small crystal egg he liked to hold whenever he thought he was about to say or do anything stupid. Its coolness seemed to draw the anger from his veins whenever he remembered to use it. Rosethorn said it worked because thinking of the stone instead of the thing that upset him simply broke the chain that fed a rising temper.

He wasn't angry now, and he could always come by another worry stone. "See this?" He held it up.

"Ooh." She reached for it with eager fingers. "It's *happy*."

Briar rolled his eyes. Why did girls get honey-sweet over things that weren't even alive? Sandry would coo like that over a spool of silk thread, Daja over a piece of well worked brass. Even Tris, who was sensible for a skirt, turned silly over a bit of ball lightning, giving the thing a name for as long as it lasted. "I don't care if it's the Queen of the Solstice," he informed Evvy tartly. "But look, it's a clear stone, you're a stone mage, right?" He fumbled for the words to guide her to do her first planned magic spell. "I bet if you really, really concentrated, just, oh, poured your whole mind into that stone? I bet if you did, you could make it light up like a lamp. A real lamp, one everybody can see."

"Oh, that," Evvy said scornfully. "That's not *work*." She gripped the crystal. Suddenly light blazed through her fingers. She opened her hand. The stone gave off a bright, steady glow.

Briar swallowed. Of his foster-sisters, Daja and Tris had learned to make crystals into lamps, Daja because fire was part of her smith-magic, Tris because lightning was part of hers. They had done it once by accident, making a night light for Sandry. After that it took each of them weeks to get the knack of it so they could do it as they needed. No one he'd known could make stone glow with no effort at all. He'd thought it would be possible, given Evvy's magic and the fact that he'd already known mages who could get stones to hold light or fire, but it was one thing to think it possible and another to see the results of "Oh, that."

"Is it hot?" he asked.

"Nope." Evvy put the stone beside the boy they were supposed to be treating.

Reminded of his patient, Briar went over him again. The leg bruise shrank under his bruise ointment, but Briar could feel a bone chip that remained under the boy's skin. Cutbane, spread neatly over the splits in his left eyebrow and cheek, drove off infection and worked to close the wounds. Next Briar put an uninjured Camelgut to work cutting the wooden staves to a proper length for splints. As he straightened the arm, Briar said to Evvy, "I thought you never used magic before yesterday."

"I didn't," Evvy said, watching him with interest.

The boy who'd cut the splints gave them to Briar. "How'd you make my stone light, if you never did magic before?" Briar asked as he splinted the broken forearm.

"I knew I could when I went home," she pointed out. "Doesn't that hurt him?"

"That's why it's nice for us that he's passed out. Elsewise they'd hear him yelling at the Aliput Gate." Finished, Briar gathered the crystal and the remaining bandage and knee-crawled to the next pallet. This patient was a girl with a shattered kneecap and a broken collarbone. "So you knew you could do magic when you got home, and —?"

"I have rocks. Some came with the place, and some I brung there. For pretty, you know?" Evvy put down her basket. "And I remembered how the junk stones I threw at the Vipers lit up, so I thought I'd try and see what stones would light for me. Some of them did. Some just got hot, though. Do you need me to make something hot?"

Briar sat back to think. He'd ordered the Camelguts to put their blankets over the injured, but what good were blankets that were mainly rags? He'd thought to ask his helpers to fill gourds with hot water to put in the beds, but stones would keep heat in longer.

"Can you make sure the heat won't burn folk?" he asked.

Evvy scratched her head. "I can *try*," she said at last.

"Do it," ordered Briar.

"I need different rocks," she pointed out.

"Don't stand there telling me about it. Sooner before later, all right?" he asked. He was taking a chance that her magic wouldn't spill out of control, but he'd seen her slip just enough power into his stone. Was it because she was used to thinking of a rock as an enclosed thing? "Do you need help?" he wanted to know.

Evvy shrugged. "I don't think so." She trotted out of the Camelgut den.

So far she hadn't once questioned his right to give her orders. Later, when he had this mess straightened out, he would have to find out why.

Briar continued to work on the injured with the Camelguts' help. When he saw he would run out of bandages soon, he instructed his assistants to dump rags into a pot of water and set it to boiling. Of the boiled water in the pot he'd fetched from home, part went for washing, part to willowbark tea, to ease the aches of injuries.

The boy with the dent in his head died by the time Briar had examined the worst hurt and had come to look at him again. Briar did a second check of the others on pallets, then got to work on the less seriously hurt. He wished for Rosethorn over and over — a second pair of experienced hands would have been nice — but knew he could manage if he just kept after things, provided the gang members continued to obey. Besides, Rosethorn was disheartened enough by the exhausted farmlands of Chammur.

*   *   *

The nice thing about Chammur, Evvy thought as she returned to the Camelgut den swinging her loaded bucket, was that it was easy to find plenty of rocks, even one particular kind of rock. Rather than work on them in the Camelgut den, with its noise and smells, she had found a rooftop where she could do as Briar had asked. It was much harder than calling light to his beautiful crystal. The core of noncrystal stones didn't like warmth. They hadn't felt warm in ages of time, and didn't see why she wanted to put it into them now. Her results were spotty, heat flickering in some of the bigger stones, but it was the best she could do. Her head was aching by the time she was done.

Briar was sewing a deep gash in a boy's forearm when Evvy reached him. When he finished bandaging the work, he inspected Evvy's creations.

She watched him anxiously. "It's not like light," she grumbled, hunching one shoulder in case he decided to hit her. "I can't do it so good. They'll stop being warm after a while, and they aren't at all steady."

"But these are lots better than gourds filled with hot water," Briar said absently, turning the stone over in his hand. "This helps, Evvy. Thanks."

A knot formed in her throat as he took the bucket from her. She watched him, blinking eyes that burned and trying to swallow that knot, as he tucked her stones into the blankets of those who needed to be warm. He'd said she helped. He'd *thanked* her.

As he placed the last of the stones he glanced at her slyly. "They don't work steadily because you don't have your power under control all the way. Jebilu Stoneslicer will teach you to get rocks to hold warmth longer, and steadier."

"He can teach, but I won't learn, not up at the palace," Evvy retorted.

Briar stood and faced her, hands on hips. "What is it with you?" he demanded. He kept his voice low, but he leaned in so Evvy heard every word. "Even you know you have to be taught now! He's the only stone mage in this whole, imp-blest, festering city!"

Evvy shrank away from him. Even if he hit her, she was going to speak her mind. "If I show myself at the palace, they'll, they'll toss me in the cells of Justice Rock for not knowing my place," she stammered. She went giddy with horror as her traitor mouth ran on. "Or they'd sell me. I've been sold once already—I won't be sold again!" She dropped the bucket and covered her face. How could she have said that? She'd told no one that before!

When he said nothing, she peeped at him through her fingers. Whatever she'd expected him to do or feel, it wasn't what she saw on his face now. What she saw looked like sorrow. Not pity—sorrow. "You're a slave?" he asked softly.

"I ran away," she mumbled. She didn't want the Camelguts to hear this. The reward for an escaped slave would tempt them; she knew that it would.

"And the collar?" he inquired, his voice softer yet. "How'd you get rid of it?"

Evvy lowered her hands. "I broke it with a rock."

Briar smiled thinly.

She guessed what he was thinking: more rock magic. "I thought it was a cheap collar," she explained, almost smiling. "You don't need a lot of iron to hold a scrawny piece of crowbait like me." It was her old master's favorite term for her. "You mean I had it" — she touched the corner of her eye in a sign that meant "magic" in Chammur — "even then?"

He walked over to a Camelgut girl who'd been seated, waiting for him. "You're born with magic," he explained. "It just gets frustrated if you get older and you don't do anything real with it, so it breaks out."

"Why can't you teach me?" she asked as he began to wash the sores on the girl's leg. "I already know you, and you know the rules and things." What she didn't, couldn't, say was that she was comfortable around him. For all his pushiness and foreign-ness, she still felt as if she'd known him all her life. He was quick and inventive, as she'd learned to be, living on her own. She might vex and puzzle him, but never once had she seen pity in his eyes, even when she'd let slip that she'd been a slave. Never once had he treated her as a child, a female, or even a *thukdak*.

"I'm not a stone mage," he said wearily. "It's important

that you get someone to teach you stone magic." To the girl whose leg he cleaned he said, "You can't scratch fleabites open like this — they get infected. Or if you do, wash the scratches out right off, with clean water — that means it's been boiled. And soap if you have it."

"Oh, sure, *pahan*," she retorted with a quick smile. "I left some under my pillow just the other day."

Briar returned her smile, looking the rest of her over while he held onto her foot. Evvy smiled crookedly. So even *pahans* weren't immune to the hug-and-kiss madness that swamped older girls and boys.

"Tell you what," Briar said to the girl. "You know the aloe leaves they sell in the market?" The girl nodded, and tried to tickle the inside of his arm with her toes. "Behave, or I'll put something that bites on these." The Camelgut girl pouted at him prettily. Evvy sighed and shifted her weight from one foot to another. He was spending more time on swollen fleabites than he did on broken arms. "Steal some aloe leaves," Briar suggested, "and when you itch, break a piece off and rub the juice on the itch. It's good for burns, too." Carefully he smoothed a salve over the sores and put a light bandage over them.

"Thanks, *pahan*," she said with another quick, sidelong glance from under curling lashes. "I'm Ayasha — if you have any more wisdom to share." She got up and walked over to a group of Camelguts huddled in a corner.

Briar looked at Evvy, who was shaking her head. "What?" he demanded.

"You want a cloth to wipe the drool off your chin?" Evvy asked wickedly.

Briefly he looked the way she felt sometimes about her old home in Yanjing, lost and lonely. Then he shed the sad look and said tartly, "Keep making sour faces and you'll need spectacles. It happened to one of my mates, it can happen to you."

"What? You aren't old enough for one wife, let alone more," Evvy objected as she followed him to the pallets.

"Not my wife, my *mate*," he said, blotting sweat from a sleeping boy's face. "It's a word we used at home, for somebody that's closer than blood family, your best friend. Don't you have mates?"

"The cats," Evvy said. "Not people, though. I keep to myself."

"Don't keep saying you aren't ganged up," Briar replied, his face mulish. He rubbed one of his salves on the sleeping boy's arm, above and below the splint. "I lived in a place a lot like Oldtown for years. All the kids were ganged up, unless they were crippled or simple. And you aren't crippled, though sometimes I wonder about the simple part."

"I'm no fool," Evvy retorted softly, to keep from catching any Camelgut's attention. How could someone as clever as he was not understand? Unless he told the truth, and he *had* belonged to a gang.

No, that was too outlandish. Old gang kids worked in inns, or peddled rags, or labored on farms or on buildings. They never became clean, well dressed anything. "Gangers always want this, and that, and some other thing. They're your friend, and why can't you help, and you'd be safer with us, and then they try to show you what you'd be safe from. Cats don't want anything from me, though it's nice if I feed them. I like that."

Briar frowned at her. "The Vipers wouldn't've grabbed you if you had a gang," he pointed out.

"No, the other gang would have grabbed me first. Grabbing's rude no matter who does it," she retorted. "Let someone try it on you sometime and see if *you* like it."

They made two more rounds of the room as Briar checked bandages, coaxed people to drink the sharp-scented tea he'd brewed, and gave out more medicines. Evvy watched him, fascinated. For all his fine clothes, he didn't mind handling the sick, as if he'd wiped away sweat, blood, and vomit all his life.

He stopped at last and looked around. "I think we're just about done," he remarked.

Someone in the group of unhurt Camelguts in the corner yelled, "I can't believe you! They killed Hammit! Pilib's dead, now, too!"

Briar frowned. Evvy wondered why. He might be caring for these people, but their squabbles weren't his.

"They'll kill us all," another boy argued. "If they don't,

you *know* Snake Sniffers and Rockheads will move in and pick us off. Look around! Half of us can't even fight!"

"The Vipers have the *takameri* to buy weapons for them," added Douna, the girl who had led Briar and Evvy here. "What's she going to get them next? Axes? Swords?"

A youth added, "If she's paying out that coin, I say she ought to pay it for weapons for us, too."

Evvy was impressed. None of the gang people she knew had the sense to think of things like this. They were too tied up with honor and protecting their ground.

"*They* want us to join and *I* don't want anybody else dying," said a male voice. "Hands. For joining?" Most of the walking Camelguts' hands rose. Other hands were raised as the kids in beds, those who were awake, cast their vote.

"Come on," Briar told Evvy, disgusted. "I'd've fought till the end of time before joining a gang that killed a mate of mine. We're finished here." He waved to those of the gang who looked at him, and led Evvy out into the open air.

She followed, dazed. Was it possible she'd been wrong, that he really *had* belonged to a gang once? That was just the kind of thing she'd expect a gang boy to say.

It was the first time that Ikrum Fazhal had visited Lady Zenadia doa Attaneh's home before sunset, but she had ordered that he was to come the moment there was word on the Camelgut matter. As her expressionless servants admitted him through the tradesmen's gate and led him to the patio and garden where the lady usually saw him, Ikrum wondered what they made of her interest in *thukdaks* like the Vipers. He could tell that they were as much in awe of her as he was, or they would have found their own ways to end his visits.

They left him standing before the couch where she usually sat. They had placed a pitcher of wine, a cup, and a bowl of fruit there for her. Ikrum was not even tempted to help himself. The one time he'd been so bold, he'd discovered that she carried a thin, bladed crop in her expensive draperies. It had left a broad scar across the back of his right hand, right between his Viper initiation scars.

Sometimes he wondered what would have happened if he and some other Vipers hadn't mistaken her for an overpriced prostitute wandering the Grand Bazaar one night. They'd grabbed her and dragged her into a nook between closed stalls, meaning to strip her of her jewels and her silks. Instead they had discovered her shadows, the armsmaster and the mute, and the lady's own tiny dagger, which she laid against the big vein under Ikrum's jaw. He had thought he was dead. Then he had told her, "Cut hard and fast and get it over with," and she began to laugh.

She liked his courage, she had said. She took him to a shop that sold coffee, buying him pastries and cups of that bitter, expensive drink. Her armsmaster and the mute sat

Ikrum's friends on the carpets in front of the shop and kept them from running away.

Terror-sweat poured from his body when he had learned that she was the *amir's* aunt, a lady from one of the great noble houses. He saw his headless corpse and those of his friends dangling from Justice Rock. Instead of calling the Watch, she asked about him and the Vipers.

She asked and listened so well that Ikrum found himself telling her his troubles. He even talked of the slight he had been dealt by the city's richest and most powerful gang, the Gate Lords, who held all the territory between the Grand Bazaar, Golden House, and the Hajra Gate. Ikrum had foolishly fallen in love with the sister of the Gate Lords' *tesku*, or leader. The *tesku* had told Gate Lords and Vipers alike that he would never allow his sister to go with the *tesku* of a pack of glorified errand boys.

"I like you, Ikrum," the lady had said on that vital night. "You are no dirt-person. You have ambition, courage, pride. I will help you." She had left with orders for him to report to her house the next day around sunset.

He had gone, because no one could refuse her. He had expected that she had lied about her address, or that she had been drunk and had forgotten all about him. Neither was true. The mute had taken him to the garden after checking him for weapons. The lady waited for him there, with plans to make the Vipers great.

"I'm bored," she told Ikrum. "My children are grown, my husbands dead. I wish no other husbands or lovers. My grandchildren are tedious. It suits me to help the Vipers to greatness, if they can make the journey. If they can accept discipline. If you cannot —" The lady shrugged. "I will find another way to amuse myself. We begin by giving your people a better sign of fellowship than that rag." She pointed to Ikrum's gray armband. "And we shall make the new token one it requires courage to get."

Ikrum was about to protest. He had killed the last Viper *tesku* for this armband, gray with yellow beads stitched to it. The words were in his mouth when a giant arm circled his neck; a slablike hand pulled his head back. Arm and hand belonged to the mute, who held Ikrum as easily as Ikrum might a kitten.

"Stand still," the lady had remarked sharply. "Will you disappoint me already?"

Ikrum obeyed. The lady's healer moved in to pierce his left nostril and thread the brass ring with its garnet pendant into the opening. Only Ikrum got his piercing and nose ring from a healer. The other Vipers got theirs from Ikrum, who added the ring supplied by the lady and a dab of ointment that both cleaned the hole and stopped its ache.

The lady did not end her interest in the Vipers with presents of jewelry. Time after time the mute came to their den with her gifts: tunics, clean and in good condition, trousers or leggings, skirts, slippers, knives, food, coins for the *hammam*. Clean, wearing better clothes, the Vipers could enter the Grand Bazaar and Golden House in ones and twos, spying out targets for theft and taking them as they left the *souks* at night. Looking more prosperous, they were hired to deliver more messages and packages, which let them scout homes and shops to rob once the residents had forgotten the messenger boy or girl with the nose ring.

He'd thought for weeks she would tire of them eventually, until he realized the opposite was happening. The more reports he brought to her of successful thefts and robberies, of the small enlargements to their territory just south of Golden House, of fights they'd won, the greater her fascination. Her reactions to their setbacks grew more heated, as if disrespect of the Vipers was disrespect of her.

Ikrum sighed now, and scuffed the courtyard tiles with his foot. He was never sure if he was glad the lady had taken them up. The sister of the Gate Lords' *tesku* was still forbidden to him. Viper life was more dangerous. Sometimes the lady frightened him.

And weren't the tiles blue yesterday? Today they were red. Uneasy, he spat on his hand to rid himself of unpleasant ideas, then carefully wiped his palm inside his trouser pockets. The lady did not like it when Vipers spat.

"Ikrum, you are early," she said, walking out into the sun. "I hope you have no disasters to report." She sat on her couch gracefully, veils floating cloudlike around her. Her skirts, sari, and head veil were dull gold today, her short blouse a pale orange. Ikrum went to his knees, then lowered his forehead until he was a hair above the red tiles. For some reason he didn't want them touching his face.

From here he could see that gilt designs were pressed into the leather of her slippers. A heavy gold ring cupped one of her ankles. She wore bracelets, too, heavy earrings, and a chain hung with canary diamonds between her nose and left ear. Why did she care about their thefts, when she wore more jewels than they might ever steal?

She reminded him of a goddess's golden statue — not Lailan of the Rivers and Rain, who was draped in blue and green and whose kindness shone form her face, but some *eknub* goddess, some distant queen of the skies. How could he worship and hate her at the same time? Ikrum wondered feverishly. Was it possible to feel two different emotions for someone? Fear and hate he knew, or he'd thought he'd known them before meeting her. But worship, admiration . . . Orlana accused him of being in love with the lady, but the thought made his skin creep. He wondered if her husbands — she'd had two — had died of natural causes. His private nightmare was that she had bitten their heads off while embracing them.

She left him with his forehead to the ground, waiting

for her maid to arrange the cushions at her back and to pour her a cup of wine. Once the maid had crossed the garden to a point where she could see if her mistress wanted her but could not hear, the lady ordered, "Report."

"The Camelguts have accepted our offer to join us," Ikrum said without looking up. "There are twenty-four of them altogether."

"You told me they had twenty-six." The lady put a slippered toe against his chin as a signal for him to look up.

"One died last night and one this morning, lady," Ikrum replied, meeting her gaze. Thick lines of kohl accented her eyes, making them deeper and more mysterious than ever. Through her sheer veil he saw her mouth curl with derision.

"Would you agree to join a gang that had killed one of *your* people?" she asked, after a sip of wine.

Ikrum knew what he would do, but he also knew what she wanted to hear. She would not be pleased if he told her he would run hard and fast. "I would never join such a gang, Lady," he lied.

"Yours is a warrior's heart, Ikrum Fazhal," she told him, setting her cup down. "We will accept these people, of course. We *did* make the offer. But they must earn our respect." She raised her hand. The mute walked out of the shadows by the house with a small leather pouch. He placed it before the lady and backed away again.

Ikrum's heart raced the moment the mute's huge body

entered his vision. He had not even known the huge man was there until he saw him: he was that soundless in his movements. If the mute ever intended to hurt him, in all likelihood Ikrum would not even know until he was dead.

The lady dug in the pouch until she could tease something out. She held it up on a hennaed fingertip: the nose ring was silver wire, the pendant garnet. "For your new members." She thrust it into the pouch and fished out a second nose ring. "For the original Vipers." It looked nearly the same as Ikrum's. The metal was a little more yellow. "You have proved your characters to be gold," the lady said with a smile.

She offered the gold ring with its garnet to Ikrum. He accepted it, but knew better than to change rings in her presence. Yoru had gotten three lashes from the armsmaster for blowing his nose in front of the lady.

"To further show generosity, I will send my healer to tend those new Vipers who are hurt," the lady said. "They will see there are advantages to their new allegiance."

Ikrum cleared his throat. "Actually, um, Lady, they're seen to. The *eknub pahan*, the one we talked to at Golden House — he brought medicine and cared for the ones that are hurt. Seems the Camel—" Her dark eyes flashed, and Ikrum backed up. "The new Vipers, they know him. He lives beside the *eknub* Earth temple, down the street in their territory."

"Now *your* territory," she reminded him.

Ikrum, who wasn't sure how to protect one territory near Golden House and one east of the Karang Gate, only said, "Yes, Lady."

"Well!" she said after a moment's thought. "If they chose to summon an *eknub* apothecary to muddle their wounded about, they don't deserve my healer." In a lesser woman her tone would have sounded peeved. "What of the girl, the one who gave three of you that unpleasant surprise yesterday? Have your Vipers found her again?"

Ikrum actually backed up an inch before he made himself stop. "She was with him," he said. "With the *eknub pahan*, helping him. She warmed stones to put in the beds of those that were hurt, and she did this. They left it behind." He fished a small, egg-shaped stone from his sash and offered it to her. Its cool white light silvered his brown palm and the lady's features as she leaned forward to give it a closer look.

"Well, well." She touched the stone lamp with a fingernail, then picked it up. "For one who had no magic two days ago, she learns quickly."

"The Ca — the new Vipers said she wants him to teach her," Ikrum explained. "And she said she wouldn't learn from *Pahan* Stoneslicer up to the *amir's* palace."

"Two days ago she fled him. Now she helps him to dab potions on our former enemies, and does magic for him, and argues familiarly with him." The lady hummed tonelessly to herself, as she often did when she thought. At last she regarded Ikrum once more. "Very well. Watch her carefully, but watch only for now." She drummed her fingers on her couch. "Since our numbers have grown, I would like to make plans for the Gate Lords. Our new members may prove their loyalty in battle."

"Lady, taking on the Gate Lords would be —" He started to say "foolish," and remembered who he spoke to just in time. "We can't trust the Camel —"

"The new Vipers," the lady interrupted. "I did not say to take the Gate Lords on immediately. I will hear your plan for it, however, in three days' time. You may go, Ikrum. Don't forget the badges for our Vipers."

Ikrum tucked the pouch full of nose rings into his sash. He was taking a chance, he knew, but he had to ask. "Lady — Sajiv never returned to the den last night."

She rolled the light-stone around the hollow of her palm. "The world is full of lesser people, Ikrum. By their errors and follies they drag the better ones, the true-hearted ones, down. When you find someone who is small in that way, it is needful to set him aside, before his taint of failure spreads. I do not like failure, Ikrum." She raised her dark eyes from the stone until they caught and held his.

He bowed low, his mouth paper-dry. She had as good as told him Sajiv was dead. "Yes, Lady."

"Here." She offered him a large silver coin. "Your Vipers

6

After leaving the Camelgut den, Briar wondered what to do next. It was nearly midday. They were filthy, smeared with dirt, blood, and less pleasant things. If they presented themselves at the palace — if Briar could even talk Evvy out of her refusal to go there, which he now doubted — the guards would laugh them off Fortress Rock.

"We need the *hammam*," he told Evvy. "More clothes for you, since we don't have decent clean things for you to put on while those are washed —"

He was talking to the air. Evvy had come to a full stop some yards back. She glared at him, thin arms crossed defensively over her chest.

"*Now* what?" cried Briar in desperation. "Can't we get through so much as a whole hour without an argument from you?"

"I'm not stealing for you and I'm not laying on my back for you, so don't think for a moment because you're spending money on me —"

"I like them prettier, fatter, and *older*," snapped Briar. He was privately ashamed that he hadn't guessed she might think this. In her world, his old world, nobody gave anything for free. "And I used to be a better thief than you, too. Jebilu will pay me back."

"I *told* you, I'm not —"

"Going to the palace," Briar said, overriding her. "I didn't forget. We'll try to find a place where he'll come to meet you. Then arrange whatever you like with him. All right? Are you happy? Can we finish this and get baths?"

Evvy glared at him, but she caught up and stayed in step with him all the way to the nearby *souk*. Luckily he'd brought extra cash in case he had to bribe the *amir's* guards. When Evvy couldn't decide between an orange tunic and a lavender one, Briar took both — they were secondhand, after all, and cheap. She ought to have more than one set of good clothes. They also found a black pair of loose trousers and a brown skirt that would fit her. Briar paid for everything, then held the clean and dirty clothes while Evvy slipped behind a curtain to change.

"She ought to have another headcloth or two," the woman who sold the clothes said idly, as if she didn't care if she earned a few *davs* more. "And a petticoat. She doesn't have loincloths, either. I couldn't help but notice."

Briar looked at her, his mouth curled wryly. "And you just happen to have them."

"Special price," the woman assured him. "Since you're getting several items."

She did finally sell the extra clothes for a lower price than she'd first asked. That was because Briar had learned to dicker from Tris, who knew how to turn a bargain. Even Daja, who was born a Trader, let Tris handle the money when they shopped.

Homesickness. Back in the spring, when Rosethorn had suggested a trip east, with new plants and new uses for them, he had jumped at it. Living in a cottage with three girls and two women, closer to the girls than even a normal boy because they were all in each other's minds, he couldn't wait to get away. The idea of months without Sandry drafting him as a dressmaker's dummy, or Daja going on at table over a new way to work metal, or Tris's swings between lost-in-a-book oblivion and maturing-crosspatch, brought him out of Winding Circle in a flash. He hadn't even minded saying goodbye to Lark. Sometimes Lark was a little too understanding, not to mention indecently aware of the thoughts that went through a growing boy's mind when a pretty novice smiled at him. Rosethorn was uninterested in Briar's changing view of girls who were not his housemates, and her own temper made it impossible for her to be too understanding, ever.

It was only after they'd been gone a week that Briar realized he was listening for the girls' voices, and wondering what they were up to. It was harder to find good books without Tris, harder to get a good round of quarterstaff practice without Daja, and pouring his troubles into Rosethorn's ears wasn't as soothing as it was with Sandry. Sandry would listen solemnly, and sympathize, and tell him how wonderful he was. Briar knew better than to even suggest that Rosethorn treat him that way. He liked his nose — girls admired it. He didn't want to give Rosethorn an excuse to bite it off.

The merchant woman took a loincloth and a headcloth behind the curtain. Soon afterward she emerged with Evvy. The girl was neatly dressed in the orange tunic and black trousers; a brown and orange headcloth covering her ragged hair. "I don't see why you bother," she grumbled.

"Because someone did it for me, four years ago. He's always got more clothes than he needs, so he said I'd waste my time giving him more. He told me just do the same for someone else," Briar said. He thrust the hemp bag with the other new clothes at her. "You get to carry 'em, though." He bundled the dirty things under one arm and marched out of the stall before she asked other uncomfortable questions. He wasn't really sure why he was doing so much for her, though what he'd said about Niko, the mage who had clothed him and brought him to Winding Circle, was true. It certainly wasn't as if he liked this rude, impudent brat.

High overhead they could hear the toll of the Karang Gate clock. It was the third hour after noon. "Time and past to eat something," he said as his stomach rumbled. Evvy's eyes brightened at the prospect of a meal.

He followed his nose to a food vendor, where they bought steamed lamb and baked mushroom-onion dumplings. Steamed quinces with walnut and honey stuffing were next. Both of them were pleasantly full when they washed their hands at a fountain and headed back to Briar's.

"How long have you been on the street?" Briar asked.

Evvy yawned. "I was six when we left Yanjing. That was the Year of the Crow," she said. "And this is the year of the Turtle." She calculated on her fingers. "Four years. Maybe nearer three. They sold me when we got here, and I escaped two moons before the Year of the Cat began."

"Who sold you?" Briar asked, before he thought he might not like the answer.

"My parents," Evvy said. "It cost plenty to come west. I was only a girl and the youngest. I ate food my brothers and parents needed. I took up space in the cart, and I couldn't do anything to bring in money." She rattled off the reasons, as if she could recite them in her sleep. "Girls are pretty worthless, even here. They only got two silver *davs* for me. I saw a boy my age get sold for twice that."

Briar looked down. Despite her matter-of-fact answer, he felt as if he should apologize — not for the question, perhaps, but because that had been her life. Kids came to the street for many reasons, as he knew too well, but at least his mother had kept him, fed him, and loved him until she was killed on a dark street for her cheap jewelry.

Evvy suddenly laughed. "I'll find them someday and show them what slipped through their fingers!" she told Briar. "Even a *girl* is worth something if she's a *pahan*!"

He'd grinned, too, until the second part of her argument sunk in. "Girl mages are worth every bit as much as boy mages," he informed her. "Believe me — I've been surrounded by them for four long years, and never for a moment did they let me forget it."

"How did you get to be a *pahan*?" she asked, curious. "Did you always know?"

Briar shook his head. "I was on the street after my ma was killed. I was four," he explained. "If she'd had magic, we'd have lived better than we did. She wouldn't have been out late the night she got killed, for certain. Anyway, the landlord tossed me. I was on my own a while, till the Thief-Lord picked me up and brought me into the Lightnings. That was our gang." Evvy nodded. "First I learned to pick pockets, because I had the good hands for it. Then they taught me climbing, and thieving inside. The third time we were caught, I was maybe ten. You know the law."

Evvy made a face. "Third arrest, hard labor for life."

It was Briar's turn to nod. "I had the two X's on my hands, so they gave me the docks. Scraping barnacles until it killed me. But this Bag was there —"

"Bag?" she asked, confused. In Chammuri the term had no special meaning.

"Money-Bag. *Takamer*. Leastways, I thought he was a *takamer*, he dressed so nice. Niko, he was. He took me. The magistrate had orders to give him anybody he wanted. And Niko brought me to Winding Circle in Emelan."

"Where's that?" Evvy wanted to know.

Talking was thirsty work, so Briar got them each an apple. As Evvy bit into hers he could see she was missing teeth. He hoped Jebilu would help her keep from losing the rest. "It's northwest of here, on the Pebbled Sea. That's where I moved in with Rosethorn, and her friend Lark." He went on to tell her of the three girls who had also come to live there. Together he and the girls had learned that their powers were so well hidden, so much a part of the natural world, that even Tris, whose magic was the showiest of all, had been passed over by other mages.

Evvy was giggling over his tale of the last of Tris's animal rescue efforts, trying to teach a young crow to fly without ever having flown herself, as they reached the house. Rosethorn was up on the roof, carefully urging the beans, corn, and clover plants into another growth cycle. Of all the gardeners in the lands around the Pebbled Sea, Rosethorn was the most successful with these new crops, discovered in the unknown lands on the far side of the Endless Ocean. Briar and Evvy climbed up to join her.

"How were the farms today?" Briar asked, sitting on his heels beside Rosethorn. Evvy perched on the bench.

"The same as the rest." Rosethorn ran a hand through the sack of corn seed she had already coaxed out of the plants. "This land is so *tired*. They've farmed it for twelve centuries. The farmers do their best to reduce the acid that builds up with too much irrigation, but some have been poor for generations and can't afford what's needed to turn the land around." A single tear oozed out of the corner of each eye. She rubbed it away impatiently. "It disheartens me, to handle dirt that's so tired."

"But these will help," Briar reminded her. "You said the beans and the clover will build up the soil." Get in here, Briar urged some of the nearby plants. She needs you. To himself he added, And she'll growl if I do anything obvious like move plants closer to her.

The plants stretched until they could rest against her. Briar had seen her worse off, but he still liked to ensure that when she was empty of power and hope, her green strength was restored quickly. After her death and revival three years ago, just the thought that she might be weary, or failing, jabbed him into action.

He glanced at Evvy: the girl stared at Rosethorn, mouth agape. Chances were that she'd never seen that much greenery on the move before, between the plants who comforted and the plants Rosethorn tended as they went from shoots to flowering growth under her hands. Of course, how many ever watched to see if plants moved? To most people they weren't alive; they were things, without needs or instincts of their own. Even when humans knew that one plant, set in the wrong patch of earth, would die, or that another would take over, forcing every other plant out, they still refused to accept that plants were living creatures.

After a while, just as Briar was starting to think of a nap, Rosethorn asked, "How did your talk with Stoneslicer go?"

Briar sighed. "We had to change our plans." He told Rosethorn about the day's work, keeping the story short. She didn't care how different people talked or behaved. Only the girls and Lark enjoyed that part of stories.

When he finished, Rosethorn sat down on the roof carefully, ordering the plants back to their proper places. When they let go of her she turned so she could look at Evvy. "So you won't visit the palace, eh?" she asked. She spoke more slowly than she did to Briar. Some people found her speech, with its hint of a slur, hard to follow. "I can't say that I blame you. Palaces are cold and unfriendly, as a whole." Evvy nodded vigorously. Rosethorn looked at Briar. "Well, you'd better ride up there and talk to him. If she's already experimenting, we can't get her a teacher quickly enough." She looked at the western sky. "It's too late now. That's for tomorrow, then, first thing. And when are you supposed to sell trees in Golden House?"

Briar grimaced. "Day after tomorrow. And I have work to do yet. That one fig tree keeps arguing with me."

"Well, go argue back," Rosethorn ordered him with a smile. "You're welcome to stay for supper," she told Evvy.

The girl shook her head. "I have cats," she explained.

Rosethorn smiled. "And they must be fed. But you'll come here tomorrow — around noon, perhaps? We'll know when you can meet with your teacher by then."

Evvy nodded rapidly, making Briar wonder if she would come back. He hoped that she would, after today, but he could tell she wasn't resigned to an unknown teacher. If she didn't come, he would simply have to collect her from her warren in Princes' Heights.

The girl started to climb over the wall, then she stopped, and turned back. "I better get my old things," she told Briar, smoothing a wrinkle from her tunic. "If I go back to Lambing Tunnel like this, they'll think I have money."

"Should have thought of that myself," said Briar, leading the way into the house. Rosethorn had folded Evvy's grayish tunic and trousers and placed them on a stool in the workroom, under a note on a slate: *Shake out fleabane before wearing*. Briar diplomatically lifted first the tunic and then the trousers, stirring the folds until the herbs dropped to the floor. He left Evvy there to change. When he returned she was gone, her new clothes folded almost neatly and left on the stool. Her sandals lay on top of the pile.

Kid's got pluck, Briar thought, remembering how he'd

hated wearing any kind of shoe at first. Not one complaint out of her, and I bet they rubbed her feet.

He went up to the roof. "She left," Rosethorn said absently as she trimmed the lively jasmine back. "Over the roofs." Eyeing the jasmine to make sure she'd cut all she needed to, the woman said, "I'd forgotten."

When she didn't continue, Briar nudged, "Forgotten what?"

"Hm?" Rosethorn asked, startled out of her reverie. "Oh, I'd forgotten what stone mages are like. Stubborn doesn't begin to describe them. I should have warned you."

Briar smiled thinly. "That's all right," he told her. "I found out myself already."

Rosethorn snorted. "I suppose you did."

Evvy trotted along the rooftop roads, bound for home. From top to toe she was trembling from the strangeness of it all. It had been such a treat to sit in hot water at the *hammam* twice that day, scrubbing until she glowed a golden peach color, feeling her hair really clean. If she had just used common sense and gone home after that . . . But she'd had to see what the jade-eyed —

Briar, whispered a part of herself. He has a name. A plant-name. Calling him something else is silly.

Of course she knew people with names: Sulya, old Qinling, who spoke the language of home, blind Ladu, who warned the street people when the slaving gangs came through. But names seemed more important with — *Briar,* and *Rosethorn.* As if the words could change her life.

I don't *want* my life changed, Evvy thought rebelliously as she crossed a bridge over the Street of Wrens. For a moment she stopped to look down at the passageway that led to the Camelgut den. She would have liked to know how they did, if they had gone ahead and joined the Vipers. She had the feeling that *Pahan* Briar had disliked their choice, but she applauded their common sense. You didn't survive in Chammur's slums unless you learned to bend before you broke. Strange that a plant wizard wouldn't know that. But that was plants, tricky, rock-cracking parasites that would break apart any stone they got their roots into. They never seemed to realize that sometimes quiet was better. As long as you were alive, fresh chances to fight would come.

Seeing no signs of Camelguts or Vipers, Evvy moved on. She felt unsettled now, even with the city's heights rising ahead, lit a flaming color by the late-afternoon sun. Always before the sight of those towering stone reefs calmed her, made her feel safe: it was why she had come here after running from her master. Let others complain of smells and crumbling walls and ceilings in warrens that had been inhabited for a thousand years. Inside those rock halls and corridors Evvy was safe.

But now she knew why she'd always been safe, and the knowing shook her. She really had magic, and could learn how to make stone like her even more. That couldn't be bad. Stone, unlike people, was constant. It was everywhere, in all its varieties. Who knew what she might be able to do with it, if she knew proper stone magic?

The only problem was that to learn more about stone, she would have to deal with more people on a steady basis than she had in years. *Pahan* Briar seemed all right, for a plant person, but he wasn't going to teach her. A stranger, one who lived in the palace, would teach her. Evvy wasn't sure that she liked that. What if a real stone mage scorned her for what she didn't know? *Pahan* Briar just told her what to do, and if she didn't know how, he showed her. He assumed she would keep up. And hadn't she done just that all day? Even when keeping up had meant such strange things, like heating stones, new clothes, and food. She wasn't sure that she liked the sandals, which had blistered the tops of her feet, but the clean cloth had felt so good against her skin, and the food in her belly felt even better.

She pulled her rolled-up headcloth from the front of her tunic, and checked its contents — an entire meat dumpling, and halves of others. She hadn't been able to finish all the food he'd bought. With the salt fish and the leftovers from yesterday's feast, she and the cats would eat well tonight.

Would this stranger mage feed her as *Pahan* Briar did? *Pahan* Briar had been a *thukdak*. He understood about meals. How would a palace man know anything about going hungry and eating scraps until a whole dumpling was a feast?

She clambered down and trotted through the Market of the Lost. Her thoughts absorbed her so much that she never realized a Viper was following her, keeping well back in case she chanced to turn and look around.

7

Briar gathered his horse's reins. "You'll be careful how you talk to her, if she comes before I get back?" he asked Rosethorn, worried. "You know you scare people."

"I won't scare her," Rosethorn told him. "I'll be as kind as her own mother."

"Don't do that," Briar said. "Her mother sold her." He clucked to the horse and set it forward, up the Street of Hares. Perhaps he shouldn't worry if Evvy would arrive before he returned, but whether she would come at all. If she didn't, he would have to root her out of those stone tunnels, a chore he didn't even want to think about. He would just hope that she would come for the free food.

His route took him through the Market of the Lost. Only a few stalls were open so early, but the signs of illegal business were everywhere. Lookouts whistled alarms when the Watch was in view; there were furtive glances and even more furtive pocketings of goods, and the few customers included the well-to-do in addition to the poor. He'd have loved to look around, but common sense stopped him. Dressed as he was, riding a good mount, he would only draw robbers and thieves. That they might get more than they realized would do Briar little good if the whole neighborhood decided to pluck him.

Instead he followed Triumph Road south, watching the stony heights on his left. They were the real Chammur, its twelve-hundred-year-old heart. So much age should have impressed Briar. Instead it made his skin creep. The city breathed exhaustion from its pores. The stone was tired; Rosethorn had said the land was tired. How long did tired places endure? On the day they had toured the city, just after their arrival, Rosethorn had commented that one good earthquake would finish the place. The Earth Dedicate who was their guide had gone dead white, and begged her not to repeat it.

Shaking his head, Briar nudged his horse into a trot. The sooner he returned to the Street of Hares, the better he would feel.

His ride up Palace Road to the *amir*'s citadel was long and expensive. Each time he was stopped by a guard Briar surrendered a silver *cham* — a coin equal to five silver *davs* — as a bribe, so he'd be allowed to pass. His purse was much reduced by the time he reached his destination and a servant guided him to Jebilu Stoneslicer's waiting room.

Once the servant retreated, Briar looked his clothes

over. He was the picture of a prosperous young man of the middle classes in a fresh cream-colored shirt and dark green baggy trousers. He'd worn his favorite overrobe again. He was glad he was dressed as well, if not better, than many nobles his age, because his surroundings breathed wealth and prestige. Stoneslicer's marble walls were carved in lacy designs and inlaid with stone flowers; silk rugs in complex patterns warmed the cold marble floor. An assortment of braziers took the edge off the morning chill. Briar welcomed their warmth: autumn was settling around the city at last, and his silk overrobe wasn't as warm as a coat.

He did note with displeasure the scent of sandalwood that rose from the braziers. Why burn a tree just to impress those who knew how costly the stuff was?

He knew the wealthy often burned sandalwood, to show their riches and power. He'd certainly encountered such customs often enough. It just seemed as if a mage ought to be more sensible and less wasteful.

Another servant arrived with a heavy brasswork tray. He set its contents — teapot, cups, a plate of pastries, and a bowl of fruit — on the low table. He filled the cups, then bowed out, walking backward. Briar scowled. He didn't like that kind of bowing and scraping, and wondered why the servant had used it on a mere *pahan*. He had his answer as a carved sandalwood door at the back of the room opened. Jebilu Stoneslicer came in, motioning for the servant to close the front door behind him.

The stone mage was fat. He did not walk as much as he waddled in a billow of gold satin robes and musky scent. His skin was sallow, more yellow than brown. If he'd seen this man in an infirmary, Briar would have found medicines to treat ailments of the liver and kidneys.

Jebilu's head looked like an egg atop his body, an egg with straggly long black hair glued to its back half. A hump on his long nose testified to a break long ago; his chin was a round bulge jutting from the bottom of the egg. His brown eyes, tucked in folds of fat, were quick and clever, his smile serene. If he had eyebrows Briar couldn't see them. Dark circles spread under his eyes, another mark of poor health.

"Forgive me," the older mage said in a high, boyish voice. "I was told a *pahan* was here to see me. . . ."

"I'm the *pahan*," Briar said, bowing to Jebilu. "Briar Moss, from Winding Circle temple in Emelan."

Jebilu clasped his hands before him, regarding Briar silently for a moment. At last he said, "Moss is not a proper mage name, and you are but a boy."

Briar listed varieties of wort plants in his head until his temper cooled. Evvy needs this bouncing ball, he told himself, and replied evenly, "I am fourteen. I picked the name 'Moss' for myself and see no reason to change it, and the Initiate Council of Winding Circle has vouched for me."

He reached into his shirt and pulled a medallion over his neck. Keeping a grip on its silk cord, he held it out to

Jebilu. The mage inspected it, touching it with a stubby finger to see the other side.

Briar and the girls had gotten the medallions nearly eighteen months before. All four of their teachers — Daja's master Frostpine, Tris's teacher Niko, Sandry's teacher Lark, and Rosethorn — had come to supper one night, as had Tris's and Briar's sometime-teacher Dedicate Crane. Afterward Frostpine had presented each of the young people with a silvery metal circle. The front of each was different: the name of the individual student and his or her main teacher was inscribed on the outer edges. At the center was an image of their magic — Briar's was a tree. On the back was the spiral symbol for Winding Circle, to indicate where they had studied.

The four were ordered never to show the pendants needlessly or even to wear them outside their clothes unless it were vital. These were mage-credentials, proof that the Initiate Council at Winding Circle had approved them to practice as adult mages.

For the most part they forgot they had them; the medallions seemed made not to be noticed by even the wearer. In the months since they had begun their journey east, Rosethorn had ordered Briar to show it to four mages, all of whom had argued about revealing how they worked to a student. The medallion had silenced them. Briar suspected they said more than just that the bearer was qualified as an adult mage, but Rosethorn refused to answer his questions.

Whatever the message of the medallion was, it did not impress Jebilu. He wrinkled his nose, as if he'd smelled something bad. "The standards for credentials are lower than they were when I was a student," he remarked. "What have you done to your hands?"

Briar turned scarlet. "I tried to tattoo myself using vegetable dyes." He put his medallion back on, tucked it into his shirt, and stuffed his vine-patterned hands into the pockets of his overrobe. "Actually, I didn't come to talk about me."

"Indeed?" Jebilu lowered himself onto a couch by the low table, and motioned for Briar to take a chair. The man spread a napkin on his lap, then took a pastry and a cup of tea. "Surely a stone mage can do very little for a green mage." He broke a tiny piece from his pastry and nibbled it carefully, allowing not a crumb to drop onto his gold satin tunic.

"Lucky for me that I'm here about a stone mage, then, isn't it?" Briar sipped his cup of tea, battling to get a grip on his dislike for this man. That wouldn't help Evvy or him. "I found this girl polishing stones in Golden House. She has magic with them. I could see it lighting up in the stones she handled, and they kept the power even after she put the stone down. Since I told her, she's been able to get rocks to hold light and heat."

Jebilu broke another fragment from his pastry and ate that busily. A crumb dropped onto his chest: he removed it carefully and inspected the cloth where it had fallen, turning it this way and that to see if the crumb had left a spot. Only when he was satisfied that his garments were still clean did he ask, "This concerns me how, *Pahan* Moss?"

"She has to be taught, *Pahan* Stoneslicer," Briar replied. "As far as I can find out, you're the only stone mage in town. The others are gone."

Jebilu broke off another bit of pastry, inspected it — for teetering crumbs? Briar wondered — then popped it into his mouth. Once he had chewed it thoroughly and swallowed it, he delicately sipped his tea. He blotted his lips dry, then said, "It was necessary for me to limit magical influences. The stone of the heights is vulnerable. Too many magics would create a disaster. My lord *amir* places his entire confidence in me."

You mean you didn't want competition, Briar thought. He regarded his cup of tea. For a moment he wanted to give it a good, loud slurp, to annoy Jebilu. He got that urge under control along with his temper and gently sipped his tea. Sandry had taught him elegant manners, though he seldom used them. He supposed he was trying to show Jebilu he was both educated and mature, if not for his own sake, then for Evvy's. When he was calm again Briar said, "That's very well, but Evvy needs a teacher right now. It'll be a while before she knows enough magic that her workings might conflict with yours."

"Send her to Winding Circle," Jebilu replied. "They seem prepared to indulge the young." He smiled at Briar.

"She'll get into trouble without a teacher," Briar said flatly. "She's run into it already. If she's scared she'll defend herself, and end up doing more harm than good."

"My dear boy, I am a very busy man," Jebilu insisted. He gave his tea another tiny sip. "My lord the *amir* keeps me busy inspecting the bridges, walls, fortresses, and dams around our fair city. With stone so ancient, problems arise. I would say, bring her here, but I am so rarely at home."

"She won't come here. She's afraid to. You can teach her while you inspect whatever you must." Briar put his cup down hard enough that the porcelain rattled.

"Impossible. I must not be distracted." Jebilu looked at his pastry, then broke off a new piece, chewed, and swallowed it. "You should try these," he said once he'd finished.

Briar got to his feet. "By the laws of Lightsbridge and Winding Circle you *have* to teach new mages in your discipline," he insisted.

Jebilu smiled. "Winding Circle and Lightsbridge are far from here. If you think they will bestir themselves for a girl of no family, you are as deluded as the stone mages who fought my lord's command for them to leave Chammur." Seeing that Briar had blinked when he'd mentioned Evvy's family, Jebilu broadened his smile. "If she had family and a proper place in the world she would not fear the palace. Neither would she rely on an *eknub* mage to present her case. Stone mages are a *dav* a bushel," he continued. "She will find one sooner or later. After she leaves town, of course. She mustn't stay and endanger *my* work."

Briar was furious on several levels. Later, when he'd calmed down, he would be the first to admit he was vexed partly because the man hadn't rolled onto his back like a defeated dog at the sight of the medallion. There was more to his anger than hurt pride, though. The thought that someone might drive away all potential rivals offended his sense of right and wrong. Rosethorn and Dedicate Crane had spent their adult lives in competition, but neither had made the other leave Winding Circle. Frostpine's apprentice Kirel had always envied Daja's magic, but he'd never even asked Frostpine to keep Daja away. Mages worked together or separately, but all had a right to work.

Worst of all was Jebilu's dismissal of Evvy. The girl could be maddening, contrary, and rude, but she was a human being, with her own heart, mind, and power. It was as if Jebilu had said that no matter what she had, she would never count, simply because she was a poor orphan. He didn't care that she survived a crueler world than that of this pretty citadel with its perfumed air and silk rugs. She deserved a chance to work her way out of poverty, as Briar had. Who was this pampered lapdog of a man to dismiss her?

About to inform Jebilu that in fact there was a representative of both Lightsbridge and Winding Circle in town, Briar stopped himself. I could argue this *kaq* around,

he thought, using an extremely rude Trader word for someone valueless. He could do it, but he knew he would be upset and unsettled for the rest of the day. That wouldn't be
any good for his trees, and he had to get them ready for
market in the morning.

I could do all that, he thought. Or I could give him to
Rosethorn. It would cheer her up to give this sniveler what
for, and she could use cheering up.

He grinned, showing all of his teeth. "I wish you would
reconsider," he suggested, his mild tone belying his grin. "If
a member of one of those councils knew of this, you could
find yourself in trouble."

Jebilu's face twitched as he thought quickly; Briar wondered what was going through that selfish brain. "Here."
The older mage searched through his robes until he found
a purse in his sash. Opening it, he counted out coins: three
gold *chams*. "I am not heartless. This will pay for her to go
to Winding Circle and to cover her fees for a year or two. If
she spends it carefully she may even get a wardrobe out of
it — No," he interrupted himself, "people like that simply
have no notion of economy." He inspected his purse, and
added a silver *cham* to the gold ones. "She must not come
back to me if she spends this without going to Winding
Circle," he told Briar, holding up a warning forefinger. "My
good nature may be imposed upon once, but not twice. If
she spends it on drugs, or fancy clothes, or drink, she will
get no more. So." He tucked the purse away and crossed his

hands over the bulge of his stomach. "I have been more than fair, I think."

Briar was breathless with rage. That this festering slug would judge a girl he'd not so much as glimpsed in the street . . . Briar's magic surged against four years' worth of barriers and controls, begging for him to loosen his grip, presenting him with images of this man as plant food or a trellis with big-thorned roses twining around his flesh. The vines in his hands rippled and twisted, looking for an exit. The trees and flowers in the garden just outside begged to come in and swamp whoever had hurt their friend.

When the servant rapped on the door and opened it, Briar's concentration snapped. Give him to Rosethorn, he ordered himself. She needs a blow up worse than you do. He slammed a lid on his power before it could escape, reminded the vines in his skin that they had no woody stems to support them outside his body, and sent a wave of calm toward the garden. Only when he'd done all that, hard and fast so his green friends and his power would remember who was in charge, did he hear the bowing servant tell Jebilu, "— required in the Pink Audience Chamber at once."

"I will not keep his highness waiting," Jebilu replied, struggling to his feet. "This *pahan* was leaving." He waddled out as quickly as his tiny feet would take him.

The servant eyed Briar uncertainly. "My lord *pahan*?" he inquired cautiously. "Shall I bring your horse?"

"Why bother to ask?" Briar wanted to know. "His royal

roly-polyness just told you I was going." He strode out of the room before he said anything worse. The servant, who looked as if he might be hiding a grin, trotted ahead of him to get Briar's mount.

After a moment in the courtyard, Briar's rage started to fade. When he could think, he realized he'd forgotten something. Stupid! he told himself. You left the money!

Anger flared again, equaled by horror with himself. Why hadn't he taken it? He should have. It had been a bribe, after all, for him or for Evvy. Accepting it did not mean he had to do as the fat man had suggested, send Evvy to Winding Circle. He could put it in his own purse. Once he would have kept the coins without worry, and told himself that Evvy needed to collect her own money.

He'd thought he was past these moments when Briar Moss, student and mage, smashed into Roach, the Hajran street rat and convict he'd once been. Even Briar Moss understood the value of money — surely temple life and mage life hadn't destroyed that for him! He could have kept it for Evvy, and be repaid for the bribes and the clothes.

But he hadn't taken it. He'd left it there, so furious at the insult to Evvy that he'd refused to touch it. Had he lost his mind? He was acting just as foolishly as some Money-Bag whose honor had been offended! He would just walk back in there and take the money. It would still be on the table unless someone entered that room. Just a few steps. Evvy would be better off, and he would be someone he knew.

Bitter orange shrubs grew along the wall outside Jebilu's palace rooms. Briar walked in among them to get a grip on himself, rather than go back for the coins. As he listened to the oranges' praise of sun, soil, and the palace gardeners, Briar's sizzling nerves cooled. Plants had no concept of money. It didn't make them crazy; nothing made plants crazy. He petted their stems and leaves, and calmed down.

When he heard the clop of hooves, he knew the servant had come with his horse. It took Briar a moment to talk the bitter oranges into letting him go. Through it the servant held the horse, gazing at his feet, as if well dressed boys talked to plants every day. Briar gave him a coin and mounted up. It was time to go home and have a chat with Rosethorn.

He returned his horse to the stable, making certain the animal had a good rubdown and an extra ration of oats. Walking down the Street of Hares, Briar was wondering if he ought to visit the *souk* when movement across the street from his house got his attention.

A girl sat on the roof of the home directly across from his. Briar knew everyone who lived nearby. If his neighbors had seen their daughters in trousers, not skirts, they would have beaten the rebellious girls and kept them inside until they forgot such folly. Briar also doubted that any of their girls knew how to twirl a dagger on one finger.

He wandered idly to that side of the street, acting as if

he hadn't seen the watcher, and turned down the lane to the *souk*. Yesterday he'd noticed ladders to the roofs along the lane; today he used one to clamber up to the road that Evvy used so freely.

A neighbor was washing clothes on her roof where he came up. When he put his finger to his lips, she raised her eyebrows, and jerked her head in the direction of the watcher two houses over. Briar smiled grimly and nodded. The woman — he had given her something for her skull-splitting headaches three weeks ago — snapped her fingers. The scruffy dog who slumbered in a corner got to his feet.

Briar shook his head. He wanted to talk to the spy first. The woman made a shooing motion with her hand and the dog lay back down. Briar crept forward through lines of drying laundry until he could see the watcher without being seen. She wore a gold nose ring with a garnet pendant. Briar scowled. So the Vipers were still about!

Using laundry, barrels, and other rooftop clutter as cover, he crept up on the Viper unseen, nodding to those of his neighbors who were present. Someone from every household was up here, puttering. They might have to live with gangs using the upper roads, but they weren't about to let anything be stolen.

One roof away, Briar watched the Viper. Her attention was fixed on his house — she definitely wasn't expecting company. The very casualness of the way she lounged by the roof's edge vexed Briar. He was getting tired of the Vipers. It was time they knew it.

The house she had chosen was perfect for his purposes. Its owners had roses planted in tubs along the back and sides of the roof. With a little encouragement, they would prevent the Viper's escape. Briar stood and stepped over the low wall between his roof and that of the watcher.

She scrambled to her feet. There were now daggers in both of her hands; she held them easily, a girl with plenty of fights under her belt. She was nearly as tall as Briar, perhaps a year or two older. He backed up three slow steps toward the rear of the roof.

Thinking he feared her, the Viper closed with him, dark eyes flashing. "I know you," she said tightly. "You're the *eknub pahan* who lives across the street."

"You're not here for me?" Briar asked, trying to look scared. It wasn't something he was sure he could do. When he was afraid, he did his best to hide it. "You want Evvy."

"That's right." The Viper advanced another step, ignoring the rustle of the roses along the wall behind her. "And you don't have a thing to say to it, not if you don't want me gutting you." She sneezed.

"I have plenty to say," Briar told her coldly, showing her that he carried a knife of his own. The girl settled into a street-fighter's crouch. Briar was about to ask the rose bushes to grab her when she sneezed twice more.

"What's your name?" Briar demanded.

She spat a curse that ended in a sneeze. Briar smiled. She had rose fever, what the Winding Circle healers called an "allergy." Just as some people got sneezes or itching spots at haying time or in a room where cats had been, others could not live with roses.

"I'm going — to — leave you for, for fire ants," the girl raged between sneezes. "I'm —" She sneezed three times in rapid succession, then wiped her eyes on her sleeve. Briar used the moment to push two more potted rose bushes forward, until the Viper was hedged all around. The older girl gasped for air, forgetting the knives in her hand.

"Wrong answer," Briar replied calmly. The roses had faded, preparing for the autumn rains. He called them to full, lively growth. Buds swelled to the size of grapes, then exploded into heavy crimson blooms. The Viper sneezed repeatedly, unable to do anything else.

He let the blooms shrink, fade, and die, calling even larger buds from their stems. Wait a moment, please, he asked them before they could open. The Viper was scrubbing her red, itching face on the hem of her tunic. Briar walked over, passing through the screen of rose bushes without even hooking his clothes on the thorns. Before she knew what he did, he coolly took her knives and replaced one with his pocket handkerchief. He then walked back through the screen of roses and sat on an overturned washtub. "Comfortable?" he asked.

He listened to her curses for a moment, and shook his head. "You know, there's kids about, learning bad ways from you," he said. "This is a respectable neighborhood — not what you're used to." When she continued to swear Briar gestured to the plant behind the Viper. It had grown as tall as she, and had sprouted a very large rosebud next to her cheek. At Briar's gesture the bud started to open, one petal at a time.

The Viper mopped her eyes and looked to see what tickled her cheek. She shrank away, only to discover the other rose bushes had closed in around her, forming a thorny cocoon that reached as high as her chest.

"Calm down and behave, or you'll have more than one of those to worry about," Briar informed her. Using one of her knives, he cleaned dirt from under his fingernails until she stopped thrashing. "You going to behave?"

The girl sneezed ferociously, then nodded.

Briar saw that there were a number of red spots on her face. "You're one of the ones who tried to grab Evvy out by the Market of the Lost, aren't you?" he asked. "One of the ones she burned with her rocks."

The girl hesitated, then nodded.

"Didn't you learn *anything* from that?" he inquired.

The girl cursed him and Evvy alike. Briar nodded to the flowerbud that bulged next to her cheek. It unfurled swiftly, a blood crimson bloom that was nearly as big as her head once it was fully open.

"Do your bidding like little scratchy lapdogs, don't they?" she demanded before the sneezes took her.

"I can't think of anything so bleat-brained as to insult me at just this moment," Briar remarked. "But then, you Vipers lost the clever race a while ago, didn't you?"

Any reply she might have given was lost in a thunder of sneezes. Her eyes were swelling shut; from her gasps, Briar realized her throat was swelling, too. "I suppose I don't want to kill you," he decided. "At least, not like this. It's not exactly fair."

Slipping off the saddlebags slung over his shoulder, he touched one of the many outer pockets of his mage kit. It opened, letting him remove a corked glass vial. As he wriggled the cork out, he made sure the rose stems were wrapped securely around the Viper's arms and legs. He then reached over them to dab one droplet of oil from the vial beneath her nose, and two more on each eyelid.

She gasped, an open-throated effort that filled her lungs. Her eyes slid open, the swelling down, though they continued to water. The sneezes stopped. His all-allergy oil was powerful: it could relieve symptoms for over an hour until Briar or Rosethorn learned what caused the allergy and blended a medicine that would help with that alone.

Once the Viper could breathe, Briar requested the rose bush at her back to produce four more of the very large buds near her head. As they swelled with growth, he asked, "Why spy on Evvy?"

"So we know where she is," the Viper replied sullenly. "Our *tesku* means her to join us sometime."

"Why?" Briar wanted to know. "She's just a kid."

"She's a stone mage," the Viper said. "She can say where jewels are hid, what's garbage and what ain't. We could be the main gang in Chammur with a stone mage."

Briar folded his arms. "When the Thief-Lord wanted me for his gang, he *asked* me first. He said I'd get food and nice goods and mates to watch my back," he informed her. "All of my mates were invited, and told why it was good to be in that gang. You, the way you do it, you don't want a mate. You want a slave. She'll never gang with you. I'll make sure she doesn't."

The girl's mouth curled. "You want us to *court* some little slant-eyed rat from Princes' Heights? She ain't even Chammuran!"

"I don't want Vipers courting her at all," Briar replied coldly. "You don't know how to act. And if I see you around here again, you'll think this" — he signaled to the rosebuds, which burst into flower around the Viper's face — "is a token of my love."

The slight amount of oil he'd given her wasn't enough to counteract the pollen from the huge flowers and the surrounding bushes. She sneezed so hard Briar thought she

8

Rosethorn heard Briar out, her slender brows coming together with an almost audible click when he repeated how Jebilu had dismissed the influence of Lightsbridge and Winding Circle. She served up midday in silence, opening her mouth only once, to call Evvy to the table. The girl had arrived that morning, while Briar was gone. Rosethorn had made her bathe, change into clean clothes, and help to harvest the new corn crop on the roof. That Evvy had obeyed didn't surprise Briar. It took a stern spirit to defy Rosethorn.

The woman ate in silence while Evvy pelted Briar with questions about the palace. The white stone walls of Jebilu's room, what were they made of? Were the inlays on the walls also stone? Did the people press such inlays into the stone as she did stones in the walls of her squat? What did the mage's pastries taste like — and what did Briar mean, he hadn't even tried them?

"Enough," Rosethorn said, throwing down her napkin. "Aren't stones quiet?"

"But I'm not a stone," Evvy replied, "I'm a stone *mage*." Her cheerful grin didn't even flicker under Rosethorn's admonishing look. Briar decided maybe Evvy's head was stone, and that was how she could resist his teacher's emphatic personality.

"You two wash up," Rosethorn ordered, getting to her feet. "I'm off to have a word with Master Stoneslicer."

"I'd like to come," Briar wheedled. He wanted hear what Rosethorn said to the fat mage.

Rosethorn shook her head. "Dishes. Then you're going to teach her something." She pointed to Evvy. "Don't let this time go to waste."

"But I can't!" protested Briar. "I'm a kid, not a —"

"Teach her to meditate," Rosethorn said firmly, cutting off his arguments. "And to get her power in a tighter grip. Don't forget to put a circle of protection around you both when you do it, either. Uncontrolled stone magic won't do my beans or your miniature trees much good."

Briar winced. "Thanks for reminding me."

"Don't mention it," Rosethorn said. "And get to work." She strode out of the house, her face set.

"Is she going to *eat* Jooba-hooba?" Evvy wanted to know. "She looks like she's going to bite him, at least."

"No — if she bit him, he'd die," Briar informed her.

"And his name's Jebilu. Learn it. He's still going to be your permanent teacher."

Evvy shrugged.

They settled in the front room for the lesson. Briar made sure Evvy was seated and comfortable before he drew a protective circle around them with a specially prepared oil. Circles came easily to him. The strength he had placed in his oil surged up and in to enclose them in a bubble of power. No matter what happened inside, no magic would escape his barrier.

Evvy's nose twitched. "What's that?" she demanded.

"It's one of my best mixes!" Briar protested of the hint that his pride and joy smelled bad. "Rosemary, cypress, and rose geranium. It holds even with five mages striving against it at once! I got a prize for it in a competition!"

Evvy propped her chin on her hand. "It smells like something died," she remarked.

Briar opened his mouth to protest, and saw her lips quiver. "Are you giving me a hard time?" he asked.

Evvy shook her head solemnly.

"I thought you were afraid of me. I thought you were afraid of everybody," he pointed out.

"You're all right," she replied carelessly. "You could've done all kinds of bad things to me by now, and you haven't."

Briar shook his head and sat cross-legged. "Now, with

meditation, you breathe special, by counting, like this." He demonstrated for her the pattern of inhaling for a count of seven, holding for a count of seven, and letting go of all that air over a count of seven. "And while you breathe like that, you empty your mind of all thoughts. Just, empty. It's hard at first, but you'll get the knack. You're clever, for a girl."

Daja would have cuffed him; Sandry would have tugged his ear or his nose; Tris would have ignored him. Evvy stuck her tongue out. Briar grinned. "Not that I've much against girls in the common way. Now, let's try that breathing."

Evvy did, twice, then shook her head. "What's that supposed to mean, clear out my thoughts? I don't have a broom for between my ears, you know. It's not like I can sweep them away."

"You have to learn to do it, though," Briar explained. "That's how you get to the place where you can handle your magic. If you don't learn, your power will cut away from you without you wanting it, and get you in trouble. Or it'll come spilling out and you won't be able to stop it, or you won't be able to find enough to do the job."

Evvy tried again. She managed to hold and release her breath three times before she cried, "But I'm thinking all kinds of things, like midday and supper and I thought I saw a Viper this morning — I can't stop thinking things!"

"Just forget about the Vipers," ordered Briar. "I'll handle

them." He rubbed his temple. "Look," he said after a moment's thought, "do stones think?"

Evvy giggled. "Of course they don't, silly!"

"Good. Do the breathing, and become a stone," Briar suggested. "Just close your eyes. Be a stone in your mind."

"What kind?" she wanted to know. "If I'm the orange stone or the salt-and-pepper stone, the sun will hit my sparkly bits and I'll notice that. Or —"

"You remember the flagstones in Golden House?" Briar asked swiftly, before she could say any more. "The ones under the main aisle? Black, not shiny at all, heavy?" Evvy nodded. "Try that stone."

She began to breathe as Briar counted. He didn't try to enter the center of his own power, feeling it was up to him to keep her on track. As it was, he wasn't sure how long he'd been counting for her before he realized she was silent. Her power shone softly throughout her body. Her eyes were motionless under their lids; her face was still. Only the tiniest shift in her nostrils and the shallowest rise and fall in her chest said she was alive. Briar rested a hand on hers, and found her skin was cool, almost hard.

"Evvy," he called, his heart pounding. "Evvy, listen, come out of it. Evvy . . ."

She stayed unmoving.

Briar wiped a hand over his circle to break it and ran up to his workroom. He needed something powerfully scented.

Finding the right plant, he broke off a stem and carried it downstairs. The smell didn't bother him — most plant smells didn't — but from the complaints voiced by others he knew not everyone appreciated its strong odor. He held the stem under Evvy's nose.

Her nostrils twitched. After a moment they flared; her chest heaved; her eyes flew open. "Ugh!" she cried, leaning away from him, a hand cupped over her nose. "Heibei's luck, what's *that*?"

Briar smiled regretfully. "It's called asafetida," he told her. "Good for lung ailments and exorcisms."

"Who'd want to breathe around that?" Evvy demanded. "I take it back about the stuff you used before. This *really* smells like, like somebody died. Why'd you make me sniff it, anyway?"

Briar gently placed the stem on the floor. "I never said turn *into* a rock," he informed her, closing his circle again. "I just said clear your mind like one. If they don't think of anything, *you* don't think of anything! Especially don't think of being one!"

"I couldn't've turned myself into a stone," she scoffed. Then she met Briar's eyes. "Could I?"

"I don't know. You looked pretty close to it," he informed her. "Now. Let's try again. Clear your mind. *Don't* be a rock."

He began to count, Evvy to inhale, hold, exhale. For a little while nothing happened. Briar continued to count as first her fingers, then her nose twitched. Suddenly she relaxed, and brilliant white light flared all around her, half-blinding Briar.

"Stop!" he cried. "Stop it right there!"

"*Now* what?" she demanded, opening her eyes. "I almost had it!"

"You *did* have it," he reassured her, breaking his protective circle. "I just wasn't ready. Wait here."

"I want a drink of water," she complained.

"Go get it, then." I'm no good at this stuff, he thought as he fetched his mage's kit and she got her drink. If I was, I'd be prepared for all these problems instead of hopping in and out of my circle. "Now look," he said when they resumed their places and he'd closed the circle again, "I want you to do it exactly like you did it before I yelled, all right? Only first —" He drew a bottle from his kit and poured a drop onto his index finger. The moment he dabbed it on each eyelid, the scene before him went darker, as if he'd put clear brown glass over each eye. Even the hard silver-white flare of the protective circle and the bubble of power around them faded to the lightest of sparkles.

"What's that for?" she asked.

"It helps me see," he replied absently. "Now, do the breathing. Try to go to that same place in your head."

Evvy closed her eyes obediently as Briar began to count. For a short while the only sounds came from outside as women talked, children shouted, and an unhappy donkey brayed somewhere in the distance. Briar watched Evvy.

First she hitched and scratched her hip. Then she sneezed. He could tell she was thinking as her eyes shuttled rapidly behind closed lids. Suddenly she went still. Her power blazed out to fill their protective bubble.

"I'm gonna touch your eyelids now. Don't yelp." Briar gently brushed her eyelids with a sight oil to help those who could not do so to see magic. "Open them. Try to keep your mind clear."

Evvy slowly opened one eye, then the other. The brilliance of the magic around them made her blink rapidly; her eyes began to tear. Slowly the blaze of her power faded as she lost the contact she had with it.

"What was that?" she wanted to know, rubbing her eyes with her fist.

"That was your magic," Briar informed her. "We're going to start you learning to grip all that close, so you don't leak it every whichway. And if you can't see it, you've got to find a way for you to know it's about, and what shape it's in, and what you can do with it. Did you feel anything before I made you open your eyes?"

Evvy yawned. "No," she said, rubbing her nose. "Am I supposed to?"

"There's something," Briar insisted. "Warmth, cold, a tingly feeling. The mage always knows. Now close your eyes and let's try it again."

"I don't want to," Evvy whined. "I'm bored."

"Sometime I'll ask you what you want. This isn't that time," Briar retorted. Then he bit his lip. *I open my mouth and Rosethorn pops out,* he thought ruefully. *Next thing you know, I'll threaten to hang her in the well.* "Close your eyes," he told Evvy firmly.

The lady nibbled a fig as she eyed Orlana. "You tried to seize the girl yesterday," she remarked. "You were burned for your pains, and you fled without taking her."

Orlana, her nose raw, her eyes bloodshot and puffy, her breath still rattling in her chest, nodded sullenly. She should have ignored her orders to report to the lady if anything happened. Ikrum wouldn't have made her come here — he was half-terrified of the woman as it was.

"And now you say you left your watcher's post because of flowers." The lady's fingers hovered over a second fig.

"You make it sound like a little thing!" Orlana cried. "I couldn't breathe, it was so bad!" Silently she cursed Ikrum in Shaihun's name. The desert winds should scrape him to the bone for having brought the lady into their lives.

"I am sure you thought the inconvenience was serious." The lady surveyed Orlana from top to toe. "And this *pahan* told you that it was necessary to court the stone mage?"

"For other gangs. He says he doesn't want Vipers courting her at all." She was thirsty, but there was no point to asking for something to drink. The lady would never permit a *thukdak* to handle her cups.

The lady inspected one of her many rings. "The courtship need not come from Vipers," she murmured. "As for your tale of giant roses — though I have warned you all that drugs will only keep you in the gutter, it is clear that you at least did not pay heed. Your tale is simply an excuse for drug intoxication, and I refuse to accept it."

"I don't care if you do or not, *takameri*," Orlana spat, fed up. "I wasn't taking drugs and that's what happened. Who are you to go questioning me and what I say? You never gave your blood to the gang. You never gave up family for the gang. You —"

The lady raised a finger. The mute walked out of the gallery and dropped his bowstring over Orlana's head, twisting it deftly. Orlana, fighting wildly, tried to get her fingers under it and failed.

As the mute stepped away from her corpse, the lady beckoned to one of the other galleries on the edges of the garden. Her armsmaster Ubayid came out of the dark room where he'd been waiting and listening. When he was close enough, he knelt on the garden flagstones and bowed his head to her.

Where the mute was big and rounded with fat, Ubayid was rawhide lean and wiry. He wore his black and silver hair combed strictly back, tightly braided. His skin was brown and weathered from hours in the sun. A long mustache framed the top and sides of a thin-lipped mouth; his cheeks were clean-shaven. His lower eyelids sagged a little, giving an emotionless expression to his brown eyes. He wore the clothes of a free man of the city — loose shirt, sleeveless over-robe, baggy trousers, boots, sash — plus a sword on his left and a long dagger on his right. He had been one of her first husband's guards, but had chosen to make her interests his own.

"Find Ikrum Fazhal and tell him to report to me immediately," the lady ordered. "Then ask questions about this *eknub pahan*. Discover where he goes. I desire to make his acquaintance, but subtly. If courtship will pry the girl from him, I shall court them, within limits. I like servants to appreciate their value. Since this *pahan* has made himself her friend, I shall make the *pahan* look upon me with favor."

As the mute slung the dead girl over his shoulder and took her away, Ubayid looked at the mess he had left. "If you keep killing them, lady, you won't have a gang left."

Her eyes widened with fury. "I give you too much license, Ubayid. They will stop offending me, and I will no longer have to punish them. These urchins simply need to learn I will not accept failure."

When Ikrum arrived, he was brought to the lady's sitting room, not the garden. The servants had not yet finished retiling the spot where Orlana had died. The lady heard the boy arrive, but did not look up from her book until well after the time he had dropped to his knees and laid his face on the floor.

Finally she closed her book, keeping her place with her finger. "Ikrum, you must inform your people I will not tolerate disrespect. Look at me."

He raised his face. Both of his eyes were black, one so badly bruised that it had swollen shut. His nose had been broken; his lips split. A crude bloodstained bandage was wrapped around his head.

The lady's book slid from her lap. She swung her legs to the floor and straightened to sit on her couch, leaning down to tuck her fingers under his chin. He let her turn his face this way and that as she inspected his wounds.

"How did this happen?" she wanted to know, her eyes flashing. "Who has done this to you?"

He tried to lick his lips and winced.

"No, wait," she ordered. To the servant who responded to the bell she rang she said, "My healer, coffee, food, and a footstool, at once." The servant ran to obey. "Say nothing until you are cared for," the lady ordered Ikrum.

The healer was there within minutes. A mage, she was soon able to reduce the swellings that covered Ikrum's face and arms, heal his broken nose and cracked ribs, and dull the ache of what she told the lady was "a truly thorough beating."

When the healer was finished, the lady dismissed her.

Ikrum carefully sipped his hot, bitter coffee. When he had emptied a cup, the lady poured a second for him with her own hands. "Who?" she asked.

"Gate Lords." Ikrum started to slide off the stool on which he sat, only to see the lady shake her head. "I — you remember, the sister of their *tesku*, I like her. Maybe she likes me. Her brother caught us together and had his mates teach me a lesson." Ikrum smiled bitterly. "He said he'd geld me next time."

"This must not be tolerated!" The lady stood and paced, her green silk draperies and veils fluttering around her. "This disrespect — that they would assault you!" She gripped Ikrum's shoulder as he began to rise from his stool. "Now do you see?" she demanded fiercely. "You did not want to deal with the Gate Lords, but do you not see we must? They heard of your recruitment of those others. They are frightened. Anyone at the top of the tree must concern himself with those below. They beat you to make you lose respect with your Vipers, so you are no danger to them."

"Tell me what to do," Ikrum whispered, head bowed. He wondered if Shaihun, the god of desert winds and the madness of crackling heat, ever wore a woman's face. Was he looking at Shaihun right now? Was it Shaihun's henna-tinted claws that bit into his shoulders, and Shaihun who breathed spices into his face? "I will do it, I swear."

"Orlana is dead," the lady whispered, her dark eyes holding Ikrum's as surely as her hands gripped his shoulders.

"She failed me twice. She let the *eknub pahan* send her scurrying. There are only two courses for us, Ikrum. Victory or death. I will not live halfway in this world. Neither will my Vipers. Here is what you will do." She spoke quietly, making sure that he understood every word. At last she let go of him. "Crush our foes, Ikrum. Give me victories."

9

Golden House echoed as market keepers opened the giant shutters, allowing sunlight to enter the building. Flinching as the sound battered his sleepy ears, Briar inhaled the steam from his tea and tried not to hate himself for having been fool enough to rent a stall. He knew it was a good idea — people had to see his miniature trees before they would pay plenty of money for them — but his body longed passionately for bed. His work with Evvy the afternoon before had tired him more than he had thought.

The last hour in particular had been a trial, he thought, and sipped his tea. No doubt he'd asked too much of her first real stab at meditation, but how could he know what was too much? He was somewhere around fourteen, just a student himself, as Rosethorn often reminded him. He would definitely be relieved when Jebilu took over.

Evvy had been surprised — Briar had not — when Rosethorn came home to say Jebilu would meet his new student at Golden House. "Don't expect him much before noon," Rosethorn cautioned, a grim twist to her mouth. "But he'll come, or I'll know the reason why." She had looked at Evvy. "Did you give my boy a hard time?"

"Your boy?" Evvy had asked with a grin. "He's no boy, he's *old*."

"I feel old," Briar mumbled as the first rays of light hit the shelves of miniature trees behind him. They chorused a welcome to the sun, their leaves eager for even tidbits of light. Only his own tree, a pine in the shape called *shakkan*, did not call. Briar had positioned it so the sun would touch it first. It was his companion and friend, a one-hundred-fifty-year-old work of art, every bit of it filled to near-bursting with magic. It was not for sale.

Others were. Five he had started from trees found in and around Chammur. Like Rosethorn building supplies of seed for the local farmers, Briar had used his power to bring those trees to perfect miniature form, careful not to weaken them as magic filled their veins. Another six were miniatures he'd bought on the way, shaping them to the point where they could be sold for ten times what he had paid. Others he had brought from home. Some he wouldn't sell unless the offered price were very good. They were samples of his expertise in the varied classical forms of miniature tree, and insurance against a need for money further down the road.

Once he finished his tea, he rearranged his charges on the shelves to take advantage of the light. He was trying to ignore a nagging voice in his mind, one that sounded like Sandry, his foster-sister. The voice tugged at his thought constantly, asking a question he didn't want asked or answered: what good will a resentful teacher do her? Or worse: what if he waits for you and Rosethorn to leave, then treats her badly?

I stank as her teacher yesterday, he argued. A teacher who knows little about stone magic and less about teaching is just as bad.

The ghost-Sandry ignored him. He knew what *that* meant: she thought he was dead wrong.

Just like a noble, he told her when she got too insistent, as the real Sandry did so often. Always worrying about future things, when right now is hard enough.

"I still say they're rock-killers."

He'd been so deep in thought that he hadn't seen Evvy arrive. Briar jumped and glared at her. "Don't sneak up on me and don't call them rock-killers," he told the girl. "They have to live, same as your precious rocks."

"My rocks don't break up your plants," she retorted, laughter in her eyes. "It's the other way around." She was clean for the third day in a row, and dressed in clean clothes. Now she let herself into the stall and perched on the tall stool. "You got anything to eat?"

He sighed. Reaching into his satchel, he found a dumpling he'd brought as a snack for later. "Didn't you stop at the house and beg something off Rosethorn?" he asked, passing her the dumpling and a clean cloth. "You're wearing your new clothes."

"I stopped and changed." Evvy tucked the cloth into the neck of her orange tunic.

You never have to tell her to do a thing twice, Briar thought, watching her settle the napkin. Maybe I *did* push too hard yesterday. "So didn't she feed you?"

Evvy pinched off some dumpling and stuck it in her mouth. Chewing vigorously, she said, "She had a pair of shears in her hand when I asked. She said if I bothered her today she'd snip my nose off, so I should pester you for something to eat when I got here," she added, taking another bite.

"She wouldn't've really cut your nose off," Briar said. He realized with a feeling of destiny that he would probably buy her a larger breakfast shortly. "Just bloodied it a bit."

"She's fierce," Evvy said admiringly. "I bet she scared Jooba-hooba plenty, to make him leave the palace."

"If he's going to be your teacher, you ought to say his proper name," Briar informed her sternly, thinking of how the stone mage might react to being called "Jooba-hooba." "Or call him Master Stoneslicer."

"I still don't see why you can't teach me," Evvy replied, jaw set. "We were learning fine yesterday, right?"

Briar rested his head in his hands. It was going to be a long morning.

Evvy finished her dumpling as Golden House came to

life. Briar placed his tree-working kit on the stall's counter, and put his willow next to it. He was training it to the spiral form, which it liked far better than the cascade form it had when he'd bought it. Working gently, assuring the tree it wouldn't feel a thing when he took off the brown leaves, he lost himself in his work for a time. So absorbed was he that when Evvy did speak again, he jumped. The willow dragged some of its branches over his hands, telling him that *he* ought to calm down.

"Now if you want a gang, that's the one to belong to," Evvy remarked. Briar looked where she did, and saw three people a year or two older than he was walk past their stall. One was a girl; the other two were boys. All three wore white, sleeveless tunics, black brocade sashes, and black trousers.

"What's the sign — the tunic or the sash and breeches?" he asked, absently checking to make sure the willow's earth was just damp enough.

"All three," Evvy told him. "They're Gate Lords. The biggest gang in the city, and the richest."

"I thought you didn't like gangs," Briar said. The three slowed to look at his wares. He kept his eyes on them. If anyone tried to steal a tree, they would soon feel as if they carried the fully grown version, but he didn't want trouble so early in the day.

"I don't, but they're the best, if you do like 'em." Evvy watched as the three Gate Lords picked up speed again. "Are you joining them?"

"*Me?*" Briar asked, startled. "Why in Mila's name would I join?"

"You keep saying people ought to be ganged."

"I meant *you*," he said firmly. "I'm a mage — I don't need protection. But you'd be safer if you were ganged up, at least till you master your magic."

"Oh, *safe*," Evvy replied mockingly. "Those Camelguts looked really safe to me, all bloody and bruised."

"But that's gang wars," he objected. "You have to keep other gangs off your ground. That doesn't happen often . . . " He fell silent, remembering times his old gang had battled to chase off another gang, or to add to their territory. As he started to count the fights, he realized they'd come at least once a week. It was not a comfortable thought. "Why didn't your local gang ever recruit you?" he asked, changing the subject. "Don't you have gangs in Princes' Heights?"

"My squat's in Crusher ground," she said, propping her head on her hands. "Tunnelers had it for a moon, then Crushers got it back. Tunnelers have been coming around again lately."

"And neither gang tried to swear you?" he asked.

To his surprise Evvy nodded. "Lots of times. They just can't seem to find my squat." She smiled crookedly. "I used to think they was stupid, but . . . " She fell silent.

"But?" Briar prodded.

"I think the rock — Princes' Heights — hides my place," she said abruptly. She paused, then asked, "What was your gang's sign?"

For some reason Briar looked at his hands, at the riot of vines and leaves that had eaten his jailhouse X's. That wasn't what she meant, of course. "A blue cloth around the right arm. I lost mine, the last time they arrested me and my mates." Suddenly he didn't want to talk about gangs any more. "Here," he said, giving her a silver *dav*. "I'd like some pears and rye bread." He pulled two cups from his satchel. "Get juice or tea or water, in these. And whatever you want for yourself."

Evvy jumped down from the stool gleefully and accepted the cups. "I like being here with you," she told Briar. "We're practically respectable and all." She trotted away, a cup hanging from each index finger.

Practically respectable, Briar thought wryly, going back to work on his willow. That's me — just as respectable as is good for me, and not one whit more.

By the time Evvy returned, carefully balancing food purchases and Briar's cup of water, three mage-students and their teacher had come to look at Briar's trees. Evvy listened as they talked to Briar about improving the yield of herbs grown for spells, fidgeting as the conversation went on. Finally Briar sent her to polish stones for Nahim Zineer so he could chat in peace with mages who came by. Most could sense the power in the trees; all asked about Briar's education. The mention of Winding Circle was enough to keep them around for half an hour, besieging him with questions. When a lull finally came, he didn't welcome it: he was in the middle of another bout of homesickness.

He'd pulled out paper and begun a letter to Sandry when a man rapped on the counter. Briar looked up. The stranger was whipcord lean and plainly dressed with black and silver hair pulled tightly back from his face. His weapons were not so plain: their sheaths were black leather, but after years with Daja the metalsmith, Briar could tell the metalwork on the hilts of the sword and dagger was very good. There was a cold watchfulness in the man's flat brown eyes. A bodyguard of some kind, Briar guessed.

"My lady Zenadia doa Attaneh would have speech with you, shopkeeper," the man said harshly. His voice was a rusty croak, as if he seldom used it.

Briar looked beyond the man. A woman stood in the aisle, watching him. She was veiled from nose to chin, but judging by the lines around her large, well-made-up eyes, she was older, in her fifties or thereabouts. Her clothes spoke softly of real money: her blouse and skirts were discreet lavender silk, embroidered with silver thread; her sari was cloth-of-silver hemmed in lavender. Seed pearls weighted the edges of the gauzy veils on her face and hair. She wore a round, green stone drop between her eyebrows — Briar, who still struggled with different *bindi*, as the stones were called, couldn't remember what green signified. She wore the tiniest hint of rosemary scent, just enough to refresh the air around her.

At her back stood a black-skinned mountain in tan linen. The cloth strained over rolls of fat and muscle. He was egg-bald and had the pudgy look of a eunuch. His eyes were a strange shade of gray that contrasted with his black skin: they were the emptiest eyes that Briar had ever seen. He carried a double-headed ax thrust through a brown sash.

"I was admiring your trees." Lady Zenadia's voice was deep and lovely, unmuffled by her thin face-veil. "They are beautiful. How did you get them to grow so small?"

Briar gave the lady a bow, touching his heart, then his forehead, in the approved eastern manner. Waiting on people had never bothered him until the man called him a shopkeeper. "It takes a great deal of tending and patience, my lady," he answered. From her clothes, jewels, and servants, she could afford his prices. "It's an art, with each tree shaped to a particular form. Aside from beauty, they are used magically to draw certain qualities or luck to a home."

Lady Zenadia stepped forward, the hard-eyed man stepping out of her path. Looking at the placard over the stall she read it aloud: "Trees by Briar Moss, Green Mage." Her beautiful voice gave his name a caress. "Who is Briar Moss?"

Briar bowed again, his hand on his heart to show continued respect. "I am, if it pleases my lady."

He could see that she smiled under her semi-sheer face veil. "But you are still half a lad! Are you truly a *pahan*?"

"I truly am, my lady."

"You have such a charming accent in our tongue," she remarked. In graceful, unaccented Imperial she added, "You come from the west, young *pahan*?"

Briar smiled wryly. He'd thought his Chammuri was improving, but apparently not as much as he'd hoped. "Summersea, my lady. In Emelan, on the Pebbled Sea."

"Summersea!" she exclaimed, still in Imperial. "Such a long way! Do you winter here in Chammur?"

"I'm not sure," said Briar. "I am traveling with my teacher. She decides when we come and go."

"Then I had best look at your wares, hadn't I? In case this is your only time in Golden House." She said it archly, eyebrows raised, almost as if she flirted with him.

That was his cue. He brought the small, cushioned chair kept in the booth for such visits and put it outside with a small, tall-legged table. It was designed to put anything on it at the eye level of the person in the chair.

The lady sat, fussing with her lavender skirts, sari, and veils until they were properly arranged. Her older man-servant positioned himself in front of the counter, the big eunuch at his mistress's back. Briar wondered if she took the eunuch along on hot days and trained him to stand where he could do double duty as a sunshade. Then he put his mind to the job of guessing what might appeal to her. With a customer who was not of the nobility Briar could ask questions to determine what tree and what sort of magic was required. With nobles he had to rely on instinct and tact. If he asked anything of Lady Zenadia directly, the best he could hope for would be a slap for impudence. It was a guessing game, one he enjoyed. He liked to draw from his knowledge of human nature to find out what this woman might want.

He showed her a succession of pines, most spelled for protection. The rich were always concerned with that. Better, those pines were older miniatures that he'd bought from Summersea. He wasn't as attached to them as he was to those he'd trained from saplings. All were over thirty years old; they had the way of being a miniature in their roots, branches, trunks, and needles. They only required the odd pinching back here and there to keep their shapes.

He was describing the benefits of a Bihan fir when he saw Evvy. She was walking toward his stall with two of the Camelgut girls: monkey-faced Douna and fiery Mai. It took him a moment to recognize Douna and Mai: their tatters and their Camelgut sashes were gone. Instead they wore tunics and skirts of clean, servant-grade cloth, and silver-metal nose rings with a garnet dangle.

Douna halted, grabbing Mai's arm. Both girls talked to Evvy for a moment, watching Briar's stall. Then they trotted away, casting frequent looks over their shoulders, as if something had made them nervous. Evvy, frowning, walked on to the stall.

As Briar returned a tree to its shelf, Lady Zenadia glanced up and saw Evvy. "Who is this lovely child, *Pahan* Briar?" she asked. "A friend of yours?"

"My helper," Briar replied. Out of the side of his mouth he ordered softly, "Go to her side and curtsy. Don't stand too close."

Evvy shrugged and walked over to stand in front of the lady. Gripping her brown skirt on either side, she gave a swift, awkward, curtsy.

"What a charming girl," the lady said. "Are you learning tree magic, little one?"

Evvy shook her head, a wary look in her almond-shaped eyes. "They're rock-killers. I don't like 'em."

"Call her 'my lady,'" Briar cautioned. He lifted down a tiny crab apple tree heavy with fruit.

"My lady," Evvy said obediently.

The woman chuckled. "Trees are rock-killers? How so, when rocks are not alive?"

Evvy shook her head and said nothing.

"Plants break up rocks, my lady," Briar explained as he put the crab apple on the table for her to inspect. "They sink roots into cracks to get to dirt, and as they grow, they split the rocks."

The lady smiled. "Why are you so passionate in the defense of rocks, my child?" she asked.

Once again Evvy remained speechless. As the silence deepened, Briar said, "Evvy has magic with stones. You'll have to excuse her, my lady. She's been living on her own for a long time. She isn't that comfortable talking to people." Even as he said it he thought, She has no trouble talking to me, or Rosethorn, or the Camelgut girls.

"But how shocking!" the lady exclaimed. "You have no family?" Evvy shook her head. Lady Zenadia sat forward on her chair. She told Evvy, "Come closer, my dear."

Evvy was about to balk when she met Briar's eyes. Guessing that he would be unhappy if she refused, she took a step forward. The woman looked her over from top to toe as Briar locked his hands behind his back. Something was not right here, he thought. His instincts were clamoring, but why? After four years of selling medicines and two of miniature trees, he knew this breed of rich, older woman. They had nothing to occupy them until their children produced grandchildren, or they didn't care to fill empty time with grandchildren. Sometimes they brewed mischief and interfered in people's lives. They shopped; they adopted pets or people; they did the rounds of their friends' houses; the more worthwhile ones did charitable work or gardened.

"You could do quite nicely," the lady said to Evvy at last. "Would you like to come to my house to live? I would clothe you and educate you, while you could keep me company and run my errands. You would eat well, have a bed of your own, warm clothing, a healer for when you are ill. I would even pay you a wage, starting now." She reached under her sari and drew out a silk purse. From it she took a gold *cham*, and offered it to Evvy.

Briar never saw himself as cold. That was his fostersister Tris, who could turn wintery in a flash. Now it seemed there was more of Tris in him than he'd ever realized. His spine turned to ice; a bitter chill flooded his brain.

She thinks she can buy Evvy, like a lapdog. Like a toy, he thought. Like a slave.

Before Evvy could reply, Briar stepped between her and Lady Zenadia with a bow. "Excuse me, my lady, but that's not possible. I mentioned Evvy is a stone mage? She is to start lessons with Master Jebilu Stoneslicer. He comes here today, in fact." Now he sounded like Daja the Trader. She could hide all of her feelings as she turned a bargain that would send away a buyer she despised while his coin stayed in her pocket. And I thought I could never learn from girls, he told himself wryly. Aloud he added, "But Evvy is grateful for the honor you do her." He turned so Evvy could see the lady, without Briar stepping out from between them.

"That's very nice," Evvy agreed, "but I have to learn magic. My lady."

Briar glanced at her again, startled. From Evvy's tone,

he might think she didn't care about the money or a decent place to live. *See that!* he told his absent foster-sisters. *She isn't even looking at that coin!*

He wished he could rub his temples — they had started to ache — but he didn't want the lady to notice. Sometimes he wished he didn't have to listen to all these people between his own ears, and think so many different things at once. It was tiring and confusing.

"Well." The lady didn't seem angry, only thoughtful. "I do not withdraw my offer — think it over. You may wish to ask Master Stoneslicer if he will teach you while you are under my roof. A stone mage in my household is no small thing, particularly not in Chammur. *Pahan* Moss, would you be so good as to show me the larch again?"

She purchased the larch after another half hour of inspection and chatter, always trying to draw Evvy into the conversation. Once she had bought the tree, and given Briar the instructions he would need to deliver it, she smiled at Evvy one last time. "When the *pahan* brings my tree, I hope you will come," she said, cupping Evvy's face in one hand. "You might feel differently once you see my home." With another smile at Briar, she and her guards left.

10

Γhe moment they were alone, Briar rounded on Evvy. "Are you daft?" he wanted to know. "You aren't stupid, so why did I see you parade through Golden House with two Vipers? Did you forget they tried to kidnap you?"

"But they aren't Vipers," argued Evvy. "It was Mai and Douna from Camelgut."

"Not anymore," Briar said. "They're Vipers now."

"Mai and Douna are still the same as they ever were." Evvy's face was as stubborn as his. "Anyway, what difference does it make? You were talking with their *takameri*."

"Their *takameri*?" Briar felt confused, a normal state when he conversed with her. "What are you talking about?"

Evvy shook her head, saddened by his ignorance. "Their *takameri*. The rich woman who gives them weapons and things. That was her, the one that bought your tree."

Briar looked at the tracery of vines under the skin of his left hand, following one stem with his right finger as he thought. Lady Zenadia was the woman who had bought the Vipers their blackjacks?

She tried to hire Evvy, he remembered. Maybe the Vipers still wanted Evvy, even though he'd told the girl yesterday that he would never let her join them. Maybe they — or their wealthy sponsor — had decided to try other ways to get her. Was that so bad, if Lady Zenadia wanted to educate her? A woman of money and power could protect Evvy if Jebilu Stoneslicer turned nasty.

No. If the Vipers didn't know how to act like a proper gang, then the Money-Bag female who sponsored them knew even less. He couldn't forget the feeling that she had tried to buy Evvy for her house, just as she had bought the miniature larch.

But she could give Evvy so many things he could not — if only she could be trusted to treat Evvy like a human being. "Do you want to live with her?" he asked, curious. "You'd eat well, get a proper education, living with someone like that."

They were interrupted as six panting slaves carrying a litter came down the aisle to halt in front of Briar's stall. The litter was elegant, every inch of wood beautifully carved. The curtains were brocade, the cushions silk. As the bearers waited, their muscles straining, Master Jebilu Stoneslicer climbed out. The stone mage wore brown satin today, a long, high-collared tunic coat crusted on every hem with gold embroidery. White lawn shirt cuffs showed under the coat sleeves. He wore black satin trousers and pointed slippers studded with jewels. All of those colors combined to make him look more sallow than ever. The bearers, relieved of their burden, sank to the ground with the litter.

Jebilu glared at Briar. "Well?" he demanded. "Where is she?"

Evvy had ducked behind Briar. Feeling like a traitor, he stepped aside. "Evvy, this is Master — *Pahan* — Jebilu Stoneslicer. The only trained stone mage in all Chammur, it so happens." He challenged the older man with his eyes, daring him to admit he'd driven off the other stone mages.

Stoneslicer wasn't even looking at him, but at Evvy. "Come forward, girl," he ordered. Fumbling in his belt-purse, he produced a round piece of obsidian. He raised it in his hand. Evvy backed up. "I need to see if you are truly gifted and how far your talents extend," he said coldly. "I cannot rely on the testimony of two green mages as to your power." The look he gave Briar would have curdled milk.

Once more Briar locked his hands behind his back. He was very unhappy to realize he didn't *want* to give Evvy up to this man. Jebilu didn't know who Evvy was or where she'd come from. If he had a kinder side, Briar had yet to see it. While none of his or the girls' teachers had ever laid a hand on them — Rosethorn's threats to the contrary — Briar knew some teachers believed that beatings made lessons stick. Could he trust Jebilu not to hurt Evvy in body or spirit?

If he beats her, I'll kill him, Briar promised himself, trying not to remember that in all likelihood he would be gone. And a real stone mage has to be a better teacher for her than a kid green mage. Doesn't he?

Jebilu pressed the obsidian circle to Evvy's forehead. For a moment nothing happened: then the stone blazed white. Its glare was as intense as the light Briar had seen Evvy give off the day before.

Jebilu muttered something and the light faded. He tucked the circle into his belt-purse and drew out an egg-shaped clear crystal. "Bring light to this," he ordered, holding it out to Evvy.

She didn't say "Oh, that" — she simply touched it. A seed of light appeared in the crystal's depths, growing until the whole stone gave off a steady glow.

Jebilu closed his hand around the crystal. By the time he returned it to his belt-purse, it had gone dark again. He offered her a small brownish-gold globe stippled with black marks. "Bring heat to this," he ordered.

Evvy took it, then handed it back. "That isn't real stone," she objected. "It's hard, but it isn't stone."

Jebilu snorted. "Petrified wood," he grumbled.

"May I see?" Briar asked. Coal, he knew, was made of plants, but he hadn't realized that wood could be made stone.

Jebilu scowled at him. "This is a delicate magical tool, *Pahan* Moss," he snapped. "Not a toy for curiosity seekers."

Briar bit the inside of his cheek. He counted silently to fifty in Imperial, to keep from telling this man to put the globe someplace uncomfortable.

Jebilu put the petrified wood in his purse and pulled out a dirty white stone. "Use this. What is your name?"

"Evumeimei," the girl replied, taking the stone. "Evumeimei Dingzai, of Yanjing." She turned the stone over in her fingers. "There's cracks in this. I might break it."

"No one can break diamond stones, Evumeimei Dingzai of Yanjing." Jebilu made her name sound like an insult. "Heat it up. *Pahan* Moss told me you can do it."

Evvy sighed, and closed her eyes. Briar saw the pale brilliance of her magic appear at the center of her forehead, lancing into the diamond stone in a tight stream. She had practiced last night, he realized. She went home and practiced, and got better. And she was still alive, so she had been able to keep her power under control. He felt an absurd sense of pride in her flower in his chest.

Her magic entered the stone. To Briar's eyes the heart of the stone shimmered with it. The light began to ricochet inside the rock, bouncing through an internal network of cracks and faces. Slowly real, visible white light began to pour from it. "It's not heating up," Evvy said. Sweat gathered at her temples.

"Try harder," ordered Jebilu crossly.

Scowling first at him, then at the stone in her hand, Evvy increased the flow of her power. Briar watched uneasily as her magic ricocheted faster through the stone's heart. "Evvy, maybe you should let this go —" he began.

"Silence!" barked Jebilu. "You are not to teach her, so let me test her as I see fit!"

Evvy flinched and lost control of her power. It flooded the stone. The crystal blazed, then shattered. Evvy cried out and dropped the pieces on the floor. She was hurt: blood welled from a cut in her palm.

Briar ducked into his stall. He yanked a bandage and a bottle of cutbane from his kit. Grasping her bleeding hand by the wrist, Briar bit into the cork that sealed his lotion and yanked it free. He poured the liquid over her wound.

Though she was trembling, she still found the nerve to quip, "Don't you make anything that doesn't stink?" The flow of blood thinned, the slashed skin in her hand closing under the Cutbane's influence.

"I like aloe, and I'll thank you not to insult my stuff." Briar wrapped the bandage firmly around her hand. When he felt he had enough layers of cloth around her palm, he ordered the linen to part, and the loose threads to weave themselves into the rest of the bandage. It wouldn't come off now unless cut.

Finishing, he saw Jebilu on his knees, holding the three diamond fragments up to the sun that streamed from a nearby window. One was smeared with blood. The other two glittered with fire like a faceted crystal, only more intensely. Jebilu's face was gray under its sallow tone. He wrapped the three pieces in a handkerchief, and stowed them in his purse.

She's stronger than he is, Briar realized, uneasy. *And he knows it.*

What would Rosethorn have done if he'd been stronger when he came to her? Briar double-checked the fastening of the bandage, stifling a snort. No one was stronger than Rosethorn. Even if Briar *had* been stronger than his teacher, he didn't have Rosethorn's years of study and practice.

Jebilu lurched to his feet. "Where are your things?" he demanded, sweat rolling down his cheeks. "I will house you with the chief palace scribe, since you refuse to live in the palace. His wife is a firm parent who knows to keep an eye on you. We have time to settle you among them —"

"No," Evvy said flatly. She ran her fingers over her freshly-bandaged hand, then looked at Jebilu and Briar. "I'm not going."

"I am the only one who can teach you, girl," Jebilu began, his face stained orange with anger. "Do not take that tone with me!"

"I don't like you and I'm not studying with you," Evvy retorted, glaring up into his face. "And nobody in the world can make me do it. I figured I'd look at you because *Pahan* Briar thought it was important. Now that I've seen you, though, I can tell it was just another of his strange notions, like belonging to a gang."

Jebilu glared at Briar. "This is what comes of dealing with guttersnipes," he snapped, trembling with fury. "They have no sense of the honor being done them, or of gratitude."

"Why should she feel grateful?" Briar inquired, curious. "You've treated her like a slave since you got here."

"*I* know your kind," Evvy told Jebilu. "You'll treat me like dirt and kiss the bum of anyone with money. I may be a guttersnipe, but you're a *zernamus*. Any learning you dish out will be as rancid as month-old butter."

Jebilu pointed a quivering finger at Briar. "This is not my fault!" he cried. "Tell that — *female* I was prepared to do my duty and was refused!" He crawled into his litter and yanked the curtains around him. The slaves picked the litter up with a grunt of effort and carried the stone mage out of Golden House.

Briar looked at Evvy with the same kind of awe as he gave to Rosethorn when the woman's temper got the better of her. If Evvy had planned every word, she could not have chosen a speech better calculated to burn Jebilu twelve ways from midday.

I'd say the guttersnipe won this game, he thought. And my problem is the same as it was before Rosethorn went to talk to old Jooba-hooba. Somebody has to teach this kid the basics, and I suppose that somebody is me. "So what's a *zernamus*?" he asked mildly.

Evvy had been watching him, one shoulder hitched up defensively, as if she expected him to hit her. Down came the shoulder; she grinned. "Someone who lives off the rich, like a tick that sucks money instead of blood."

Briar shook his head. "He would have been a rotten teacher anyway."

"I thought so. Can we eat?" asked Evvy cheerfully.

"You don't understand," Briar said, trying to make her see it as he did. "The only rocks I ever studied were the kinds that could be spelled to make plants grow better, like malachite. Even that way it's easier to lay magic on the fertilizer or the seed, because the stone fights me."

"Well, malachite's a lesson," Evvy said, perching on Briar's high stool. "You'll think of something, *Pahan* Briar. You're awful smart. And you don't think you're better than people just because there's silver in your pocket."

She doesn't know, Briar thought, bewildered and scared. *She thinks I'm an adult who knows things. She sees a pahan, not a fourteen-year-old kid who's spent the last four years with his nose in the dirt.*

Had Rosethorn ever felt this way? As if he thought her perfect, and might be disappointed if he found she was human after all?

Talk Evvy around, argued a cooler part of himself. *Talk*

her around and talk Jooba-hooba around. You could maybe do it. You talk a fair stitch when you want to.

Did he want to?

She needs to learn to read and write, he thought; I can teach her that. I remember how Tris taught me. Same with sums, and learning the stars, and how to use paper and ink. I can teach the meditating. Earth temple has to have some books about stones and stone magic, and we can find her a stone mage once we leave Chammur.

It could be done. But how was he to tell Rosethorn? He knew it was good for the student to live close to or even with the teacher. Rosethorn definitely would not like it, if he brought another resident into their home. She might say he should have made Evvy listen to Jebilu.

"We ought to live in the same place," he remarked quietly.

She had remained silent on her perch for as long as he'd been thinking, not distracting him with chatter. Now he saw worry in her eyes. "I can't leave my cats," she replied. "I just can't. Please don't ask me."

He and the girls had all agreed that their dog Little Bear should go with Tris, who would have missed him the most. Still, it had hurt Briar to see Little Bear walk onto a ship without him, and Little Bear was a shared dog, not his alone. What would it be like, to be forced to give up a pet?

He chewed on a thumbnail. I could find another house, maybe near Rosethorn, he decided, reviewing the amount of cash he'd left with the Earth temple treasurer. He had plenty, but he always liked a plump money cushion, just in case. It was a good thing Lady Zenadia had bought the larch, or at least, it would be good once Briar had the coin in hand. Nobles often changed their minds when they got home and added up their accounts.

"You're more trouble than you're worth," he informed Evvy tartly.

She shrugged. "I'm a girl. That's my job."

He grinned at that — it fit the girls *he* knew — then sobered. "I didn't mean that," he apologized. "About you being trouble. I'm just not sure I'd be a very good teacher."

"You have to be better than Jooba-hooba," she said.

"Not like that's saying much," he retorted. "That —"

"Hey — tree people!" someone said sharply, interrupting.

Briar and Evvy looked up. Two of the three Gate Lords who had passed by earlier had returned. Their morning's good mood had vanished: they looked hot and cross as they walked up to the booth.

The female, a black girl of Briar's age, pointed to Evvy. "What did they do with him?" she demanded sharply. "Your two friends? We saw him talking with them, and that's the *last* we saw of him."

"They're just people I know," Evvy protested. "And who's 'him'?"

"Our *tesku*, brat," said the male Gate Lord, a brown-skinned youth of seventeen. He reached over the counter and grabbed Evvy's shirt-front, dragging her toward him. "And if you're friends with Vipers, you're a Viper —" He looked to the side, to the dagger Briar had gently laid against his face.

"She isn't a Viper and you just annoyed me," Briar told him softly. "If you don't want a third nostril, let her go."

"She runs with Vipers," objected the girl. "Or gutter slime that let go their true gang to join Vipers."

Briar saw the girl was moving to the side, ready to grab Evvy's arm when her mate let Evvy go. Briar woke the willow and the fig trees, releasing years' worth of growth into their branches. As soon as the Gate Lord girl was within reach of the miniature, he turned them loose.

Wire-thin branches twined around her arm and neck as Briar called on the essence of the full-sized tree at the heart of each miniature. Though the girl's bonds were flexible, slender branches, she felt as if she were locked in the limbs of a full-grown willow and a full-grown fig. "*Pahan*," whispered the girl, her dusky skin gone ashy with fright.

"Now back off," Briar told the male Gate Lord. "I get any more vexed and I can't promise what I will and won't do."

The youth released Evvy, held up his hands to show they were empty, and waited for Briar to lower his knife. When Briar did, the Gate Lord took three slow steps back. "If she ain't a Viper, does she know what those two done with our *tesku*?" he asked. "He was talking to them, and no one's seen him since."

Evvy shook her head. She smoothed her blouse with a shaking hand. "They just wanted to say hello to *Pahan* Briar," she mumbled.

"Let my friend go," the youth told Briar. "We'll be about our business then."

Sweat came to Briar's forehead. It was much harder to get miniature trees to reabsorb all that wonderful new growth and return to being small again. Even though he drew away the strength of their sprouting, letting its power spill into the air, he would have to do serious pruning to return them to their original state. The fig, sensing his plan, instantly started to complain.

When the trees let her go, the female Gate Lord scurried off with her friend. Both of them looked back over their shoulders at Briar to make sure he didn't follow.

"Are you happy?" Evvy demanded, her lips trembling. "This is what happens with gangs. You don't have to belong to one — just be in the way when they get a notion into their heads. And if you do belong, it's worse."

He would have told her she was wrong, but he knew she wasn't. He remembered the times he and his mates would charge through a market, overturning baskets, scaring donkeys, and pulling down awnings. They would single out a man or woman walking down the street and flock around that person, cutting him or her off from other passersby, tugging on clothes, pinching or patting, giggling as their prey grew more and more frightened. As part of the gang, he'd thought it funny. It didn't seem amusing just now.

"You don't understand," he replied at last. "Your gang's who you have when you don't have anyone else."

"For you, maybe. For me, it's one more pack of wild dogs looking to tear me apart." Evvy brushed away something that looked uncomfortably like a tear and smoothed her blouse again.

Rather than defend it, knowing he couldn't, Briar went for food, leaving Evvy in the stall with the trees. They would keep her safe if anyone else bothered her. Making his purchases, Briar kept his eyes and ears open. The Gate Lords were everywhere, making guards edgy as they searched behind curtains and stalls. The Vipers appeared to have left the *souk* — Briar didn't see any of them.

He and Evvy ate their midday in silence. She stayed close for the remainder of the afternoon, while Briar worked on trees and talked to people. A second noble and a wealthy mage both expressed interest in trees, and told Briar they would send word if they chose to buy. He thought the mage would follow through, though he wasn't sure about the noble.

Finally it was time to go. Evvy retrieved the donkeys he'd rented from the market stables and helped him to load his trees in their special carry-baskets. After making sure they'd left the stall as clean as it had been when Briar arrived that morning, they led the donkeys outside. The sun was already below the western wall, though higher buildings still got plenty of light.

They hadn't gone far from the *souk* when a woman in the full-length veil-cocoon worn by the strictest Mohunites walked up to them. "*Pahan* Briar, may I walk with you? Just 'til we're out of Gate Lord territory?"

He glared at her. "I don't even know you," he snapped. He was tired, headachy, and not at all ready for his talk with Rosethorn.

The woman unhooked the section of pale blue cloth that covered all of her face but her eyes to let him see her: Mai. Her eyes were red and puffy from weeping; tears had made tracks down her dirty cheeks. Parts of the veil-cocoon were still wet — she must have stolen it from a drying line. "Please, *pahan*, don't send me away. The Gate Lords killed Douna." She began to weep again. "If they find me, they'll kill me, too."

Briar went cold all over. Just a day ago Douna had fetched him to the Camelgut den. He wanted it to be a story, but he knew it wasn't. He knew the look of someone who'd just lost a mate. "Evvy already got threatened by Gate Lords just for being with you two," he said, trying to sound cold. "See if your *takameri* will protect you."

Mai wiped her eyes on her sleeve, then fastened the face veil again. "I don't want anything from that —" The word she used was so raw that Evvy yelped and covered her ears. "Just let me come as far as Cedar Lane."

Briar had been as tough as he could be when a girl he liked stared at him with heartbreak in her eyes. "All right," he said gruffly. "Walk on the side of that middle donkey. Put a hand on the basket like you're holding it steady."

Mai did as she was told. There were Gate Lords everywhere in the crush of people leaving Golden House and the Grand Bazaar. Two of them started toward Briar's donkeys, but the girl who'd been captured by the willow and the fig stopped them. Briar, Evvy, and the disguised Mai walked away from the gang searchers in safety.

Briar waited until he hadn't seen a Gate Lord for five blocks before he walked up beside Mai. "Why'd they kill Douna?" he wanted to know. "Didn't you tell them you had nothing to do with their *tesku?*"

Mai looked away.

"Lakik Trickster take you both!" he snapped. "You did it, didn't you? You snatched the head of another gang! Nobody does that!"

"It wasn't us that took him," Mai replied sullenly. "We just lured him to Ikrum and the others. They said we had to, to prove we were worthy to be Vipers. If you'd ever been in a gang, you'd know."

Briar *did* know. But the gang hadn't saved Douna, had it? The Vipers had let her and Mai wander off alone, outside the safety of the group. They'd let them go, knowing the Gate Lords would remember who had been seen last with their leader.

Evvy, on the lead donkey, glanced back at them. Suddenly she asked, "So *Pahan* Briar, if I get ganged up, I could end like Douna someday, right?"

"You aren't in a gang?" Mai inquired, startled. "Where do you live, in the palace?"

Briar, who'd gotten the point of Evvy's artless question, glared at her. "Enough," he told her. "You made your point."

"I hope so," Evvy retorted.

When they reached the Cedar Lane fountain, Mai let the Mohunite cocoon slide off her hair. "I've got to tell Douna's granddam," she said grimly, her eyes hard. "And then I'm going back to the Vipers. Gate Lords killed Douna. We'll make them bleed."

"Mai, don't." Briar reached for her. "What good —"

"Blood for blood." She turned down Cedar Lane, walking away from them without a backward glance.

"That's gangs for you." Evvy's voice was bitter in the growing dark. "Good at hating."

"*Evvy*," Briar started to say warningly. He stopped himself. She was right.

They finished their ride in silence as Briar tried hard to think of nothing at all. He wanted Sandry, and Daja, and

Tris. He wanted to be in Discipline Cottage at Winding Circle, with his own garden, his dog, his foster-sisters, and Lark. He wanted to hear Rosethorn and Crane squabble. He wanted to eat Dedicate Gorse's cooking again. Chammur was a hard place, with no love for the people that lived among all this stone. He wanted the rains to come and wash the city right out.

When he saw the night-lantern hanging over his door, he remembered he hadn't planned what he would say to Rosethorn about Evvy's refusal to study with Jebilu. "Oh, pox," he whispered as he led Evvy and the donkeys to the Earth temple stable. It was not a good idea to say just anything to Rosethorn. Desperately he planned as they helped the hostlers to care for the horses and donkeys, and promised to return for most of the miniatures in the morning.

He and Evvy carried the *shakkan*, the fig, the willow, and Briar's kit home while his mind raced. He'd tell her he'd rent a house. That would blunt the worst of her anger; even Rosethorn could live with Evvy for a few days. He had to remember to say that it would just *be* for a few days, before he mentioned the cats. But first he should tell her about Jebilu, then give her his plan for the new house.

What *had* Jebilu said to make it so clear that Evvy would be miserable with him? Or was it something that Evvy had said? Briar was too tired and too depressed about Douna to remember the conversation word for word.

He and Evvy walked into the dining room, where they

put the trees and the saddlebags on the table. Evvy collapsed into a chair. Briar stood with his hands in his pockets, gathering his wits for battle. He could sense Rosethorn as she came down the stairs from the workroom.

The direct approach — Evvy's going to be my headache, not yours — was a mistake. It would just spark Rosethorn's temper. He had to come at things sidelong when she was involved. When a disruption of her routine was involved. She —

Rosethorn walked in, carrying three fat, leather-bound books. She dumped them on the table between Briar and Evvy with a sigh of relief. "You'll need these," she said breathlessly. "To start with, anyway."

Briar read the lettering on the spine of the topmost book. He was so tired it was hard to focus. It took three trials before the title made sense: *Of Stones and Their Magic, Inherent and Retained.*

When he finally understood, he gaped at Rosethorn. She had gone to fetch covered pots from the warming oven under the kitchen fire. "I cleaned out the front room and bought a pallet. The cats can do their business in the backyard, and *you* get to clean it up," she added, looking at Evvy. "Start earning your keep. Dishes and bowls in that cupboard." She pointed, and went back to the kitchen.

As Evvy brought out plates and bowls for the three of them, Briar sat heavily on a chair. She had known. Rosethorn had known, and she'd made her own decision.

"You could have said something," he called to Rosethorn, vexed.

She emerged from the kitchen, hands on hips. "For all I knew, he would see it was time to do the right thing, and act like a man instead of an egg gone bad. I'm too hard on people — Lark's always telling me so. I had to give him the chance to act properly."

"He did," Evvy remarked, setting plates on the table. "I said no. He was going to be a pig about it anyway."

Rosethorn smiled crookedly. "I admit, I did also think you might take that attitude."

"So I guess I was the last to know," Briar grumbled.

"Of course you are. You're a man, aren't you?" Rosethorn asked evilly, ladling lamb and rice pilaf onto the plates. Evvy giggled, and Briar rested his head on his hands.

Not only am I doomed, but they're going to laugh at me while doom happens, he thought, contentedly morose. Whyever did I leave Summersea?

11

The next morning Briar and Evvy went to Princes'
Heights to fetch her cats. Wearing racks that supported
covered straw baskets, Briar and Evvy passed through the
entrance to her part of the Heights, a black stone arch that
some wit had named Sunrise Gate. It opened onto a broad
tunnel into the rock. Briar looked around as Evvy led the
way: he could see wood and stone shoring everywhere. Part
of the tunnel roof was covered by a wooden ceiling. In
places the wooden planks had fallen; heaps of stone and
dirt lay under them.

"Don't you worry about cave-ins?" he asked.

Evvy shrugged. "They happen all the time. Nobody
thinks much about it."

Briar shuddered and decided he wouldn't ask any more
questions.

In the wider tunnels the air was reasonably fresh. Shafts
cut through into open air above, creating a breeze. It carried

a rich bouquet of scents: wood smoke, burned food, rancid oil, burning fat, mildew, and rot.

Leaving the large tunnel, they turned into a smaller one, then a third. Now serious odors flooded Briar's sensitive nose. The jelly-thick reek of too many people in a space for much too long a time made his eyes water. The stone itself had absorbed years of old urine and dung, cookfires, blood, cheap food, and death.

Briar was gasping as they entered their fifth tunnel. His nose had stopped up completely. Tears flooded down his cheeks. The light thrown off by a few torches and burning knots of wood or manure showed air filled with a gray haze.

He stopped to rearrange his burden, settling the rack lower on his shoulders. The roof was not very high in the depths. "How can you *bear* it?" he asked Evvy.

She frowned, confused. "Bear what?"

"The *smell*!"

Evvy shrugged. "I don't smell anything." She raised her flat-ended nose and sniffed. "Oh, all right, somebody was cooking goat last night. Don't you like goat?"

A heap of rags by the wall cackled and turned into an old woman who struggled to sit up. "You live here long enough, my lad, and you won't smell nothin' either. Got anything for an old lady, Evumeimei?"

Evvy knelt by the old woman. "Maybe I do." She pulled two rolls from her pocket: they looked suspiciously like some of the ones Rosethorn had bought for breakfast. "Qinling, chew careful," she cautioned.

"Don't go worrying about me," Qinling replied. She gnawed a roll eagerly.

Evvy walked on. "I'll miss Qinling," she murmured just loud enough for Briar to hear. "She's the only one who speaks Zhanzou with me."

"What's za — what you said?" he asked, wiping his dripping eyes on his sleeve.

"Zhanzou. The language we spoke in my province. Qinling tells me stories in it sometimes, if she's not too drunk. This is Lambing Tunnel, what we're on." She led him around a turn.

Briar stopped and looked back for a moment, trying to tell if they were followed. They had passed doors and windows on the way, openings barred with wood, rags, or even bead curtains. He'd sensed people behind those barriers, peering at them, sizing them up. He half-expected them to follow, like starving rats. Flexing his hands, he realized his wrist daggers had dropped out of their sheaths and into his palms. He kept them there. All along he'd felt less and less plant life as roots on the ground overhead reached their limits. There would be no calling on plants for help in this sunless place. Only mold grew down here, and mold wasn't much good in a fight, though he supposed he could use it to make attackers sneeze themselves blind. He hadn't felt so naked of friends in years.

Evvy stopped in front of a shallow niche formed by one chunk of stone overlapping another. She rested her forehead against the stone, her back to Briar. "I know he's a stranger, but he's a *good* stranger," she murmured to the stone. "He'd never hurt me. He's my teacher. He's safe."

Briar shook his head — his foster-sisters would laugh themselves sick to hear him called a teacher. He still felt not like someone who deserved the title, but an imposter. Once we get her a proper teacher, she'll know I'm not one at all, he told himself. If that idea pinched him a little, it was overtaken by shock. What he'd thought was a shallow niche was really a passage. How had he seen a wall there?

I'm starting to think the rock hides my squat, she'd said yesterday.

She was right.

Briar followed her into the narrow passage. It was just wide enough to admit them and the baskets they carried on their backs, though Briar had to crouch to keep from banging his head. Ten yards down they began to climb steps so old they were worn like bowls in the middle.

"I think there was a cave-in, long ago," Evvy remarked quietly. "It sealed off my place in front. This was the back way, originally." She passed through an opening at the top of the stair to be greeted with a chorus of yowls. Briar sneezed: the aroma of cat urine blended with the funk of the passage. He didn't even try to blow his nose. The worst thing he could imagine just now was a nose clear enough to smell everything afresh.

Evvy's home was a two-room chamber carved in orange stone. The light was better than it had been in any of the tunnels. It shone steadily from five opaque or cloudy white crystals that were sunk into the stone of the walls.

At first it seemed as if the floor crawled with cats. They meowed and twitched their tails as they mobbed the girl, who knelt to pet each one. A second look sorted them out. There were indeed seven, all as thin as Evvy. They came in a mixed bag of colors: blue-gray with apricot patches, brown-black with orange patches, two brown masks and feet with gold fur, two cinnamon masks and feet with gold fur, black-and-white. Evvy crooned and handed out the contents of a cloth bag she'd pulled from the front of her tunic: chunks of beef and what looked very much like half of the breakfast ham.

Briar inspected their surroundings while Evvy tended her friends. A pile of rags in the corner seemed to be her bed. Directly under a hole in the ceiling was a rough fire pit, with a bucket and a battered pot beside it. A collection of cracked and chipped pottery was stacked by the wall. In a niche he saw a much-battered god figure: a smiling fat man with shriveled flowers at his feet. A thick coat of cat hair covered everything. A ripe drift of scent from the other room told him it served Evvy and her cats as a privy.

The most remarkable thing about the place was the walls. In some areas the rock had been planed smooth, though enough chunks had fallen out that the effect was irregular. That he expected. What he hadn't expected was the stones embedded everywhere, small ones the size of a *dav*, others the size of his palm, even some polished rounds and eggs that were probably stolen. Their color and texture varied. One thing was the same for all: They had been pressed into the wall as if it were soft butter, not stone. Briar tried to pry one out, and couldn't.

"You put these in?" he asked Evvy as the chorus of yowls quieted and the cats ate.

She nodded. "Ria, let Mystery have that. You have your own," she chided the black-and-white cat. "I thought maybe it's just dirt, the walls, and that's why I could push them in."

Briar rapped the wall around one stone and grimaced. "It's rock, Evvy. You made the rock act squishy."

She shrugged. "I didn't think it was anything special when I did it." She ducked her head suddenly. When she spoke, her voice was wry. "Though I stopped after I kept getting headaches. I think the Heights were telling me, enough, please."

Briar surveyed the room again, hands in his pockets. "Can we take some of these back with us?" he asked. "Including your light-stones. We'll look them up in the books, find out what they are and what-all you can do with them."

Evvy scratched her head. "Right." She scrabbled in the rags of her bed, drawing out a large section of cloth. Once she had laid it flat, she began to pry various stones from the walls. They came easily for her. When Briar tried it, they remained stuck fast.

"What *I* don't see is how we're taking the cats," Evvy commented as she placed stones on her cloth. "There's ways out of here they can use once we start try loading them, you know."

"Don't you get rats through those ways?" Briar asked. He placed Evvy's basket and the two that he had fetched on the floor and opened the lids.

"No rats," Evvy said firmly. "The cats gang up on them. They let the rats get in and then jump 'em." She bent to scratch the nearest cat's chin. "They're good friends to me." Her lower lip trembled. "I don't want to leave them."

"Girls. Always fussing," Briar said. "Leave it to me."

The cats finished devouring their food and started a post-feeding wash. Briar slid an oilcloth packet from his shirt pocket and opened it to reveal three catnip leaves. He placed one leaf in each open basket, then woke the power in them. To feline noses it was as if a huge bed of fresh catnip had sprouted in the baskets. They scrambled to get at it.

The moment two cats were in each of the small baskets and three in the largest, Briar closed the lids and fastened them. He lashed one to the rack Evvy would carry, then put the remaining two on his. Once they were set, he changed the power of the leaves to make the cats sleepy. The baskets rocked as the occupants curled up for naps.

"How did you do that?" Evvy wanted to know, awe in her wide brown eyes. "Can you teach me?"

"Not with catnip," Briar replied with a grin. "Maybe us rock-killers are good for something after all."

Evvy blushed, grinned, and flapped a hand at him. She wouldn't say he was wrong, but she wouldn't admit he might be right.

"Hurry up with the stones," Briar ordered. "I have to see Lady Zenadia to deliver her tree, don't forget."

Evvy tied her rag bundle shut. She had left only one stone in the wall, to light their way out of the room. The others shone through her cloth, rays of light poking like fingers through openings and holes. "I'll have to wash before we go." She tied the rock bundle to her waist and let Briar settle her rack on her shoulders.

"You're not coming," he said, securing the ties. "I'm going by myself."

Evvy scowled at him. "Why can't I?" she asked. "She said I could. I'd like to see a *takamer* house."

"Not this one," Briar said firmly, checking the bindings on his baskets. "She might just try to keep you and give you to the Vipers. Better not to risk it." When she opened her mouth to argue further, he said, "You wanted me for a teacher. That means you have to listen. If you don't like it, I'm sure Jebilu Stoneslicer would let his student visit any *takamer*'s house in town, carrying messages and such-like."

"No he wouldn't," grumbled Evvy. "He'd put me under a bushel basket and send a cobra in to keep me company." She pried her final lightstone from the wall, then led the way out, holding the stone up like a lamp. They had re-entered Lambing Tunnel and passed the lump of rags that was Qinling before Evvy remarked, "You thought me living in the *takameri*'s house would be good yesterday."

Is this how parents live? Briar thought a bit wildly, as frustrated by his own lack of answers as he was her questions. Do kids go on asking the same questions even after the answers change? Do they question everything out of a person's mouth? "I changed my mind," he retorted.

"So you don't want me to work for her. And you don't want me to join the Vipers. And you're sure this time."

"Right," Briar said flatly. "*Exactly* right." I think, he added to himself.

It was close to midday by the time Briar was able to set out for Lady Zenadia's home. He bought food and ate on horseback rather than lose more of the day. He was starting to feel a little scraped and brittle. It was time to work on his trees, to brew medicines and weed the rooftop plants, before he forgot who he really was in all this running around.

Before that, he had a larch to install. It took five people to direct him through the maze of the city and into the less maze-like, but still confusing, web of streets that made up the monied parts of town. At last he came to Attaneh Road in the part of Chammur called the Jeweled Crescent. These homes were notable for their large gardens, the wealthy flaunting their spacious residences. The city's oldest families lived here, those who grabbed the best land between the heights and the river when they finally spilled out of their rocky fastnesses.

He knew better than to enter through the front gate. He'd learned early that the rich viewed mages not so much as honored guests but as very expensive servants. Instead he rode to the tradesman's entrance and told his business to a blank-faced man-at-arms. Once he passed through the gate, he was met by a chamberlain who guided him through winding galleries, halls, and courtyards.

Briar cast an expert's eye over the gardens they passed through: like many houses in the east, it included small gardens within the larger one that wrapped around the house. Each of the small gardens was laid out to create certain moods. He was impressed by what he saw. Lady Zenadia's gardeners knew the futility of trying to create too many lush, green spaces in so dry a climate. There were green oases, miniature water falls and ponds, but they were carefully tucked into corners to shelter them from Chammur's dry, hot winds. The remaining gardens held a rich variety of desert and hot country plants, showing the bountiful life that flourished in country most people thought of as wasteland.

Passing along part of the garden that encircled the house, Briar paused. Some of these trees and shrubs were gleefully vigorous, pulsing with strength. What would do that? Surely the gardeners didn't fertilize with fish heads — fresh fish was a costly delicacy in this water-poor country. Offal, perhaps, or animal leavings, chopped fine and mixed with normal fertilizers? He would have liked to ask the gardeners, but the chamberlain was tugging his arm.

Briar hesitated, curious still. *What are they feeding you?* he asked the fruit trees by the rear wall. *What have they put in your earth to make you so alive?*

Good food, they chorused, leaves fluttering. *Rich food!*

Briar sighed. How could he expect trees to know what went into the dirt around their roots? He was trying to formulate another question when the larch complained. They were in direct sunlight and the miniature was already dry so it could be drawn easily from its present earth to be repotted. The larch wanted Briar to stop talking to these great, overgrown plants and tend to *it*.

Briar shook his head and followed the chamberlain. Clad all in white — white breeches, white shirt, white turban — but for his green overrobe and sand-colored sash, the man seemed like a ghost. Only near the end of their walk did he speak. "Will you require anything of the house, *pahan*?"

"Only a pitcher of water," Briar replied, shifting the weight of his saddlebags on one shoulder. They contained his tools, as well as a selection of pots in various colors. He never knew ahead of time what colors were in a house — bringing a variety solved more problems than it created, even if it did make for a heavier load. The tree was cradled in his other arm; with it he carried a bag of fresh soil.

The man bowed him into yet another open gallery. This one opened onto a green garden, a pocket oasis with a fountain at its heart. Briar laid a hand on the stone wall that ran around the gallery at waist height. He had a dish that would go nicely with the green-veined black rock that formed it and the columns that supported the roof here. Placing the larch here would ensure that it got sunlight while still being somewhat sheltered from the hard winds that swept the city from time to time. "Shaihun's Breath," they were called; they snatched moisture from any surface they touched.

Briar found the dish to match the setting and placed it on the wall, checking it on either side. There was no need to build a shelf to support it, as the wall was the right width. That was a relief. He'd spent time in Winding Circle's carpentry barns, but he still preferred not to have to cut and hammer wood if he could help it.

He placed the larch in its carry-box on the wall and began to lay out his tools. Clearing his mind of the many plant-voices from the garden, he began to layer compost in the dish to prepare it for the new occupant.

That done, he asked the larch to free its roots from its soil. The tree obeyed, glowing in his mind with resignation: he had repotted it twice before. While it didn't care for the process, it knew fresh earth and the change of space would feel good once it was settled. No tree liked to be lifted free of its dirt, but Briar's trees, old and new, trusted him to make the operation fairly painless.

He was inspecting the roots for any sign of blight or damage when he heard Lady Zenadia's voice. "*Pahan* Briar, so this is where you got to!"

I'm to think you didn't order your servants to bring me here? Briar wondered, turning to bow to the lady. Servants padded into the garden to set a long chair, a table, and two upright chairs on the tiles. Lady Zenadia, majestic in dark red top and bronze silk wrap, reclined on the long chair when it was ready, crossing her sandaled feet before her. Servants moved to adjust the pillows that propped her up; another servant poured three cups full of some dark liquid; a maid put out bowls of fruit and napkins. One of their number took position behind the lady with a long-handled fan of cloudy white feathers.

Her companion, to Briar's vexation, was Jebilu Stoneslicer. The fat stone mage, trying to conceal a pout, sat in an upright chair. He wore dark green silk today, heavy at the hems of his tunic and leggings with gold embroidery. A constellation of jeweled rings winked from his plump fingers. Once settled, he placed a napkin on his lap. He did not begin to eat; instead he occupied himself with finger-pressing the fine linen into thin pleats.

"Where is your assistant, *Pahan* Briar?" Lady Zenadia inquired, her heavy brows knit. "That dear child Evumeimei. I had wished to see her again. I did invite her."

The lady appeared out of sorts, Briar thought. Too bad. "She's home, settling in," he replied, returning to the larch's roots. "She doesn't know anything about miniatures, anyway."

"That is the *bunjingi* form, is it not?" inquired Jebilu. "The calligraphy form?"

Briar was impressed. Not everyone knew the correct names of different miniature shapes. "Quite right, Master Stoneslicer," he said. "Do you study miniature trees?"

Jebilu sniffed. "In the imperial court of Yanjing, where I lived for a time, those who did not know the forms were considered untutored barbarians. I was forced to learn, to appear to advantage at tree-viewing parties."

"This talk of trees is all very well," the lady remarked sharply, "but I particularly desired to speak of Evumeimei, *Pahan* Briar. Surely you know that she cannot receive a proper education under the roof of a green mage who is young himself. And surely *you* have better things to do than instruct a young girl."

Briar carefully trimmed a few roots. "I don't understand my lady's meaning," he murmured, thinking, She's like a terrier with a favorite toy. *How can I make her let go of all this about Evvy?*

"I mean that Chammur must offer many distractions to a handsome young man," the lady said, delicately peeling an orange. "Unless our young women have gone blind. Bring your Evumeimei to my house. Master Jebilu has agreed that he may have been overhasty in his dealings with her. He has offered to teach her while she is under my protection. I will see to it that she is fed, clothed, and educated properly."

Briar looked from her to Jebilu. The stone mage busied himself with carefully sipping the contents of his cup, blotting his lips dry after each sip. He refused to look at Briar. She muscled him somehow, Briar realized, and he's *scared* of her. "I think there's been a misunderstanding, my lady," he said, returning to his inspection of tree roots. "Evvy won't study with Master Stoneslicer. Her mind is made up."

Lady Zenadia chuckled warmly, real amusement in her voice. "My dear *pahan*, if nothing else betrays your youth, this does! Young girls cannot be allowed to order their own fates! They have neither the experience nor the fixedness of purpose of their elders. This is why I would be more fit to undertake her education. I have raised three daughters, and each married well. Once Evumeimei is under my roof, her childish attempts to order her life, rather than to fit obediently into her proper place, will end. She will thank us both for that, one day."

The bleakness of the vision — of the life — she had just proposed made Briar's breath catch in his throat. She wants to break Evvy to the rein like a, a horse, he realized, suddenly furious. Battling his temper, knowing he would kick himself for it later if he opened his mouth now, he rested the larch on its original earth and met the woman's large, dark eyes squarely. "My lady, if you bought this tree because you thought I would force Evvy to live with you in exchange, I'd better take it home," he said, his voice flat. "She's settled with my teacher, *Pahan* Rosethorn, and me. We're headed to Yanjing in the long run, and we're going to take Evvy back to her home province when we do." They'd discussed no such plan, but Briar thought it might give this high-and-mighty pair an excuse to back off before things got truly ugly.

Lady Zenadia sat up straight and planted her feet on the ground. Bracing her hands on her thighs, she asked in a cold, chilly voice, "Do you think to defy me, *boy*?"

Briar didn't even blink under her hard stare. "Shall I take the larch home, my lady?" he inquired, rather than answer so foolish a question. Of course he was defying her. He would do it with pleasure and an overturning of all her carefully raked and planted greenery, if it came to that. It was time she learned that people who came from poorer homes were not toys to play with.

Moments that felt endless passed as she silently tried to

break his gray-green gaze with her dark one. Jebilu actually shrank back in his chair. Finally the lady flapped a hand in disgust. "No. I have purchased that tree, and I will keep it."

For a single copper *dav* he would have taken the larch home anyway, but caution stopped him. Whatever he might think of Lady Zenadia and her dealings with humans, she had very fine gardeners. They would tend his tree well. No doubt she would even hire another miniature tree expert to serve only her. Also, he had made the bargain, and registered the sale with the keepers of the *souk*. He didn't want to get a reputation for bad dealing.

The conversation, at least as far as he was concerned, was over. He quit the staring contest and returned to the larch. Eventually the lady and Jebilu discussed about events and people Briar had no interest in. He worked carefully, not allowing his fury to distract him from making sure his charge would flourish. At last the larch was settled and eagerly drinking the water he'd given it, wriggling its roots around to fit its new dish. Briar cleaned up, stowing everything neatly, then shouldered his bags.

A black silk purse had appeared on the wall beside the larch. Briar opened it and counted its contents, aware that Jebilu and Lady Zenadia watched him. All of the money was there. He poured out the coins and put them into his bags, leaving the silk purse empty. He wanted nothing of this female other than his rightful payment. He bowed to the lady and to Jebilu, then walked away.

On the way out, he stopped once more at the arch that offered the best view of the big garden, looking at its plants and trees with a careful eye. There was freshly turned earth near the bases of two trees, a prickly juniper and a short-leafed cedar, he saw.

What do they feed you? he asked them silently. What makes you grow so well in such tired ground?

They still had no words for it. Briar shook his head wearily and followed his guide to the servants' gate.

12

As he loaded the donkey and mounted his horse, all Briar could think of was home. Visions of soup, fruit, maybe a roasted cook-shop chicken floated before his mind's eye. A bath would be good, too. He wanted the scent of the lady's house off his skin. He didn't know why, but the place had given him the crawls. It was as if he'd been asked an important question while he wasn't listening.

I don't *want* to know the answer, he told himself as he nudged his horse through the gate. I'm no Sandry, forever wanting to solve the world's troubles, or Tris, poking about for secrets. Daja has the right of it: keep business to yourself and your clan, and get on with life. There's no point in sticking my neb in things around here.

He held to that policy of godlike detachment right up to the moment when the gates closed behind him. It was then that he saw five Vipers squatted in the small, unsheltered bay in front of the tradesman's entrance. One of them was

206

the dimpled girl Ayasha he had flirted with the day the Camelguts joined the Vipers.

"What are *you* doing here?" he demanded, scowling.

She got up and came over, smiling to show her dimples. "*Pahan* Briar, you certainly get about." She lifted her skirt above her knee, showing him a round, tanned and ruddy leg free of blemishes. "See what good work you do?"

Briar looked — she had very pretty legs, particularly without sores from scratched flea bites — but his heart wasn't in it. He also didn't like the silver ring and garnet in her nose. Did that mean she was expendable to the Vipers, like Douna?

"Why are you here?" he asked again. "This isn't Viper ground."

Ayasha shrugged. "She sent for us and we came, wagging our tails like good puppies. Will you be here for the Festival of First Rains? It's at the next full moon, and I haven't got a partner for the dancing."

Briar didn't hear her invitation. The knowledge that the lady had summoned the Vipers in broad daylight — and they had come — burned him like acid. Would she step in if they were picked up by the Watch? Would she care if any of them rotted in the prisons of Justice Rock for being in a part of town where gangs were not welcome?

Fury raced through Briar's veins. He dismounted, wrapping the horse's reins in one hand. The donkey, its lead rein tied to the horse, grumbled and dropped a pancake of dung on the dirt before the lady's gate. The horse did the same.

Briar glared at the Vipers. "What kind of gang are you?" he demanded. Ayasha sighed and went to sit with the others. Briar paid her no attention as he went on, "You come in daylight and sit on your heels out here like so many tame dogs. How stupid can you be? It's folk like *her* that keep folk like us poor. She —"

"Folk like *us*?" repeated the short, black-skinned youth Briar had seen before. "What do *you* know of being poor? Who are you to talk to us of gangs?"

"I spent ten years in Deadman's District in Hajra," Briar said tightly. "Six of them in a gang, the Lightnings. I fought rats for bread and stole to keep the Thief-Lord from whipping the skin off my back. Once I had a chance to get out, I took it. All I have, I earned. I didn't get it waiting for the scraps from a *takameri*'s table! She's the enemy, her and all the nobles like her —"

"She is Shaihun's creation," interrupted one of them as he stood. He was tall, lean, and familiar, the youth who had told Briar that something that talked and walked like a dog was probably a dog. Fading bruises circled his eyes. "No *eknub* can understand submission to Shaihun."

"Besides, she's going to make us the top gang in the city," added the short, black Viper. "Gate Lords are already milling like scared sheep. They don't know who's next since their *tesku* went missing."

"If you had any weight as a gang, you wouldn't need anyone but your mates," Briar informed them bitterly. "Doesn't it shame you, taking orders from the likes of her?"

He'd allowed himself to be distracted from the tall Viper, who had drifted closer. Now he leaped on Briar, seized him by the shirt, threw him to the ground and landed on top of him, hands around Briar's throat. At least Briar's hands had not been napping, unlike his brain. He dug the points of his unsheathed wrist knives into the Viper's sides. The taller boy ignored them, despite the tiny rounds of blood that flowered on his shirt.

"She has graced us with her attention," he snarled at Briar. "Don't talk about something you don't understand." He relaxed his grip on Briar's neck.

"What I understand is that you're a sworn member of the daftie guild," retorted Briar. Mentally he kicked himself for letting this fellow get so close. "Don't you see you're in a tight place, tighter maybe than you can escape?"

"Ikrum, no." Ayasha wrapped her hands around the thin Viper's arm. "The *pahan*'s all right. He just don't understand." She tugged Ikrum's arm. "He's a friend in a pinch, though. Yoru, help me," she told the short black youth.

"He doesn't respect her," Ikrum protested.

"He don't have to. He isn't sworn to her." Yoru took Ikrum's other arm. Carefully he and Ayasha pried their *tesku*'s hands off Briar's neck. To Briar, Yoru said, "Sheath your knives. He didn't even bruise you."

"Get him off me first," snapped Briar. "Before I teach him a lesson none of you will forget." Yoru and Ayasha pulled Ikrum to his feet.

Briar wiped the bloody points of his knives in the dust as he sat up, then resheathed them. He looked up at Ikrum, still in the grip of his two followers.

"If you want *my* opinion, you'll get away from *her*." He nodded toward the gate. "She's no goddess, just a *takameri* who's mad with power. She'll eat you all if she gets the chance." Briskly he removed his over robe and shook the dust from its folds.

"He's a good *tesku*," snapped another Viper, a golden-skinned boy. "We've done better with him than any other."

"If he's done you so much good," Briar replied, slapping the dirt from the seat of his breeches, "why are you out here in the sun like a pack of hounds?"

"I'm all right," Ikrum snapped, jerking himself away from his keepers. He strode over to Briar, pressing his hands against the small wounds in his sides. Holding up his blood-marked fingers, he licked them clean. "You stuck me," he said casually, and gave a toothy smile. "You won't do that twice."

Briar stood on tiptoe to glare into his eyes. "You won't

get another chance at me, play-toy boy," he said quietly. "Now, rethink your life, before she takes it from you and leaves you on a garbage heap." He thrust a foot into one stirrup and mounted his horse. "Because you aren't one of hers, no matter what she says, and unless you're one of hers, you're just a thing to be used." Briar surveyed the other Vipers. "And you're a bunch of sheep if you let him do it." He urged his horse into a walk.

An image of his past had come into his mind at the mention of garbage heaps. He'd been five or six, perhaps, when he stole a fine scarf. Two older boys had taken it, leaving Briar to grub in the garbage behind an inn, hoping to find a morsel of food. The Thief-Lord had met him there. He'd offered food, and a gang, and mates who wouldn't beat him up and take his prizes. By the time Briar learned that the two older boys belonged to another of the Thief-Lord's gangs and that they often set things up so street kids would be grateful to the Thief-Lord, he was being trained as an all-around thief.

So what makes me different from the Vipers? he wondered gloomily, studying one of his palms. The inked green vines had not managed to conquer his right hand entirely. The scarred welt that crossed his palm would not take the dyes, forcing the vines to twine around the three deep pockmarks where thorns had marked him for life.

Long before Niko had taken him to Winding Circle, Briar had scaled a rich man's wall. When he touched a thick, woody stem on top, the thing had wrapped around his hand, snake-like. Its thorns had clung to his flesh well after Briar cut the stem free. The Thief-Lord had sent him up there, to steal a white stone statue that he wanted for himself. It hadn't put food in the mouths of Briar's gang. Not only that, but he'd suffered for days after prying out those thorns, until the Thief-Lord had grudgingly paid a cheap healer to see to the wounds.

Only difference between the lady and him was that she's born noble, Briar thought gloomily as he came to the intersection of the Attaneh Road and the Karang Road. I was just as stupid as these Vipers. As all of us in kid gangs. There's always someone older around, telling us what to do, who to rob, beating us when we don't do or say or think what they want. We put up with it because they tell us we mean something — but we don't. Not to them. All we are to them is a tool for making them important.

And I wanted that for Evvy?

So preoccupied was he that he didn't realize he had company until his horse shied. Briar fumbled to get a better grip on the reins and brought the horse up with a firm hand. Five horsemen waited ahead, blocking his advance. They wore the orange shirts and trousers and the black turban of the Watch, the city's law enforcers. All had weighted batons tucked into their black sashes. One carried a tall lance with a flag at the tip: an orange sun on a black field, the badge of the Watch and of its commander, the *mutabir*. He was the *amir*'s right hand and the law inside Chammur's walls.

Briar looked behind him. Five more horsemen of the Watch rode out of a blind alley to cut off his retreat.

One of the men ahead rode forward until he was a yard from Briar. "*Pahan* Briar Moss of Winding Circle temple and Summersea in Emelan," he intoned in a wooden voice. "You are invited to speak with *Mutabir* Kemit doen Polumri. At once."

Old instinct and new learning fought bitterly in his head. Instinct told him to leap from his horse's back and *run*, as far and as fast as he could. He clenched his teeth and fought it, sweating. He wasn't a thief anymore, wasn't a street kid, wasn't meat for the Watch to grind up and spit out. He was a citizen, a *pahan*, not a criminal. Citizens didn't run from the Watch.

Still, what did he do to get the notice of a *mutabir*, who governed the Watch and courts of Sotat? Unless they thought he was stirring up the gangs?

"Why?" Briar demanded. "I'm an *eknub*, just passing through."

"The *mutabir* will explain, when you are presented to him," replied the one who had spoken first. The pale white wall on either side of Attaneh Road now sported green crowns, as trees and vines stretched and grew over the top.

Rosevines snaked down the street side of the wall. Had the Watchmen noticed them?

Stop it, he told the plants, putting all of his will into the command. I'm fine. "Very well," he said, wanting to get these men away before they noticed the greenery's odd behavior and tried to do something about it. "But this had better be important."

He nudged his horse forward; the Watchmen ahead wheeled their mounts and led the way. Briar glanced back to see if the rest followed: he might still escape if they didn't. No, they were moving forward, all but one. That one was bent in the saddle, listening intently to two people. One was a woman dressed like a local servant, the other a man whose sand-colored clothes made him look like part of the walls or of the dirt underfoot. The woman finished first. Hoisting a large jar on her hip, she trotted up the road and out of sight around the bend. The man faded into the blind alley, and the Watchman they'd spoken to caught up with the rest.

Who are they watching on this street? Briar wondered as he faced front again. He knew the look of police informers and official stakeouts. The *mutabir* was looking at someone on Attaneh Road, looking hard.

The ride to the *mutabir's* residence, at the base of Justice Rock, was a short one. Briar used the time to let the plants that grew along the way know he'd been there, in case

Rosethorn had to come after him. There was nothing to distract him from talking to them — the Watchmen were as closemouthed as stones.

Ordinary folk got out of their way quickly. Briar wasn't sure if that meant the Watch were respected and appreciated, or simply feared. Either way boded ill for a former street thief. He checked his hands often to reassure himself that his arrest tattoos had indeed been consumed by the green vines under his skin. As if they sensed his unease, the vines on his left hand sprouted gaudy blue and yellow blooms. The ones on the right sported tiny black roses.

Servants at the *mutabir*'s residence took Briar's horse and donkey, while his escort led him on foot through an outer courtyard. On either side stood the Watch commanderie and Justice Hall, crouched like guardian dogs, the shuttered windows staring blindly at one another. Both were massive structures of some kind of granite, rare stone for that part of the country. Briar shivered as he walked between them.

Passing through a gate on the far side of the courtyard, the Watchmen led him through a beautifully arranged desert garden. Briar felt a softening in his attitude — it was hard to dislike people who enjoyed gardens like the Chammurans did — and hardened his heart. Gardens or no, he didn't like the way things were done here. Duke Vedris's fair, if heavy, hand in such matters back in Emelan had soured Briar on Sotat law and courts.

From the garden he was shown into a sprawling house. Immediately to their right as they entered was a large and airy chamber, walled and floored in cool white marble, with green and red stone vine inlays along the ceiling and floors. The shutters were open, but the insides of the windows were covered with carved wooden screens to keep people from seeing into the house. Pillows were scattered on the floor, for supplicants, Briar supposed. At the far end of the room, bracketed by Watchmen who carried long spears, was a marble dais covered with long, flat cushions; other small, plump cushions were heaped on it.

A man sat there, sipping from a tiny coffee cup. As he did so, he turned papers over with his free hand. Papers and coffee pot were placed on two short wooden tables.

A second person — was it a man? — sat on the edge of the dais, legs crossed under him. He wore the head-to-toe veil of a Mohunite; only dark eyes showed through the slit left for them. Unlike the blue one Mai had worn to hide from the Gate Lords, this veil was dark gray. The wearer would be a Mohunite initiate — a mage.

A third person, a veiled scribe, sat at a full-sized table in the shadows at the rear of the dais. Briar could only see hands and painted eyelids: the scribe was a woman. She wrote busily, her work illuminated by a brass lamp.

The sight of her made Briar feel slightly more comfortable. He wondered if he would ever get used to the way that women east of the Pebbled Sea were expected to keep to homes and families. Few were encouraged to work in the larger world as the women he knew did. The *mutabir* must be all right, if he hired a woman for a sensitive job like this.

The head of the Watch detachment came to attention and said, "This youth, who our contact says is a *pahan* named Briar Moss, an *eknub* from Summersea, came to the house of Lady Zenadia doa Attaneh this morning, Lord Mutabir, as did the *pahan* Jebilu Stoneslicer. This youth was inside the house for a period of two hours, in the matter of a miniature tree. When he left the house, we followed our orders and conveyed him to you. *Pahan* Jebilu remains at the house."

"Very well, *Hedax* Yoson." The coffee-drinker's voice was deep and melodic, a huge voice for a slender man. "You and your squad are dismissed." The *mutabir* dressed simply for a Chammuran of power in loose breeches of dark green linen, a white shirt, black sash, and a long-sleeved, dark green overrobe. He had no jewelry or embroidery; no braids hung below his crisp, white turban. He watched the Watchmen file from the room and nodded to Briar. "You may approach."

Right then Briar knew he'd been with Rosethorn, Sandry, and Tris for much too long. Their part of him demanded that he stay where he was, prop his fists on his hips, and demand to know what was going on before he

went any further. They did that a lot, no matter how much
trouble it caused. Against them Briar put his street rat self.
He had survived ten years by smiling, bowing, agreeing,
mouthing "your highnesses" to anyone and everyone, and
running the moment a chance was offered.

The street rat won, in a way. "May it please your highness, I'd like to know what the charge is." He smiled, trying
for charm.

"Have you done anything worthy of a charge?" the *mutabir* inquired. He sat up, putting down both coffee cup and
papers. Whites and blacks had crossed on his family map
often, Briar decided. His face was very light brown and
splattered with freckles. It was impossible to see his hair,
covered as it was by his turban, but his moustache was dark
brown and full.

"Never did anything lawless, never will, highness," Briar
answered.

The gray-veiled mage raised a small crystal orb in
fingers painted with henna designs. Red light danced in the
orb's depths. "He lies, my lord." The voice was female.

The *mutabir* raised his eyebrows. "Interesting," he
mused. "Would you like to answer the question a second
time, young *pahan*?"

Briar glared at the mage. "I haven't done anything re-
cently," he amended. The red lights in the crystal winked
out. "I'm all respectable now." Something shimmered in the

depths of the stone and was gone. "Is there a truth spell on that thing?" he asked the mage. "How'd you put it on? Most truthsayers just look to tell if they're lied to or not."

The mage looked at the man on the dais, who nodded. She replied, "I purchased this device ready-made, from Jebilu Stoneslicer. The spells must be renewed every three years, but the procedure is simple enough."

"Huh!" exclaimed Briar. "So the old pickle had some juice in him, once."

"Why did you go to Lady Zenadia's house?" asked the *mutabir*.

Briar looked at him. "I sold her a miniature larch — it's a kind of pine, good for protecting against fire. I had to install it in a new dish and in the right place in her house."

The *mutabir* searched through papers until he held one up. "According to our observers, you met the lady in the Golden House *souk* yesterday."

"That's when she bought the tree," Briar explained.

"Did you see anything unusual in her house?" the *mutibir* wanted to know. "Hear anything, smell anything?"

"I wouldn't know," Briar pointed out. "I've never been there before, to know what was usual and what wasn't." The *mutabir* said nothing, but regarded him steadily. After a moment Briar added, "She has a good gardener." The *mutabir* continued to stare.

Briar scratched his head. Surely the lady's troubles,

gang, or habits were no supper of his; the same was true of the *mutabir*'s concerns. He certainly wasn't inclined to start tattling to the law in this stage of his life.

"Where are you from?" the mage asked, her voice breaking the silence so abruptly that Briar twitched.

"Summersea in Emelan," he replied without looking away from the *mutabir*.

"Partially true," the mage announced.

Briar glared at her. "Don't that thing tell you when answers are complicated?" he demanded. "I was born in Hajra, but I went to Summersea when I was ten."

The mage's hand held up the crystal globe. "Stones are simple creations — rather direct, as most mages learn. You claim to be a true *pahan*. How can you not know this?"

Briar sighed. "I *am* a true *pahan*. You don't know how true. Just not with stones." He walked up to the mage, drawing his pendant out and holding it so she could see. As she leaned in to look at it, he showed her the far side as well. Without warning, she grabbed his hands and inspected them, tracing a vine with a hennaed fingertip. The vine moved under Briar's skin, following her fingertip like a fascinated snake.

Freeing him, she made a noise that sounded a great deal like "hmpf." She straightened and nodded at the *mutabir*.

With a flick of the hand the man sent everyone else, guards and scribe alike, from the room. Only when he, the mage, and Briar were alone did the *mutabir* tell Briar, "This is *Pahan* Turaba Guardsall. She is my aide."

Briar nodded to the veiled woman. "I still don't see why I'm here."

"Lady Zenadia doa Attaneh is the *amir*'s aunt," Turaba said. Her voice was curt and slightly muffled by her veil. "She bought our prince his first pony. She is godmother to his oldest son and daughter. There are Attanehs in the army, all three priesthoods, the *amir*'s council, and the council of nobles. She is even a distant cousin of the king who reigns from far Hajra."

Briar, about to spit at the mention of the Sotaten king as he always did, thought the better of it. It was possible that they might *like* the monarch. Besides, Briar's insides were prickling. These people wanted something from him. Whatever it was, he doubted he would like it.

"When so important a person is concerned, any attempt to discover the truth of ugly rumors must be handled with care," the *mutabir* said, choosing his words slowly. "Any great family would be sure to renounce one of their own as criminal, should rumors be proved. Alas, a noble family would be quicker still to attack the Watch if it were to learn that the Watch is investigating one of them."

"What rumors?" Briar asked, his voice sharp. "If you mean her taking up with a gang, I bet everyone from the Street of Wells to Triumph Road knows that."

Turaba was shaking her head. "Deaths have been rumored, over the last ten years," she replied. "Deaths and disappearances."

"Our last four Watchers in that house have vanished," the *mutabir* informed him. "We can find no trace of them."

That was why Briar had noticed the spies reporting to the Watch when they picked him up — the house was being watched from the outside, if not from within. "So," Briar said, inspecting the vines on his scarred hand, "would you have grabbed me at all if it hadn't been four of your own gone missing? You haven't exactly stopped her from giving weapons to a gang, have you?"

The *mutabir* raised his eyebrows. "Gangs have been at war since Mohun crafted the dark spaces within stone," he told Briar. "If they kill one another, it is hardly of concern to me or mine."

"She wants that street girl you found," Turaba added as Briar thought longingly of punching the *mutabir*. "She offered the girl employment, suitable teachers, a place in her home. Why do you refuse such an opportunity for the child?"

Briar scowled. How close had some informer been to his booth yesterday, if they knew so much? "Do you also know how many times I get up in the night to make water?" he demanded crossly.

"Information is the key to order," the *mutabir* replied, his mellow voice amused. "My people gather as much as they can. We would like some from you, *pahan*. Why does she want that girl?"

"Scry your own answers," retorted Briar. "You must have seers in the Watch."

Turaba shook her head. "House Attaneh has owned land in that part of the city for over six hundred years," she informed Briar. "The outer walls and the houses themselves are protected with old and new spells from common nuisances like burglars and seers. Forgive me if I am the first to explain," she added with mocking kindness, "but the wealthy like to keep their secrets. Will you please tell us why the girl is important to her?"

Briar shrugged. Of course he knew the wealthy bought magic to protect their homes: he'd dealt with plenty of it. There were always counter-magics available to negate such spells. On the other hand, layers of spells, laid down over centuries, could be much harder to beat.

"Lady Zenadia says she wants Evvy to run errands and keep her company, but really it's for her toy gang, the Vipers," Briar told them. "They'll do better at thieving if they have a stone mage, and Evvy's the only other stone mage in Chammur. The Vipers tried to get Evvy and failed, so Lady Zenadia tried going through me. I'm Evvy's teacher for now." Inspiration struck. "You could lock her up for criminal business," he offered. "If she runs a gang, she benefits from the fights and the stealing, right?"

"One doesn't bother the *amir*'s aunt with petty charges,"

Turaba replied. To the *mutabir* she said, "The rumors weren't so persistent until she met their *tesku*, Ikrum. He's been a bad influence. So has the gang."

What about the influence she's been on them? wondered Briar.

The *mutabir* looked at Briar. "What *did* you see in her house?"

Briar grimaced. "A chamberlain. A lot of rooms. Gardens — nice ones. A few servants. What did you expect me to see, dead Watchmen hanging from the rafters? Loot the Vipers turned over to her?"

"I do not appreciate impertinence, even from a *pahan*," the *mutabir* informed him. "We desire you to allow the girl to go to Lady Zenadia. She will then report to us. She is clever in the way of street people, and, better still, too young to be suspected as a Watch informer —"

Briar backed up a step, angry again. "No," he snapped. "Send a kid to spy in a house where four of your own grown Watchmen have gone missing? Not while I'm her teacher, and not while Dedicate Rosethorn is *my* teacher. I don't care if it makes your life easier." They blinked at the mention of Rosethorn's name. He'd risked their not knowing who she was, but it seemed like a small risk. If they knew his conversation with Lady Zenadia in the *souk*, they had to know Rosethorn had talked to Jebilu, and that she'd forced their wonderful stone mage to bow down. He continued,

"If you meddle with Evvy, you won't like what happens. Rosethorn will back me up. Evvy stays with us."

The *mutabir* glared at Briar. "I do not like threats."

"Briar Moss," Turaba remarked. "I have heard stories of four young *pahans* in Emelan, one of them named Briar Moss. The stories are — astonishing."

Briar shrugged. "Stories get stretched when they travel."

"But you are that *pahan*, are you not?" Turaba pursued.

"Maybe," Briar said with another shrug. "Me and the girls always get talked about."

Turaba looked at her master and made a flickering signal with her hand. Tentatively she asked Briar, "Can we not reach an accommodation?"

"I don't appreciate people using street kids as pawns," Briar told them. "Evvy's scraped to live in this wonderful city for years. You owe her better than sending her into that house, if there's a chance she'll be risking her life."

The *mutabir* sighed. "There have been poor since the birth of humankind, young *pahan*. It speaks to the generosity of your heart that you have taken this girl in, but know this: for every girl lifted from poverty, there are twenty more to take her place. No one could save them all."

Not that you ever bothered, Briar thought, but he kept it to himself. He'd already pushed this man as far as was safe.

The mage inspected the crystal globe she still held.

"Will you at least keep your ears open for more information? You have been seen with members of the gangs involved — you may hear something. You may be invited to the lady's house again."

"Why bother?" asked Briar. "Her kinfolk will hush it up, no matter what."

"If she has committed truly serious crimes, her own kin will want an end to her activities," the *mutabir* replied. "Even nobles answer to the law. She cannot murder without consequences."

"I'll think about it," Briar said flatly. "Can I go now?"

The *mutabir* drummed his fingers on a tabletop, then nodded. Briar turned and walked out, the skin on the back of his neck prickling. He was surprised at their restraint. Most law officials he'd known would bruise people first for defying them, then apologize later. He knew that lawkeepers tended to walk softly around mages — why risk creating problems they might not be able to fix? — but this was the first time he'd experienced it personally. Which stories about him and the girls had filtered to this far place?

13

The house on the Street of Hares was quiet when he arrived late that afternoon. A lone cat — Briar thought it was the brown tortoiseshell Asa — napped in the middle of the dining room table. Looking at her in decent light, Briar realized she was pregnant.

"Wonderful," he muttered, dumping his packs and parcels on the table. "Rosethorn?" he called. Asa looked at him, meowed a complaint, then went back to sleep.

"Workroom," shouted Rosethorn.

"Evvy?" He walked toward the kitchen.

"In my room," Evvy called. She sounded cross.

Briar reversed course and went to the door of Evvy's new room. An invisible force halted him at the threshold. He looked down. A thin line of green powder lay across the sill. Touching it with his magic, he found it was the Hold-all mixture Rosethorn kept in her stores. There were also lines of it across the windowsills.

Evvy sat against the far wall in the middle of a nest of

cats. She was toying with the stones she had brought from home and pouting.

"What did you do?" asked Briar. He fought to keep a grin off his face.

"I didn't *mean* anything by it," Evvy whined.

"She had her nose in the mouth of a jar of Must-Sleep powder and was about to inhale," Rosethorn said tartly from the top of the stair. She stood with a jar braced on one hip. "I *told* her not to go poking in the workroom."

"I wanted to know how it smelled," grumbled Evvy.

Briar shook his head. "And if you'd taken a big whiff, you'd be asleep for months," he informed her as sternly as he could. "You have to obey Rosethorn. She mostly doesn't give orders without good reason."

"Mostly?" Rosethorn murmured, coming down the stair. Briar stepped aside to let her pass. "Just mostly?"

"Sometimes you give orders to be crotchety," Briar whispered as she went by. He watched as she put the jar by the front door. "What's that?"

Rosethorn stretched, hands pressed against the small of her back. "I'm about set for those farmers," she explained. "I've packed every last seed for the fields. You can help me bring it down here. Her, too." Bending down, she dragged a finger through the line of powdered herbs across Evvy's door. "Come make yourself useful," she told the girl as the freed cats raced out. "And *don't* get into anything."

"I just wanted to see how it smelled," Evvy grumbled as she followed Briar and Rosethorn upstairs.

The fruit of Rosethorn's rooftop endeavors, the clover, bean, and corn seed harvested and mage-dried to keep them from rotting, had been packed into jars and sealed with wax. They had to be carried downstairs. So did a dozen sacks of grain. Rosethorn had poured her magic into them, giving them the strength to become a fast-growing winter crop, hardy enough to survive the rainy season. Last of all were small kegs of a growth potion, a small drop of which could fertilize an acre of land for years.

As soon as everything was clustered before the front door, they set about preparing supper. Briar had bought his cooked chicken on the way home; Rosethorn had made lentils and noodles during the day. Once the food was served, Rosethorn worked a protective circle to keep the mewing and yowling cats from climbing on the table.

"They'll get fed," she told Evvy, who seemed much chastened. "But we work hard for our food here, so we get to eat first."

Once he'd devoured a bowl of noodles and lentils and a chicken leg, Briar asked, "Won't you need me to help you in the fields?"

Rosethorn shook her head. "Most of the work's done. I'll be gone three or four days. You two will have to manage without me." She glared at Evvy. "I'm putting wards on the workroom to keep you out. You don't go in until you learn to read."

Evvy nodded, eyes wide.

"Aww, you're getting soft," Briar teased Rosethorn. "Time was you'd have skinned anyone who fooled with your pots."

"I may do that yet," Rosethorn replied, with an extra glare for Evvy. "A mage's workroom is *not* a spice merchant's shop. Our brews can kill people, or worse. When do you start teaching her to read?" she asked Briar.

"Tonight," he replied, carving more chicken. "I got her a surprise at the market."

"Just make sure it isn't a surprise for me, too," Rosethorn said, wiping her lips. "Will you two be all right the time I'm gone? Earth temple would probably let you move into the guest house —"

Briar shook his head. "We'll be fine."

"Did the lady ask about me?" Evvy asked Briar. "What was her house like?"

Rosethorn propped her head on her hands. "Yes — what was it like?"

"The gardens are . . . very healthy," answered Briar. "Especially the biggest one. And it's fancy inside, all marble and stone inlays, expensive wood, silk, velvet, gilding. She asked about Evvy again, but I think she listened this time, when I told her no." He added more details about the art he had glimpsed and what the lady wore, used to such descriptions after four years of living among females who wanted to know how others lived. He didn't mention his conversation with the *mutabir* and his mage. The more he thought about it, the more it troubled him. Rosethorn would need a clear mind to do the work she intended to in Chammur's fields. It could wait until she returned.

"I've been thinking," Rosethorn drawled, when Briar finished. "It might be possible to reach Laenpa, across the border in Vauri, before the rains. An old friend of mine from Lightsbridge settled there — she's written she has plenty of room for us, and that she'd like the company."

"I won't leave my cats," Evvy announced nervously.

"I'm not asking you to," Rosethorn informed the girl. "They'll have to go in baskets, and we'll need two camels, I suppose, for all our gear, but that can be done."

"What about at night?" Briar asked. "And won't the cats fight, or get sick, being in baskets all the time?"

Rosethorn looked at him as if she wanted to ask if he'd been drinking stupid tea. "We draw a circle around them at night," she explained patiently. "They don't go out, only Evvy goes in. They'll be safer than we will. And it's not a long haul, only about a week. I spoke to the man who runs the last eastern caravan of the season. They leave in six days. He must have some weather magic, because market gossip is that he's never been caught on the road by the rains."

"You mean it?" Evvy asked, her chin and voice wobbly. "You won't leave me and the cats here?"

Rosethorn took the napkin from her lap and folded it precisely. "I won't leave the scrawniest, most vicious of those troublemakers in this bloodless, dying place, let alone you," she said quietly without looking at Briar or Evvy. "I can't wait until I can scrub the dust of Chammur from my skin." She rose and broke the circle on the table. The cats remained where they were, keeping an eye on her. "I'm off. Keep things quiet down here — I need to be up well before dawn, so I'm going to bed soon." She walked out of the room and climbed the stairs.

Briar scrubbed his tired face with his hands. This was the second time that she had anticipated a problem he wanted to discuss and settled it before he could speak. Relief flooded his mind. Laenpa was further east, another land entirely. They would all be safe from the lady, the Vipers, and perhaps even the *mutabir*. When he looked at it that way, even the fun of carting seven cats in wicker baskets for a week didn't seem too high a price to pay.

After he and Evvy cleaned up and washed dishes, Briar settled her at the table once more. After some thought he'd decided to teach her to read and write in Imperial. The books that Rosethorn had borrowed from the Earth temple were in that language, since the Pebbled Sea and the lands around it were the center of the Living Circle faith. Evvy already knew a number of words in Imperial, as she did in a handful of other languages, to get along in Chammur's marketplaces. Moreover, the three of them wouldn't be staying so long that a knowledge of how to read and write Chammuri would do Evvy any good.

On the way to the lady's house, wondering how he could teach Evvy in a way she would like, Briar had been struck with inspiration. Now he put out a slate and chalk, a dampened cloth, and one of the books of stones and crystals Rosethorn had brought. He added a sheet of notes he'd made during a long visit with the crystal merchant Nahim Zineer. Last of all he put down the heavy roll of cloth he'd purchased, undid the ties, and opened it until it lay flat on the table. Its white inner surface was covered with a number of small pockets. He'd put a stone or crystal in each as he bought them from Nahim.

"This is yours," Briar told Evvy as she bounced in her chair, staring at the cloth with bright eyes. "None of these stones have any magic. I made sure of that. You want to start with something that's never known magic, so any changes or spells you put in will be yours, and nobody else's. Don't let anyone else handle these, either. And you're not to do any magic with these stones at first. Keep your magic in your skin, understand?"

"All right, all *right*," Evvy said impatiently. "But what are they? What will we do with them? Are they really mine?"

Suddenly it was worth the time he'd taken after his

meeting with the *mutabir* to purchase all of this at Golden House. "They're really yours, but they're for you to learn with. And the first thing you'll learn with them is how to read and write. You —"

Evvy threw herself across the gap between her chair and his and hugged him fiercely. "Thank you, thank you, thank you!" she cried. "Nobody ever bought me anything so nice!"

"Stop that," Briar protested, untangling her arms from around his neck. From the heat in his face he knew he was blushing. "Girls. Always wanting to hug somebody." He gently thrust Evvy back toward her chair and picked up the slate and chalk. "Here we go. Reading and writing in Imperial, and some thoughts for stone magic." Carefully he drew the big and small versions of the letter A on the slate. Pointing to the first pocket in the cloth, he said, "Take that one out."

Getting up on her knees on the seat of the chair, Evvy reached out and slowly, carefully, drew a purple crystal from the cloth. She put it on top of its rightful pocket. "This is amethyst," she breathed.

"Yes. A — see here, that's this letter, big A and little a — A is for amethyst." Briar opened the book and leafed through to the proper entry. "According to this, it's good to ward off nightmares and calm people down. Seers use it because it makes visions clearer. Now, take the chalk, and draw both A's."

As Evvy slowly copied the letters on the slate, Briar read

on. "It gives folk courage and keeps travelers safe on the road. Guess we'll need that soon, eh? Now, tell me the uses for amethysts."

Evvy recited them solemnly. Briar inspected her A's and asked her to draw them several more times. He read out even more uses for the stone and had her repeat them. Rosethorn had done this same kind of teaching with plants during formal lessons in the first winter they'd spent as teacher and student. That was purely magical learning: Tris had already taught Briar how to read.

"All right," he said when he got thoroughly bored with amethysts, "put the stone back and wipe the slate clean." He looked at the paper Nahim Zineer had given to him. "Next pocket over. B is for bloodstone." As Evvy drew out her bloodstone, Briar wrote the letter on the slate. "Big B, little b," he said, making sure that she looked at the slate before he continued. "They're supposed to help stop bleeding. Also good for physical strength . . ."

They got as far as G for garnet. Once Briar saw Evvy was struggling to concentrate, he ended the lesson and ordered her to bed. She replaced the garnet in its pocket and slowly, carefully rolled up the cloth kit. Once the ties were secured, she hugged it to her thin chest.

When she looked at Briar, there were tears in her almond-shaped eyes. "I never knew anyone with anything as fine as this," she whispered. "You won't be sorry you got me as a student, *Pahan* Briar. I promise you won't. Good night." She walked into her room. Her cats left their various watch-and-nap places in the dining room to follow her.

Briar closed and locked the doors, banked the kitchen fire, and blew out the few lamps burning downstairs. He stopped for one final look into Evvy's room. She was already asleep, her cats distributed around her. She still clutched the roll of cloth with her stones to her chest.

The orange-patched blue-gray Mystery left the group of cats and trotted upstairs ahead of Briar, squeezing through Rosethorn's barely open door. In his own room he found one of the cinnamon-masked golden cats, the one with a crooked tail. Apricot, Evvy had called her. Apricot had curled herself up on Briar's pillow. Briar put on his nightshirt, cleaned his teeth, and got between the sheets.

"You'd better not snore," he told Apricot. Just before he drifted off to dreams of stones of all colors, he heard her start to purr.

In the morning, Briar rose when Rosethorn did. Together they loaded her things onto the camels brought by the farmers she was helping: the sky was just barely pink over the cliffs of Chammur Oldtown. He watched her go, then went back inside to put on water for porridge and tea. There was no sense in returning to bed; better to tough out the day and return to normal sleeping hours that night. As he stirred porridge, he made lists in his head. He would start packing while Rosethorn was gone. If they were to leave in less than a week, they didn't have much time.

While the porridge finished cooking, he brought his *shakkan* down from his room to the dining room table. It needed attention, and working with it soothed his last uneasiness over the sale of the larch. He always needed time with his *shakkan* after parting with another miniature. Reaching for the larch with his power, touching it on its ledge in the lady's house, he could feel contentment. He knew he hadn't given it to a bad home, at least not for trees. Still, the *shakkan* soothed him. It reminded him that the trees were not simple creatures, but as complex in their ways as the humans who shaped them. He wasn't their creator, only their caretaker, one who was expected to pass them on in time.

He was sweeping dirt and trimmed branches from the table when Evvy emerged from her room, yawning. Under one arm she still carried her stone alphabet. Briar shook his head when he saw it. "Are you going to bathe with that?" he wanted to know, pointing at the roll of cloth.

Evvy smiled. "Probably. Look." She got the slate and chalk and carefully wrote out each letter they had studied, both in capital and small form without mistakes. Watching her, Briar felt something warm and funny in his chest, something that made him want to clap her on the back and take her out for an expensive breakfast.

He was proud of her.

"Pretty good," he said, not wanting to get all emotional. "Can you match them to the stones?"

Evvy undid the ties and rolled her cloth out flat. Starting with the top, left-hand pocket, she drew out the proper stone for each letter and recited its name. She even listed its uses, with only one or two small errors.

Briar corrected them, then ordered her to wash her face and hands and clean her teeth. She's smart, he thought as he spooned porridge into bowls. Where would she be right now if someone had started her learning things years ago?

He didn't know, but he would make up for that lost time. He could read ahead in the stone books at night to help her learn. It was worth an hour or two less of sleep, if he could teach her enough to keep that proud feeling inside. They'd show Jebilu what a fine student he'd missed.

They cleaned the dining room and kitchen together. "See, I think about my lessons when I do chores," he explained as they scoured pots. "Practice them in my head, see if I have any questions about things. Be sure and ask questions. Your teacher doesn't know if you're learning right unless you do ask."

Once her bed was made, Evvy went to the *souk* with a few coins for cat meat — some of the cats had already tried porridge, with mixed reactions. They went out to the rear yard as Briar fetched some traveling boxes from the storage shed. He would start packing in the workroom.

He walked into the barrier Rosethorn had laid on the room, forgetting she had put it there to keep Evvy out. It was one he could pass, once he remembered the right unlocking words. Rubbing his toes, he spoke them, and carried the boxes in.

On Evvy's return, Briar let her feed the cats, then took her up to the roof. There he enclosed them in a protective circle of his own. "Show me what you learned from meditating yesterday," he ordered.

With the same steady attention she brought to everything she wanted to learn, Evvy sat cross-legged and began the pattern of breathing. Immediately Briar could see the silvery glow that was her power, set loose from whatever bodily stronghold it was kept in. Today it stayed inside her skin, which impressed him. She learned so fast!

He talked her through drawing her power in, compressing it to make it stronger, then releasing it to fill her skin again. There were slips and escapes, but she seemed to understand better what he asked of her. At last Briar settled into his own meditation, coming out of it only when she stretched a cramped leg.

"More letters now," he said as they clattered downstairs, cats all around them. Since she'd moved in, he felt as if he took every step in this house as part of a river of fur. "At least a couple of stones before midday, and then maybe a break for a time. You're working harder than I did at my first lessons."

"But didn't you like it?" she asked, hugging the cloth roll to her chest. He'd made her leave it outside his protective circle when they'd meditated. The first thing she did when they got up was grab it, as if she'd thought it might run away. "Didn't you like learning the magic?"

"I wasn't sure why I was learning it, or what use all that sitting and thinking and breathing would be. And the first plant thing I did, the first thing I thought might be magic, was trim my *shakkan*. That hurt. It's hard to think magic is fun when clipping bits off a tree hurts." He smiled as they walked into the dining room. "But the gardening. I liked the gardening, even if it was mostly pulling weeds. Any garden that Rosethorn works in is happy. Well, except for the weeds. We try to make it quick for them." He pointed to the chair. Evvy sat, undoing the ties to the cloth roll with eager fingers. Briar got his sheet of notes and the book, pushing the slate and chalk over so Evvy could reach it. "Hematite," he read, and drew the large and small h on the slate. "Healing. It helps you concentrate on the real world," he began.

They had gone as far as lapis lazuli, and Briar was planning lunch, when a flurry of knocks sounded at their door. It was Ayasha, the dimpled girl who'd been a Camelgut. She was flushed, tousled, and gasping for air, clutching her chest as she tried to slow her breathing. Briar hesitated, not sure he wanted anything more to do with the city's gangs. She grabbed his arm, her brown eyes huge with fright. Her thick lashes fluttered like butterflies as she sagged against him. He could feel her trembling. Against his better judgment Briar let her into the dining room to sit, then fetched her a cup of water.

"We got caught by Gate Lords, Mai and me and some of the others," she told Briar when she could speak clearly. "The Lords beat Mai bad, worse than the boys with us, because of their *tesku* talking with her. The boys went to tell Ikrum, but I stuck with Mai. She's really hurt, and she doesn't trust anyone but you now." Ayasha grabbed Briar's hand and kissed it. "Neither do I," she whispered, looking at him with pleading in her face.

Briar ran upstairs to fetch his mage kit. "There's meat and bread and cheese in the pantry," he told Evvy when he returned. "I'll put a warding on the windows and door so nobody comes in. That means stay put, understand?" He was fairly sure Lady Zenadia and the Vipers had given up on chasing Evvy, but there was no harm in taking precautions. Quickly he drew a protective line around the doors and windows. When he returned to the dining room he told Evvy, "Have the cats do their business in the back hall — they can't go out. We'll scrub it before Rosethorn comes home."

Evvy nodded, eyes wide.

Briar tugged her nose gently. "Stay out of trouble," he ordered. To Ayasha he said, "Let's go." Walking out with her, he stopped to put a final ward on the front door.

Ayasha took Briar's hand and led him through the streets and up along roofs, into the middle- and lower-class neighborhoods south of the Street of Hares and east of the Hajra Gate. Briar was well and truly lost after the first three or four turnings. "No wonder you were breathless," he told Ayasha as they climbed down to the street once again.

She glanced at him. "I needed to put her someplace safe," she explained. "I know the lads had to tell Ikrum, so they could get back at the Gate Lords, but I wish they'd stayed until I fetched you. I couldn't manage her alone. Here." She walked through a narrow passageway that pierced yet another blank stucco wall. It led into a dead end courtyard between five houses. There a rickety wooden lean-to stood against the wall on one side of the entrance. Ayasha struggled with the door, finally getting it open.

"In here," she whispered. Mai lay in the dark inside, on a pile of sacking.

When he got a clear look at Mai, for a moment Briar was speechless with rage. She'd been beaten hard, her nose broken, her arms and legs dappled with bruises.

He knelt beside her and gently felt her arms and legs. Her left leg was broken near the foot. Next he checked her ribs and collarbone. "You need a healer," he told Mai softly. She shook her head, grunting. Did they break her jaw? He felt it, and the rest of her skull. As far as he could tell, they were whole. "Did you lose teeth?" he asked, gently prying her swollen lips open. Her teeth were coated with blood —

he saw cuts in the flesh of her lips — but they didn't seem broken. "Mai, why can't you talk?" he asked, tugging on her lower jaw. "Lemme see your tongue."

When she opened her teeth, he smelled cloves and lavender. That scent — he should *know* that scent. Her tongue was undamaged. He felt her voice box, but it too was normal. He extracted medicines from his kit to ease the pain of her broken nose and broken leg, and to reduce her lumpiest bruises. While he tended those, memory told him the source of that odd smell. He sat back on his heels.

"*Numbtongue?*" he whispered, baffled. Numbtongue was only barely legal: a substance that could stop people with broken jaws and teeth from talking could also keep people from shouting for help. "Why in Lakik Trickster's name —?" He looked around for Ayasha.

She was gone.

Briar smelled something far worse than numbtongue — a trick. He looked at Mai for a moment, wiping his hand over his dry lips. She wrapped her hands around one of his wrists. Her eyes begged him for something; what, he didn't know.

"Only one way *to* know," he muttered grimly.

The back of his mage's kit seemed to be of a piece with the front. Only someone familiar with it, or someone with sharp eyes, would guess that the apparent back on the inner compartments was secured by tiny buttons. Briar undid them and opened out the secret compartment, revealing a row of small vials, each carefully sealed and labeled. Everything here was hazardous; possession of these substances was limited to recognized mages and healers. With his mage's credential he was allowed to carry these things, but he hid them from thieves.

He cracked the vial of Loosetongue syrup, and dabbed it on Mai's tongue. It was good for several uses, including interrogations. Few people remained silent with Loosetongue in their mouths. It was also the antidote to Numbtongue.

Mai swallowed, once, twice, her eyes watering. She gasped and said, "The Vipers did this — not Gate Lords. It was to bring you. They went to take your Evvy!"

Briar straightened with a curse, and bumped his head on the shed's low roof. He cursed again and lunged for the door. Mai's yelp as she fought to sit up halted him.

He couldn't leave her in this place with a broken leg. The Vipers might beat her again, to punish her for telling. If not, there were plenty of people who took advantage of girls who could not run.

But Evvy! his mind shouted. She'll be scared! She'll — wait. The cooler Briar took over, the one in control of his thinking, most days. I put wards on the doors and the windows. They won't be able to get past those.

He'd splinted Mai's leg with boards from the lean-to and was wrapping a length of bandage around the splits when he saw he'd forgotten something. It was stupid, in this city, and if anything proved he was truly an *eknub* it was this: he hadn't warded the roof. Hadn't even thought of it, not when he was at the house, not even as Ayasha led him across roofs to this place.

"I've got to get you to a healer," he told Mai, helping her to stand on her good leg. "And then I've got to get home. Are there healers nearby?"

Mai shook her head. "I only know the ones around home, our old territory," she said. "Besides, I haven't any coin. Look, *Pahan* Briar, you've done enough. I don't want you losing her because they used me. Go find her."

Briar smiled crookedly. "If you knew what my teachers would do to me, if any of them heard I left you with no healer, you wouldn't even suggest such a thing. I can find Evvy if need be. Let's go."

In the house on the Street of Hares, Evvy found plenty to do with Briar away. She practiced her letters until she got bored, then leafed through the book of stones they were using, gazing in wonder at the colored illustrations. She couldn't wait to read what stone each beautiful picture represented, and tried to guess their names by using the letters she'd learned so far. When that grew tiresome, she tried to interest her cat Ball in playing with a round of hematite from her stone alphabet.

Was that a noise on the roof? She listened sharply, but heard nothing. Suddenly wary, she put the hematite piece back into its pocket, rolled up the stone alphabet, and took it into the pantry. Once it was hidden, she emerged from the pantry, walking straight into a hand covered with smelly cloth. It covered her face. She clawed at whoever held it, but the fumes burned through her nose into her head, pulling darkness into her.

It was a long, hard trip to the Water temple, with plenty of stops to rest. At last Briar was able to turn Mai over to the Water temple healers. They assured him they'd give her the best of care, and assured Mai that there was no charge. After she gave him directions to the Viper lair, Briar said his goodbyes to Mai. He was about to go when something made him ask, "What will you do after this? Go back to the Vipers?"

Mai, pale-faced and sweating, shook her head. "That's a joke. I'm out of gangs, any gangs. Nobody knows how to act any more. My sister's been after me to work in her cook-shop. I'll try that instead."

"If you don't mind?" snapped the healer appointed to care for Mai. "The sooner I treat her, the better she'll feel. You can talk later."

Briar wasn't sure they'd have a later to talk in. From the look on her face, Mai felt the same way. "Walk carefully with the Vipers," she told him. "Keep an eye out for the lady's mute and the swordsman. Especially the mute. He's noiseless when he walks, and he likes to get behind people."

Briar saluted her and strode out of the infirmary, his mage kit over his shoulder. Once outside, he sorted through his magical ties. Here were Tris, Daja, and Sandry, his connections to them stretched over so much distance that they were as fine as hairs to his magical vision. Here were his bonds to Rosethorn and to Dedicate Crane back at Winding Circle. Crane's, too, was thinned by distance. And here was Evvy's, strong and steady. Right now she was closer physically than even Rosethorn — but she was not in the north and east, where the house was. Her tie led south of his present position, in the direction of the Vipers' den. The tie was also warm with Evvy's rage. She wasn't frightened or in pain, but she was definitely angry.

That makes two of us, Briar thought grimly as he set off down the Street of Wells.

Evvy woke, gasping for air, and panicked. Everything was black around her, black and lightless. Had she been caught in a cave-in? But she always knew when stone was about to give way . . .

She tried to feel in front of her with her hands, to find they were tied together behind her back. Her feet were tied as well. Vipers, she thought, panicky and livid at the same time. The pus-filled, leeching, dung-faced Vipers had caught her at last.

"She's awake," a female voice called. "I saw her thrash."

"Good," drawled another voice, male. "The little crawler needs her exercise."

"Lemme give her water," a second female said. "You know sleepy juice dries your mouth."

"Females — so tender-hearted. Leave the blindfold on," the male voice ordered. "Don't let her see anything to work magic with."

Hands helped Evvy to sit up. She felt a cup at her lips. Ignoring the pain in her hands and arms, which were trapped under her, Evvy gratefully slurped water until her belly was full. When she finished, hands lay her down on her side again.

They had come over the roofs, she realized. *Pahan* Briar had forgotten to magic the rooftop door, not remembering how much Chammurans used the upper roads. I'll give him a hard time about it when I see him again, she promised herself. She refused to believe she might never see him again. He would get her out of this — if he could.

Is that what I've learned in four years? she wondered, gnawing her lower lip. Somebody else will come and help? Nobody helps me.

Except *Pahan* Briar. She had never known anyone like him, had never heard of anyone like him. He talked like a sensible person, for one thing, not like the *pahans* of the *souks* and stories. He knew what it was like to be poor and afraid. She could see it in his eyes.

Am I a lily-footed princess of the imperial court, unable to walk on my own? she thought, remembering the noblest ladies in Yanjing. She had always felt sorry for them because they couldn't run from trouble. Well, now *she* couldn't run away, either, but she hated to think that *Pahan* Briar would learn she hadn't done something to fight the Vipers.

Master High-and-Mighty Viper was wrong about her magic. If she felt it working, like the *pahan* said she could, she might be able to do something. Anything.

She was on bare, pounded earth. No help there. The nearest stone was in the wall, two feet behind her. It was old stone. It had been here for a very long time after it was cut from its bed. It had lasted for three houses built on its foundation, each new building setting it more firmly in its ways. Getting that stone to move, hundreds of years after it had been cut and placed here, would take work, hard work.

It was fizzy, her magic. She'd felt it that morning, during meditation. It fizzed inside her brain, and kept on fizzing when she reached for something, as if it were an arm that had gone to sleep. Evvy sent a stream of magic down into her hands, straining it through her spread fingers. Now she had six cords of her power. She thrust them at the wall, twining each one around a stone. She hoped she didn't pull the house down on herself, but she had to do something, and this was all she had to work with.

Taking a breath, gripping her power, Evvy *pulled* on her stones. Within moments she was soaked with sweat, though she hardly noticed it. She pulled again, and again, dragging on her power while the stones in the wall grumbled and groaned. The habit of long years was hard to break. She felt as if she tried to walk down Triumph Road dragging this house and its old, mulish foundation.

"Yoru, look at her." It was the female's voice, the girl who had brought water to Evvy. "I think the sleep-stuff made her sick."

"Fussing over the *thukdak* again?" The male voice drew closer. Evvy felt air move, and a hand touched her face. "Sweating. What's the matter, princess, scared?"

Evvy went cold with fury; her grip on her magic slackened. Please, she thought to the stones, believing she had failed. Pretty please? she thought, hating that bit of childish silliness.

In the stone she felt an answer that seemed uncomfortably like, You could have just *asked*.

Rock grated; Evvy smelled dust. People yelled. A handful of stones exploded from the wall, just over Evvy's body. One struck the boy in front of her; he grunted and hit the ground with a thump. Evvy drew up her legs and kicked out, shoving him away from her.

Someone was babbling a prayer to Mohun for quiet and peace. A boy cried, "Get me a rag; Yoru's bleeding."

"Ikrum?" someone further away cried. "Ikrum, you'd best come!"

"What happened?" The young man's voice came from outside the room. When he spoke again, Evvy could tell he wasn't far from her. "Shaihun eat it, what did she do?"

A babble of voices answered him. Evvy heard the boy near her moan. Not dead, she thought savagely. Too bad.

"We thought she couldn't do magic if she was blind-folded!" cried the girl who'd given her water. "She'll pull the house down if we keep her here!"

"Yoru?" The young man's voice sounded now close to Evvy, as if he crouched about three feet away.

"Brained me," said the cruel boy's voice, slurred and filled with pain. "Li'l *belbun* threw stone at . . . me."

"Well, your skull's in one piece." There was no sympathy in the crisp voice.

Please? Evvy asked the rocks in the wall near those she'd pulled out. Please help?

They thought about it.

Hard fingers grabbed her ear and twisted. She lost her hold on the magic between her and the rocks in a wash of pain. "I think we'd better take you to the lady, Yoru's *belbun*," the crisp voice said. "She'll know what to do with you, or her mage will. And if I were you," he added in a whisper, "I'd think of ways to keep the lady happy. If you don't, you'll never see daylight again." To someone else he called, "Gimme the sleepy juice."

Evvy fought to concentrate on the stones, tried to grip

14

By taking Mai to the Water temple, Briar had dealt himself a bit of luck. The street on which the Vipers laired was close to the temple. Better still, the turning onto the Vipers' street, Oleander Way, was clearly marked. He had not gone far down that twisted road when he saw that other visitors had come to call. Ten Gate Lords clustered around a blank doorway over which a snake was painted. The gang members were armed with clubs and daggers.

Briar looked at the Gate Lords coldly. If they attacked the den, Evvy might get hurt. That was unacceptable. He had to deal with the Gate Lords first.

As soon as he had made the seed balls he and Rosethorn used for protection on the road, Briar had stowed his share in his mage kit. Reaching into an outer pocket, he slid out two wrapped in yellow cloth. He sprinkled them with a few drops from the kit's water bottle.

A Gate Lord looking around noticed he was there. He

pointed a club a Briar. "Stop gawping and take off, if you know what's good for you!"

Briar glanced at the club: it sprouted leafy twigs and sent roots searching for the ground. As the Gate Lord yelped and dropped it, Briar hurled a ball into the midst of the gang. It opened when it hit, scattering seeds. Briar followed it with a surge of power. The seeds he had so carefully prepared exploded in frantic growth.

Vines shot from the ground in all directions, as if they meant to do twenty years' worth of growing in an afternoon. They were a mixture of grape and five-finger plants, tough, flexible and strong, spelled to twine rope-like around the target Briar chose. He directed them to the Gate Lords. The vines obeyed, whipping around gang members, trapping arms, legs, and weapons. Three went sprawling, to be bound where they lay. The remaining seven were dragged back by their green captors, away from the Vipers' door. Some vines shot across the street. They wrapped long stems around door handles and window gratings, tying four Gate Lords to it. Some plants reached out to one another, yanking the remaining three captives into one green bundle.

Once the Gate Lords were secure and yelling curses in voices that shook with terror, Briar plucked weapons from helpless fingers, placing them in a heap out of harm's way. "Be good, children," he told his captives. "I won't be but a minute."

He rested his palms on the wooden door to the Vipers' den and called to a memory deep inside it, one of growth and strength, not dead endurance. It wrenched itself off its hinges, falling to one side as it groaned, creaked, protested, and sank new roots deep in the ground. Branches forced their way out of planed boards. The Vipers might find another den one day, but it would not be this one, not when Briar was finished.

Just before he passed through the open frame, he threw his second damp packet into the room beyond. With it he sent another surge of magic.

Vipers charged as he walked out of the bright street and into the lamplit shadows of the den. They'd been preparing for the Gate Lords' attack. They had their own weapons in hand, including lead-weighted blackjacks. The contents of Briar's seed packet dug into the bare dirt floor unnoticed as the Vipers closed on him.

Mind the lamps, he ordered silently as his seeds began to grow. They burn.

Vines wriggled around and past the lamps like green snakes, reaching with eager tendrils to snare human beings. Briar ducked a swinging punch from the nearest Viper and called three vines to trap the youth's arms: it wasn't that he couldn't or didn't want to punch back, but that Evvy came first. The smoky, garbage-scented air of the cellar changed as more vines sprouted and threw out leaves. Briar took a deep breath of cleaner air and faced the boy who had tried to punch him. It was Yoru, the short black Viper. He was now bound in a web of green ropes, gasping for breath. A bloodstained rag was wrapped around his forehead.

Briar pulled away the stem that clutched Yoru's throat, letting him breathe. "Sorry to interrupt that war you started with the Gate Lords," he said with false good manners. "Tell me where Evvy is and I'll let you get back to it."

The other boy spat in his face. Briar grimaced, wiped the spittle on his sleeve, and ordered the vines to hang the Viper upside down. They grew, anchoring themselves on the posts that supported the building above, taking Yoru with them. Briar went to the next Viper, and the next. Those who didn't spit on him cursed him. By the time he'd reached the far door, the vines had borne fruit: a crop of dangling, trapped Vipers.

Briar stepped across the doorsill into the next cellar. It looked to be the room where they slept: mattresses and sacking beds lay on the floor. The front room vines were already here, snaring the feet of any Vipers present. Briar, tired of being polite, took a crimson packet out, wet it, and tossed it onto the floor. Thin, whippy vines punctuated with hooked thorns jumped from the seeds as they sank roots in the dirt floor.

A Viper rushed Briar from the side. Briar dropped to his knees and grabbed the gang youth's arm, using his leverage to toss his foe into the wall. The Viper hit with a grunt, the wind knocked out of him. Before he could sit up, Briar was on his chest. His knees dug into the fallen youth's ribcage as he held a knife to his throat.

"You people took Evvy. I want her back," Briar told the youth softly. He sent a command to the nearest rose. A thorny vine lashed out to furl itself around one of the Viper's hands, forcing him to drop the knife he'd meant to stick into Briar's ribs. "You didn't answer," Briar chided. "Stabbing isn't an answer." The youth looked at the room beyond them, his eyes wide at the sight of his friends battling with vines and roses. Briar gripped his chin and forced his captive to look at him. "Now harken to me. She's ten, skinny, has Yanjing blood in her, and she's my *student*. Where is she?"

"Threaten all you like," the youth retorted breathlessly. "Torture us, kill us —"

"Why would I do any such thing?" Briar inquired. "What I *will* do is leave you Vipers wrapped up tight. That way you just stay here until the locals come to laugh at you. If laughing's what they feel like. They might just want to get back at you for every bruise, broken jar, and free meal you took from them."

The youth glared at him and clamped his lips shut.

With a sigh Briar left him for the roses and walked into the third room of the den, which filled the cellars of several houses. Its cook-fires were already hemmed by tall green weeds that had felt his magic and sprouted from the dirt floor. The room was empty of Vipers. He saw a pot of boiling water, overturned teacups and bowls, and oddly enough, a tumble of stones that appeared to have exploded from the wall. He smiled grimly at the stones: it had to be Evvy's work. She was a fighter. She wouldn't let these idiots treat her like a helpless kitten.

This was the final room in the hideout. The only other door in here opened to the world outside. Briar frowned and groped for his connection to Evvy. It led through the door and — southeast? Southeast. Toward Justice Rock or Fortress Rock.

Or toward Lady Zenadia.

Sheer spite made him waken the back door, helping the dead oak to return to life. By the time its growth slowed to normal, both it and the front door tree would be large enough to bar the entrances permanently. As long as the vines planted here could get runners into the sun, the den would be filled with a thorny tangle of greenery that would not take kindly to any attempt to clear it out. He and Rosethorn had thought that was fair, when they crafted plants that would be in danger of hurt from the moment they put out runners. They had given them a strong hold on life, to thank their creations for defending them first.

He left the Vipers and Gate Lords as they were, trapped by his plants. If they were not cut loose first, the plants would free them at dawn. Then the new growth would search underground until it found yards, courtyards, and other open spaces to grow.

Briar followed his connection to Evvy into the afternoon light and up onto a roof. Keeping to the upper road, he began to trot, laying his plans as he followed her captors.

Only once did he change course, when he spotted a team of Watchmen in the street below. He climbed halfway down a ladder to the street and waved to get their attention. "I have a message for your *mutabir*," he called when they looked up. "Tell him *Pahan* Briar Moss says if he still wants a look inside the house of Lady Zenadia doa Attaneh, he'll be able to see anything he wants in a couple of hours. Tell him she's kidnapped my student, and say I asked, '*Now* will you act?'"

"Mind your manners!" banked a Watchman.

"We're supposed to believe you're a *pahan*?" asked one of them, a woman in the short, sheer, yellow face-veil worn by some nomad tribes to the south.

Briar was done with manners and patience — look where they had gotten him! A seed that had escaped his packets clung damply to his hand. He flicked it out, feeling — rather than seeing — it drop onto the street before the squad. "Believe what you like," he said. Two cobbles went flying in advance of a stout, woody-trunked grapevine that leaped from the ground.

Briar climbed back up to the rooftop road, too angry to care if they were so vexed that they tried to shoot him full of arrows. They didn't. He looked down from the roof. Most of the squad had gathered around the vine, caressing its trunk in wonder and awe. Two others raced up the street toward Justice Rock.

Before he moved on, Briar strengthened the vine he'd just planted, stopping its absurd growth in time for it to fit in with the cycle of winter rains to come. If the city didn't cut it down, it would remind people he'd been there.

The trip to the Jeweled Crescent and Attaneh Road took a long two hours afoot. As he made his way through the city, the sun dropped lower in the west, casting long shadows along the roofs. It was autumn; the days were shorter. Luckily for him, the seeds of his arsenal didn't require sunlight to do what he asked of them.

His connection to Evvy stretched, then firmed: she had settled. He still felt only anger in the bond, which reassured him. She didn't seem hurt or frightened. Did she know he was on her trail? He hoped she did.

Finally he reached Crescent Rim, the broad street that was the inner edge of the Jeweled Crescent. Beyond this point there were no rooftop roads. The houses of the Crescent lay smugly behind ten-foot-tall stone walls and guardian spells, protected from the likes of common folk.

Even the Crescent Rim shops were proof that things changed here. They offered custom-made jewelry, delicate porcelains, and fragile cloth the rival of anything sold in the Grand Bazaar. Dropping into the street, Briar noted discreet signs that advertised mages and upper servants for hire, pawnbrokers, shoemakers, and healers. He felt watched, but no one tried to stop him.

It was a long trudge to find Attaneh Road, since he hadn't gone there from this part of Chammur. His tie to Evvy was of little help — it simply passed through buildings he had to go around. At last he reached familiar surroundings, and made the turn into House Attaneh's personal street. The shadows were deepening, granting him cover as he followed the road's turns. At last he reached Lady Zenadia's home.

An alley circled the lady's house outside the ten-foot wall. Smiling grimly, Briar drew a thick gray packet from an external pocket in his kit. With the opened packet in one hand and his water bottle in the other, Briar walked the circuit of the wall, first laying a thin line of seeds at its base, then wetting them with a trickle of water. He left no breaks in his sowing, placing a steady line across the one-man gates used by the gardeners when they carried out trash, across the tradesman's gate he'd used on his last visit, and across the bay that ended in the wrought-iron main gate, until he reached his starting point. As the short autumn day began to end, he could see spells in the walls, from the dimmest hint of the oldest ones to the deep silver sheen of the newest. They looked beautiful as they shifted under the wall's creamy stucco, forming patterns and ripples of magic. Of course, they would be useless now. They kept away thieves and baffled spy or curse magic. Plants were real, common physical things. The magics in the wall were not made to treat plants or green magic as a threat.

This seed mixture was different from that used in the Vipers' lair. Its plants were those kinds of green life that grew into cracks in stone and looked for a place to cling. They were destructive if left to grow for too long, weakening walls and loosening mortar. Rosethorn and Briar just speeded — and strengthened — what they did naturally.

Briar rubbed his hands together and woke the seeds up. As vines popped out of the ground, he felt through his magic until he grasped a connection stronger than any of the others. It went straight to his *shakkan*, his storehouse of extra power. The tree was elated to be called on: it often complained that too much magic in its trunk, roots, branches, and needles was not comfortable. The best word to describe the tree when it had not been tapped for a while was "itchy."

"Let's scratch your itch," he said. He drew on that pent-up magic, hurling it into the trees, bushes, and grasses inside the wall. The sheer strength of his power, added to the inability of protective magics to recognize green magic as a threat, meant that the spells on the wall didn't slow him.

He found his larch and woke it to its full strength, feeling it crash out of its shallow dish. Its growing roots lanced through tiles, grasping at the earth beneath. On the far side of the house he felt vines rip the service gates from their hinges. In the kitchens dill seed, fennel, pepper, star anise, and cardamom forgot their dried existence as spices. They sprouted and groped with new roots for a bit of earth. Sensing it beneath the kitchen flagstones, fueled by Briar and his *shakkan*, their roots burrowed into cracks between the flags and shot into cool dirt. All around the walls his ivy climbed, webbing them in green, sending tendrils into each and every crack, anchoring itself firmly. As it grew, stucco began to flake from the walls in patches, baring pale orange stone and mortar. The ground quivered under Briar's feet. His plants were shaking things up.

"Hey, boy!" someone inside the main gate yelled. "Your sort doesn't loiter here! Move on your own, or we'll move you along!"

Briar ignored the guard and sat cross-legged before the gate as he continued to pour strength into all the green life within the walls. Nearby something cracked, and grated. He glanced toward the sound as a piece of the wall's upper rim dropped off. The vines swarmed through the gap it left, now attacking the wall from both sides.

He heard the rattle of keys and looked up. A guard was opening the main gate to come after him. Briar reached into his mage kit, found a rose-seed cluster, and tossed it at the guard as he approached. The cluster leaped into growth in midair, sinking roots as it twined around the man's legs. It gripped him, biting in with its thorns. The guard struggled and went deathly still as the plant wrapped his thighs and hips.

"Good decision," Briar told him softly. "I hate to think of all the tender places that thing will hook if you move."

The guard turned white and began to sweat. Briar stood and walked toward the open gate. As he went by, he patted the man on the shoulder. "Don't go away, now."

"You'll regret the day you were born," the guard snapped. He shouted, "Filyen, Osazi, alert! Get Ubayid!"

"Over a *boy*?" someone called. "You take care of it!"

Briar looked in the direction the voice had come from: a watchman's box just inside the gate on his left. A lamp shone through the lone window. The men inside couldn't see he had walked through the open gate.

The watchbox was made of wood. Briar started to let his magic go, then called it back. I'd best save this, he thought — waking dead wood used power he might need. Instead he called on the vines that had come over the wall and the jasmine that grew inside of it, both running riot under the magic he'd already put in. They twined into ropes, then reached out. Some grabbed the flat wooden roof of the watchbox, some went lower to grip two of the walls. At an unspoken command, the vines yanked hard. The walls flew out, the roof dropped. The men inside yelled. The lamp went out; when no flames came after, Briar drew a breath in relief.

The quickest way to Evvy was around the house, by his reckoning. If he went inside, there would be fewer big plants to help him, and more of the lady's men-at-arms. Already a fistful of them came running from the side nearest the tradesmen's entrance, buckling on swords, some with napkins tucked into their collars. Their attention was on the men yelling in the ruined watchbox and the man at the gate, not on the boy strolling to the left of the house. Noise had started to come from inside the main building as glass shattered and voices cried out.

Briar walked as if he had the right to be there, hands in his pockets, following the large garden around the house. Grasses sprouted in his wake, the burst of soaring green life rustling like the sweep of an imperial cloak. As he enjoyed the growing cool of the evening, Briar roused every plant and seed around him. People rarely crossed mages; it was his duty to remind the lady why tonight.

Evvy stirred, her head banging. She lay on some kind of mattress. When she sat up, she discovered that her hands and legs were free; the blindfold was gone. She was in a dark room, but the door had a panel in it that was carved. Flickering light shone in from outside.

She heard footsteps in the distance. ". . . don't know how much juice she's got." It was crisp-voice; Ikrum, the Vipers had called him. "She was shaking and all over sweat after she pulled those stones out of the wall."

"If she is strong, we must keep her drugged, until she sees reason. She will destroy no walls *here*."

Evvy would never mistake this lovely female voice. It was Lady Zenadia's, and she was not far from the door.

Life as a slave and a *thukdak* meant learning to think fast at bad moments. She wanted her power for later; she did not want to be drugged again. Evvy thrust her magic away, into the stone of the floor, the wall and the ceiling of her room, into stone walls above her room. She saw her power in her mind's eye, fizzing its way through marble and slate: it built a picture of the house above for her. She thrust and thrust at her magic, sending away as much as she could, leaving her body with just a trickle of it while voices murmured outside, and keys jingled, and the door swung open.

Evvy shaded her eyes against fresh lamplight. When she could see past the glare in her vision, she saw the lamps were carried by a tall, thin Viper and a servant woman who bore hers on a tray. They followed Lady Zenadia and a pale white woman whose clothes were styled like those worn by the *eknubs* west of Chammur.

Evvy moaned and collapsed onto her pallet again, keeping her eyes covered. "My lady, I'm sorry," she said in a tiny voice. "My head hurts."

A billow of some unusual scent washed over her; expensive silk rustled. Evvy uncovered her eyes. The lady sat on a low chair she had drawn up. She watched the girl over her veil with concerned eyes.

"Ikrum, you may have given too much potion the second time," the lady said, resting a cool hand on Evvy's cheek. "My dear child, welcome to my home."

She had seen people around the nobility often enough to know how to act like one. She grabbed the lady's hand and kissed it, struggling to sit up. "Thank you! I thought the Vipers would kill me, and *Pahan* Briar wouldn't let me come live with you! If I'd known they were bringing me to *you* I wouldn't have been so bad . . ." She kissed the lady's hand again, and promised she would scrub every part of her that touched the lady with strong soap when she was free.

The lady gave a small gasp of polite surprise. "Do you mean to say you *wished* to accept my offer?"

Evvy nodded briskly, then clutched her temples. That was no show for the lady: her head banged like a drum.

"Something for her headache, if you please?" The

warmth fled the lady's voice as she looked at the healer, a mistress giving an order to a servant. The healer took a cup from the tray held by the maid, looked at Evvy, then added something to it from a vial on the tray. She swirled the contents of the cup, then crouched beside Evvy.

"How strong is her power?" the lady asked the healer.

The healer shook her head. "I feel only a residue, mistress. There are medicines I must give her to offset the magical draining. Did that boy teach you nothing?" the healer asked Evvy. "Young mages must not overextend. The damage could be permanent."

"I thought they were going to hurt me," Evvy grumbled. There was no help for it; she would have to drink whatever was in that cup, or the lady would be suspicious. She prayed it wasn't a drug that would fuzz her mind again. "Is that for my head?"

The healer passed the cup to Evvy, who drank its contents with a prayer. The banging in her temples slowed; the headache eased.

"Would you like to stay?" the lady asked again. "I was told you were unwilling —"

"*Pahan* Briar and his teacher were mean to me," Evvy complained, keeping to her role of greedy *thukdak*. "They made me do servant work like cooking and cleaning. I want the things you offered, and to live in a nice house. They couldn't even teach me my own magic!" She thought of the look on her mother's face when she told the auctioneer to get as much as he could when he sold Evvy, and her eyes filled with tears. It was a trick that never failed. "I think they were going to sell me for a slave!"

"Well, you are safe here," the lady assured her, once more cupping her cheek with a cool, hennaed hand. "No one has the power to take you from me. Now. You must rest, and take the medicines the healer brings to you, and eat. You will stay here for the night, I think, and tomorrow you may choose your own room in the house."

Evvy yawned. "I'm tired," she admitted. "And awful hungry."

"Very hungry," the lady corrected her with a kind smile. "Only *thukdaks* say 'awful hungry,' and you are no longer a *thukdak*, my dear." She rose from her chair.

Evvy knew what she had to do, and she did it. Rolling from her pallet, she crouched before the lady and kissed her slippered foot. "Thank you, great lady! May Lailan of the Rivers and Rain bless you!"

The lady smiled. "Healer, see that she gets those medicines and food." She swept out of the room, Ikrum and the maid following her.

The healer remained, staring down at Evvy as the girl crawled back onto the pallet. "Soup, I suppose," she commented dryly, "and it will take some time to assemble the medicines to restore your strength. Use the chamber pot in the corner for your business — the lady doesn't like it when people just pee on the floors. You won't be allowed to leave this room tonight. It's magically shielded, in case the plant mage comes looking for you." She walked out. When she closed the door behind her, Evvy heard the jingle of keys, and the clack of a turning lock.

Evvy stood and spat on the floor to get the taste of the lady's shoe from her lips. A pitcher of water and a cup sat on a table: she drank straight from the pitcher, not caring if water spilled over her face and onto the floor. Then she sat cross-legged on the pallet, and began calling back the power she had hidden in the stone all around her.

This ought to be easy, she thought, smiling tightly. The stone around her was fairly new, not stubborn with ages of sitting in the same place. She would need much less effort to make it move.

As he walked down the side of the house, Briar caught the first ripples of unpleasant scent. Rotten meat, he judged after a sniff. Maybe they used fish as a fertilizer after all.

The walk between the outer wall and the long side of the house showed him the upper half of the wall was buried in green and going to pieces. Chunks of stone dropped off it on either side. In one spot, where a clump of deodar pines stood, the wall was shifting as the pines expanded outward. Briar went over to pat them and tell them they had done well. If the trees had been young girls they would have blushed at his praise; they quivered instead, and continued to grow. A large section of wall beside them collapsed into the alley beyond.

Briar halted: there was a glint of light beside the deodars' roots. Their earth turned and tumbled with the trees' swift growth, casting something out. Briar picked up the pale thing that had drawn his eye, and hurriedly dropped it.

It was a skull — a very small skull. A very small, *human* skull. In his years at Winding Circle, Briar had studied anatomy, animal and human, as backup for his lessons in healing. He knew a human skull, however small, from a monkey's.

One by one, he picked up other bones thrown to the surface by the deodars' surge. A thigh bone, an arm bone, ribs and back bones, all child-sized, old enough that no tissue remained to keep them attached to one anther. He also found a ball, and a silk scarf. Who had buried a child's remains under the deodars? How long had the child been dead? Was this one of the murders which the *mutabir* had mentioned, or something more ordinary? Cemeteries, particularly the small ones attached to most nobles' houses, were sometimes dug up for new buildings, the bones placed elsewhere. Or perhaps a servant's child had died. Briar knew that if he were dead he would rather be buried under trees than in Chammur's hard sun.

All the same, he didn't order the plants to cover the

bones, or the trees to open a hole so they could be tucked back into the earth. Some instinct made him place them a little way from the still-growing pines and draw a cypress oil protective circle around them. Only then did he wipe his fingers on his handkerchief and continue his walk.

15

The stench of rotting meat grew as Briar approached the back of the house. It was particularly strong in the corner where a stand of almond trees grew by the wall. The trees, like every other green thing on the grounds, were doing their best to outrace their proper growth, pitting slender trunks and roots against the wall. It was giving way, pushing into the lane behind the house. Inside the small grove, thrown from the ground by clamoring trees, was a bloated, reeking body. The clothes were blackened rags; a deep cut passed all the way around the neck, separating it into two parts. The swelling was so great that it was impossible even to guess the sex of the body. About a yard from it Briar saw another corpse, this one so far gone in decay that only scraps of skin clung to the bones. A knotted cord hung around the neck.

The stench of rotten flesh was so bad it made his stomach roll. While he hadn't been sure the child's bones were a sign of murder, it was harder to think of legal reasons why

273

these newer bodies would be here, among dainty almond trees, rather than in a proper burial yard. Most gardeners didn't like the thought of walking on the dead when they did their work.

Briar retreated from the six-tree grove. He turned straight into another pocket of stench, wafted into his nostrils by the mild breeze from the east. There were more dead to be found in this largest of Lady Zenadia's gardens, he realized. He wiped his sweaty forehead on his sleeve.

Suddenly he froze. His connection to Evvy pulsed: she was angry, furious. A surge of magic rolled through their bond, leaving Briar without breath in his lungs. He sent his power back, as if she were one of his foster-sisters, but it was no good. She couldn't even feel it, let alone use it. Her magic was too different and not mixed with his. Briar had the feeling that it was only because he had a little earth and metal magic in him that he could sense anything more than where she was.

From inside the house he heard the thunder of falling stone. It went on for a breath, then stopped. A puff of dust rose in the air over the roof like smoke. Briar forced a query to Evvy through their bond. What he got back was savage satisfaction and a calming of her rage. Whatever had taken place, she was pleased.

A fresh series of rumbles began in the house as green voices called a warning to Briar. The lady's mute certainly was silent in his movements, but the grasses on which he walked were not. The mute had come around the house to take Briar from behind. Using his right hand the boy slid a cloth bundle out of his kit, a special mix he had worked on for a long time. In his left he already grasped a wrist knife.

The bowstring settled around his neck, then wrenched cruelly tight, cutting off Briar's air. He tossed his small bundle behind him, where he guessed the mute's feet to be, and slid his knife under the strangler's cord. The knife bit into his neck as it cut the bowstring — Briar didn't mind a little blood if it meant he could breathe again.

He smashed a booted heel into the mute's bare foot, hearing bone crunch, then lunged away. Turning to face his attacker, Briar coughed, his throat aching from the pressure of the cord. Now he gripped knives in both hands.

"How many of 'em did you do that to?" he snarled when he could speak again. "Did you *like* it? Did you have fun choking them and burying them as fertilizer?"

The mute bent over, trying to massage his foot. He didn't even look at Briar.

The second assailant didn't try to be quiet. Behind him Briar heard the hiss of a drawn sword. With his power he tapped the bundle he'd left between the mute's feet, and faced the swordsman. The man leveled his weapon. Sharp metal gleamed in the scant light cast out here by indoor lamps. Another sullen rumble came from inside the house, drawing closer to them. Neither the man nor Briar risked a look to see what caused it.

Instead the swordsman laughed when he saw Briar's knives. "I have the advantage of you, boy," he told Briar smoothly. "I have reach and expertise."

The mute shrieked, his tongueless mouth freeing a sound more animal than human. He screamed a second time; the third cry broke off in the middle. After that the only sounds were the rattle of branches growing rapidly, tearing flesh, and a slow, wet drip. The swordsman could see it over Briar's shoulder. His eyes widened in horror.

Briar didn't turn. He and Rosethorn had once defended Winding Circle from pirates, using mixed seeds of thorny plants; the girls had given him use of their magic to make the plants extra lethal. A similar mix of seeds had been in the packet he'd tossed at the mute. Now Briar told the swordsman in a chatty tone, "Four years ago it took me and my three friends to work this bit." He had to raise his voice to be heard over the crunch of falling stone in the house. "The trick is to make this stuff grow so fast it just goes clean through anybody on top of it." He grinned, showing teeth. "I've learned a lot since then. I can do it by myself."

The copper tang of fresh blood drifted on the desert wind. The swordsman stood motionless, eyes bulging at the nightmare behind Briar. The boy sheathed one of his knives. His foe didn't look as if he wanted to attack anymore.

"I can do it to you," Briar said quietly. "In fact, maybe I should." He reached into his kit. The swordsman fled, stumbling and thrashing his way through the rioting garden plants. He ran not for the house, but for a gap the vines had torn in the back wall.

Now Briar made himself look at the mute. He had killed the man, after all; he owed it to him to face his work. There was little of the mute to see. The thorns and vines had covered him completely, gouging him in a thousand places and sprouting through his flesh, holding him in a massive, woody, bloodstained sheath. Briar nodded to his creation, his mouth trembling.

It was him or me, he thought, turning away. I knew he could kill, and he was going for me.

Evvy, he told himself. She's all that matters.

Now he spared a look for the side of the house closest to him. The wall trembled. There seemed to be holes in the roof. Grit rose above them in clouds, given a sulphur-yellow glow by lamps casting light through the gaps.

The wall closest to Briar blew outward, spraying stone fragments in the hip-high grass. A small, dark figure appeared in the opening left by the collapse, petting the stone on either side of the gap like one would pat a trusty dog.

"Evvy?" Briar called softly.

The figure froze, peering at him. Briar stepped into the light that streamed through the hole in the house.

"*Pahan* Briar!" Evvy croaked. She threw herself across the ground between them and hugged Briar tight, burying her face against his chest. He hugged her back, feeling her thin shoulders quiver under his hands. Wetness that he was fairly sure wasn't sweat dampened his shirt under her face.

"I guess you've learned a way to feel your magic," he said after a few moments.

Evvy nodded against his chest and let go, stepping back. She rubbed eyes that ran with tears. "I'm not crying," she said defensively. "I'm washing out the dust. I don't think I can do any more with stones. I feel all — empty."

"That's all right," he reassured her. "You've done plenty of damage already. And don't rub your eyes — that just grinds dirt in. Let the tears wash it out." He offered her his water bottle. Evvy drank half of the contents and poured the rest over her head.

Briar wiped grit and wet mud from her face with his handkerchief. "Better? We've a bit more to do, here."

Evvy nodded. "I know. I just wish I could help."

Briar grinned. "I think you've done plenty already," he said, tossing a packet of rose seeds at the gap she'd made in the house. They scrambled to life, weaving their stems as they grew to bar the opening. No one would escape that way.

When he looked at her again, she was staring at the

huge-thorned tree that had cut its way through the mute. She turned huge eyes to him. "*Pahan* Briar," she breathed in awe. "What you *did*."

"It doesn't make up for all the folk he killed for her, but it's a taste," he said grimly.

Evvy nodded. "I can't do anything like that. I wish I could," she said, approval in her voice and eyes.

"That's my girl," he said, giving her a one-armed hug around her shoulders. "Now, let's finish up."

Working through the date palms, aloes, junipers, tamarinds, and fruit trees at the rear of the house, they found eight more dead, all but one fairly recent, all with a bowstring knotted around their necks. Briar was sure that the *mutabir's* four missing spies were among the bodies he'd found. One dead girl wore the Viper nose ring and garnet; one looked like the boy who had followed Briar from Golden House. A third, the freshest, still wore the black and white of the Gate Lords: their missing *tesku*. The wind shifted twice as they walked, sending a cloud of dead gases into their faces. Twice they had to stop for Evvy to vomit; when she finished, she walked on with Briar, her face set in hard, angry lines.

The crack of stone nearby made Briar look up. The outer wall was coming to pieces along its length, assaulted by vines outside and trees within. Earth shifted and writhed as the plants surged, bringing down the last of the stone structure that had hemmed them in. There were torches outside. In the distance someone shouted, "Halt for the Watch! In the *amir*'s name, halt!"

Another voice cried, "We're slaves! We didn't know!"

"Halt for the Watch!" the first voice ordered again. "Or we will shoot you where you stand! Hands in the air!"

"Should we go?" Evvy inquired, worried. "I don't want to tangle with the Watch."

"Don't fret," Briar assured her. "They're on our side, mostly."

They came to the rear of the house. The courtyard gardens had rebelled, tearing chunks from the walls that separated them from the living quarters. Vines and shrubs had combined to block every window and door on this side of the building: the slaves had to be escaping from the front of the house.

"Stop that man!" someone behind Briar and Evvy cried. "Stop him!"

Briar rubbed his mouth with his thumb, thinking. There was no way out through the rear of the house: his plants had blocked those exits. The front windows and doors were easier to escape from — few large or tough plants had been planted on that side of the house. If he knew anything about Lady Zenadia, though, she would not run with the slaves, and she could not escape out the back without some hidden tunnel he didn't know about. Reaching with his power, he made a request of the trees. They thrust their roots as widely and as deeply as they could, sifting through the ground. There were no tunnels.

She would be inside, then.

They walked forward. Plants moved aside to admit them to a passageway. Once they went by the plants drew together to create a living wall.

He led Evvy down a stone gallery now soft with grasses, moss, and flowers that grew from seeds blown into cracks and corners. It led to an inner garden that had become an impassable thicket of shrubs and short trees. Even the tiles that paved the ground had vanished, thrust aside by rioting plants. When he saw the larch on the other side, Briar realized that he'd talked with the lady and Jebilu here. The larch, freed at his bidding to become its normal-sized self, blocked the door into the main house.

Creaking anxiously — it knew it wasn't supposed to be this big — the larch moved just enough to let Briar and Evvy pass. He stopped for a moment to pet it, to assure it he still loved it, even if it had lost its *bunjingi* form and gotten huge. He gave it his blessing, then walked on.

The house was no longer cool and elegant. There was greenery everywhere; he frankly thought it was an improvement. Tiles, flagstones, and walls had been knocked out of place, chipped, even cracked by an explosion of growth.

"Do you know where she is?" Evvy inquired, worry on her dust and tear-streaked face. "She won't get away?"

"She won't." Briar reached throughout the house, asking its plants where he might find Lady Zenadia.

The lady was to his right, they reported. He and Evvy followed their directions, walking toward a door painted with the image of a burning lamp.

Halfway down they crossed an intersection with another hall. The Viper *tesku* Ikrum leaped from its shadows, daggers in both hands.

Briar ducked and rammed sideways, catching the older boy in the gut. He thrust up with his back and shoulder, tossing Ikrum into the air. The older youth landed with a thud and lurched to his feet. Like him, Briar wobbled, trying to get his balance as the hall floor rippled. Ikrum staggered and went down on one knee.

Briar realized what was happening and darted toward Evvy, getting onto solid ground. With a grating rumble the floor under Ikrum collapsed, dropping the Viper into the cellar below. He screamed curses up at them for only a short moment. Then the ceiling above the hole in the floor collapsed. Stone and wood rained into the cellar, knocking Ikrum down, then burying him, until there was no trace of him to be seen.

When Briar looked at Evvy, she shrugged. "I guess I had a bit left after all," she told him. She walked to the hole in the floor to spit on Ikrum's wood-and-stone tomb. "And *that's* for kidnapping me," she snapped.

Briar put an arm around her bony shoulders. "You do good work," he said with approval. "Come on, now. We have one more thing to settle."

They sidled around the hole in what was left of the floor, and continued on to the door with the painting of the lamp. Briar opened it. Inside was a sitting room, part of what Briar guessed was the lady's personal chambers. Ornately carved sandalwood screens perfumed the air. Carved ebony screens covered two small windows. Sprigs of greenery poked through as the plants outside looked for a way in. They clamored their welcome to Briar.

The lady did not. She sat on a backless chair, as regal as a queen in red-and-bronze silks. She gleamed with gold jewelry: ankle cuffs hung with bells, armlets and bracelets, heavy earrings studded with rubies, a nose ring and a jeweled chain to connect it to her earring under her semi-sheer veil. Lamps had been lit and placed around the room as if she were prepared for a night spent reading at home. There was a pitcher beside her, and a cup. To all appearances she could have been welcoming guests. Briar saw past that, to the blank rage in her eyes, the trembling hands posed gracefully in her lap, and the brittle way she held her head.

"You disappoint me, *Pahan* Briar," she said, her lovely voice tight. "You have played the destructive child here. What did you hope to accomplish beyond the ruin of my house? Will you dare to harm me? My family will avenge all that you have done. You should never have set yourself up to oppose me."

Briar shook his head, amazed. To Evvy he said, "You wouldn't think she did anything worse than borrow my student without permission." Evvy nodded.

"I don't think you understand," Briar told Lady Zenadia slowly. He knew an explanation was probably a waste of time, but he had to try. "Your family won't protect you, not after they see your garden."

Her smile was tiny, but a smile all the same. "Do you think they will care about dead *thukdaks*? The children of the streets are without value to anyone."

Evvy growled. Briar stilled her with a hand on her shoulder. "The *mutabir* will care about his dead spies. We had a nice talk about that yesterday, him and his *pahan* and me. Ask him yourself — he's outside with the Watch. And I bet some of those other bodies aren't as unimportant to him as they were to you."

Lady Zenadia blinked. "He would not dare," she whispered, but the tremor in her hands got worse.

"Your mute's dead." Briar inspected a scratch on his hand. "So's Ikrum. I don't know about your swordsman. I think maybe the *mutabir*'s people picked him up when he made a run for it."

This time the lady swallowed hard. In someone less refined, it would have been a gulp. "Ubayid would never betray me."

"How's it betrayal if you can't be touched?" Briar asked pleasantly. "If you can't be harmed, then it isn't betrayal, just — gossip."

She flinched.

Briar continued, merciless. If he couldn't make her sorry for the ruin she had caused, he wanted to make her deeply sorry to be caught. "If I were your family, I'd think you've gone too far. If I were the *amir*, or the *mutabir*, I'd think the common people will be angry when they find out nobody cared how many poor folk and slaves you murdered. Lots of the *mutabir*'s Watchfolk come from poor districts, I bet. He can order them to shut up about what they see here, but how many will do it? How long before riots start? How long before your family thinks maybe it's time to wash their hands of you?"

"You'll be the first relative of the *amir* to see the top of Justice Rock," Evvy put it. The top was where executions were done in Chammur.

"Or maybe they'll just hand you to commoners," Briar remarked. Sound reached his ears: people were shouting inside the house. "That sounds like the Watch." He held Lady Zenadia's eyes with his, showing her no warmth or mercy. She hadn't shown either to anyone — none to those pitiful bodies, shoveled without ceremony into dirt to serve as fertilizer. Normally he approved of fertilizer, but not, it seemed, when it came to human beings. Even the poorest had a right to be mourned by someone.

"Excuse me for a moment," she said, getting to her feet. "Inform the *mutabir* I will be with him directly." She walked into an inner room.

"*Pahan* . . ." Evvy whispered, tugging on his sleeve. "She'll get away!"

"She can't go anywhere," Briar replied softly. "The house is shoulder-deep in plants and the Watch." He knew what he had thought he'd seen in the woman's eyes. If he was right, it would save a great deal of awkwardness. As he waited, as the sound of searchers came nearer in the house, he tinkered with the ebony and sandalwood screens in the room, guiding them to set down roots through the marble floor and sprout. Finally, when he heard approaching feet just outside, he walked into the lady's bedroom.

She lay on an opulent bed that was draped in silks and heaped with damask-covered cushions. Her eyes were closed, her clothes neatly arrayed, as if she had gone to sleep. Briar lifted the simple pottery cup on her bedside table, to sniff its contents. It held the quickest-acting poison money could buy.

Despite Lady Zenadia's attempt to look as if she'd felt no pain, there was a trace of foam at the corner of her mouth. He rested his fingers against her throat. There was no pulse.

He thought for a moment. Then he spat on her, and walked away.

Three days later, the plants around the Karang Gate told Rosethorn where Briar and Evvy could be found: the huge caravansary by the Aliput Gate, outside the city's southern walls. Concerned and confused, she went there rather than home, arriving exhausted, disheveled, and covered with road grime.

Briar sensed her approach but said nothing to Evvy. Asa was giving birth to kittens under the girl's watchful eye. Even the door slamming open couldn't distract the girl. She shushed the world impatiently without looking around, intent on the latest arrival.

Rosethorn glared at her, then at Briar. "Why in the name of the Green Man and scrub pines are you here?" she demanded. "We aren't leaving for three days. While you're gone the house is probably being looted. . . ."

"No, because it's all here," Briar said calmly. He patted cushions next to him and poured out a cup of the tea he'd set to brewing the minute he'd felt her ride through the Aliput Gate.

Rosethorn sat in a puff of dust and accepted the cup. "Everything?" she demanded, suspicious.

"Everything," he replied, voice and eyes firm.

"But rent for this place costs a fortune. We're already paid at the Street of Hares until the full moon." She sipped the tea and, despite her wrath, sighed gratefully. It was her own blend, a morning pick-me-up tea that could help the dead to cast off weariness.

"Actually, the *amir*'s paying the bill," Briar said. "The least he could do, since they kicked us out of town."

Rosethorn sipped her tea and fixed her eyes on him. "Tell me," she ordered.

He did, keeping it brief. She had a second cup of tea while she listened. When he finished, Rosethorn put down her cup and lurched to her feet. "This I have to see," she remarked, and walked out.

It was dark when she returned. At some point she had visited a *hammam*, bathed, and dressed in a clean habit from her saddlebags. From the way she settled on the cushions, Briar knew she must have eaten as well. He still had pomegranate juice, bread, olive oil in which herbs and garlic had been steeped, and cheese set out for her. Rosethorn tore a piece off the bread and dipped it in the oil, then put it in her mouth and chewed thoughtfully, her eyes on Evvy. Asa had finished producing four kittens, a first litter. She and her newcomers were asleep in the basket bed Evvy had made for them, while Evvy herself curled up beside it, as soundly asleep as they.

"Well," Rosethorn said quietly, after swallowing and drinking some juice, "*I'm* impressed. They'll never clear the grounds, you realize. You put too much of your power into it. The Watch *pahan* says for every bramble they cut, four more sprout. They fight the people who try to cut them back. It looks like the Watch actually tried to burn it all, but the plants won't catch fire."

"Maybe next time they'll think of that, when they ignore a murderess." Briar knew he sounded cold. He felt cold when it came to Lady Zenadia. "The rich folk here sure don't care about what's right. Just like Jooba-hooba saying how far away Lightsbridge and Winding Circle are. They think they're in the middle of nowhere, so they can do things civilized folk can't. Now they know different."

Rosethorn smiled thinly. "I forgot to tell you, I wrote to Lightsbridge and Winding Circle. They'll be sending harrier mages to Chammur, to explain to Master Stoneslicer why he can't chase other mages out of town. To remind him of the vows he took in exchange for their learning."

"Good," Briar said. "Let them sweat him a while." He fiddled with a piece of flatbread.

A cool hand cupped his cheek, lifting his head so he met her level brown eyes. "What is it, Briar?" she asked in their native Imperial, her voice kind. She stroked the skin under one of his eyes with a thumb. "You haven't been sleeping. I can see it. Tell me what's wrong, and we'll weed it out." She drew her hand away.

He swallowed hard. Picking up his cup of juice, he turned it in his hands while he thought. She ate a bit, and lay flat on the floor, propping her head on a cushion. He knew better than to think she had forgotten her question. She was simply waiting for him to grow into the answer.

Finally he had it. "I thought Tris was a baby, waking up with nightmares all the time, squalling about those drowned slaves," he said haltingly in Imperial. "I couldn't see why she fussed so. They would have died in a normal battle anyway. I mean, I hugged her, but I thought she was just carrying on."

"But she's not like that," Rosethorn commented softly.

"No. I know she isn't." He put down the cup without drinking from it. "I've been dreaming. I'm back in the garden again, only this time it's day. All those dead people are out in the sun, just rotting. I keep trying to bury them, so they can be decently under ground, but I can't empty a big enough hole. And whenever I turn, they're staring at me. I didn't even *kill* them. I never dream about the mute, and he's the one I did for." He swallowed hard, rubbing his eyes to stop their burning. "They were the saddest thing I ever saw in my whole life."

She reached over and gripped his arm firmly. "No," she told him gently. "The saddest thing would have been if you and Evvy had joined them."

"I know that," Briar admitted. "I do. But I keep waking from the dreams. I want to scream, but I don't." He put his free hand over the one that held his arm, golden brown hand over ivory wrist. "Will I dream about them forever?" he asked, his voice cracking.

"I don't know," she replied. "I have such dreams of my own."

He let her go finally. She sat up, twisting her head from side to side with a crackle of neck bones.

"They never tell you some things," Briar said bitterly. "They tell you mages have wonderful power and they learn all kinds of secrets. Nobody ever mentions that some secrets you don't ever want to learn."

"All you can do is learn good to balance the bad," Rosethorn told him. "Learn and do all the good within your reach. Then, if you wake in a sweat, you have something to set against the dream."

Two days later the caravan to Laenpa rolled out of sight of the flame-colored cliffs of Chammur. They had entered a mountain pass where the stone colors were tan and gray, without so much as a hint of orange. When he realized he'd seen the last of the ancient city, Briar felt as if a weight had fallen from his shoulders.

"Let's take another route home," he called to Rosethorn as she rode ahead. "South or north, I don't care."

She nodded without looking back. Her attention was on the tumble of dirt and gravel to her right. She was seeking plants she might not know.

Briar's own search for new growth in ground frequently scoured by floods and avalanches was interrupted by Evvy's giggle of delight. He dropped back to where she rode, a scruffy student queen on camelback. She reigned from the top of her beast's hump, Asa and the kittens in an open basket on her right, where she could keep an eye on them, and a traveling desk on her lap. Her stone alphabet was open on it. She showed the slate to Briar. On it she had written the large and small Q shakily.

"Q is for quartz!" she cried gleefully as her camel gave her a reproachful glare. In her other hand she held the surprise Briar had left her for when she got that far: not a single stone but a cloth strip to which six small quartz stones were fixed. "Crystal, blue, rose, green, smoky, and roo-rootle — rutilated!"

Briar grinned up at her. It was fun to make her happy. "You are easily amused," he informed his student.

"I'm learning to read," she replied gleefully, fingering her quartzes. "And I'm going to be a *pahan* of stones. Who wouldn't be amused?"

"Your camel, for one, if you keep bouncing," Briar reminded her. "Do you know what things you can do with quartz, young *pahan*?"

"Nahim Zineer told me some. You can see, you can have peace, it can help for love spells . . ." She continued to recite. Briar listened contentedly. Listening to his student, he felt as if life were an adventure for the first time since he'd left Chammur. The only drawback was that with Evvy, there was no way of telling what the adventure would be —

but that wasn't such a bad thing. It would put some interest into those long hours on the road east.

He couldn't wait to introduce her to his foster-sisters. He'd finally met another girl who was every bit as difficult as they were.

ACKNOWLEDGMENTS

I can't always do a set of acknowledgments for every book. The things that create ideas are sometimes so hidden in my past that I often don't remember where I started to think about them. This time I do have a concrete set of people and sources to thank.

First, my thanks to Kate Egan, Liz Szabla, and Jennifer Braunstein at Scholastic in the U.S., and to Kirsty Skidmore, Holly Skeet, and Ben Sharpe at Scholastic in the U.K., for encouragement, help, and ideas which profoundly shaped this book. Thanks also to my agent Craig Tenney, who made sure Evvy had a more active role in the finale than she did at first.

Thanks again to my sister Kimberly Pierce Bagby, paramedic and nurse, who advised me on head wounds. If there are any errors here, they are mine. My thanks, too, for the intellectual loan of a few cats; Ellen Harris and Jessica Scholes also supplied some, though they may not recognize them in their new incarnations.

Mapping an Arab-like city is tricky. My thanks first to Richard M. Robinson, who first explained that older Arabic cities don't follow Western grids. I also owe a debt to Knopf Guides and Cadogan, whose travel books for countries heavily influenced by Islam provided me with a rough idea of the layout of the older parts of many cities.

I owe debts to three men I can't thank in person: James Michener, whose mention of a city of rose-red stone in Jordan in THE ADVENTURERS set up echoes which still shake my imagination; T. E. Lawrence, who introduced me to Islamic culture, and Scott Cunningham, whose books on plant and stone magic have been invaluable sources for ideas.

I'm not sure if it's thanks I owe to the University of Pennsylvania School of Social Work and the Philadelphia Public Defender's Office of Social Services, Juvenile Court, for introducing me to gang culture and sociology. I found my work and education experiences to be, well, instructive.

ABOUT THE AUTHOR

TAMORA PIERCE is a full-time writer whose fantasy books include The Circle of Magic, The Song of the Lioness, *and* The Immortals *quartets as well as* Magic Steps *and* First Test, Page *and* Squire. *She says of her beginnings as an author that "after discovering fantasy and science fiction in the seventh grade, I was hooked on writing. I tried to write the same kind of stories I read, except with teenaged girl heroes — not too many of those around in the 1960s."*

In her Circle of Magic *quartet, Ms. Pierce introduced the four unforgettable mages-in-training who are now four years older in* The Circle Opens — *Sandry, Briar, Daja, and Tris. She began the new quartet at the urging of her many readers, who encouraged her through letters and e-mails to explore the mages' lives further. She chose their next turning point to be when they each acquire their first students in magecraft.*

Ms. Pierce lives in New York City with her husband,

their three cats (Scrap, Pee Wee, and Ferret), two parakeets (Zo-rak and the Junior Birdman), and a "floating population of res-cued wildlife." Her Web address is www.tamora-pierce.com.

GLOSSARY

amir — prince, ruler of Chammur

belbun — Chammuran term for four-legged rat

bindi — paint, metal, or jewel placed between the eye-brows

bunjingi — miniature tree form in which trunk is long, with a few branches balanced at the upper end

cham — large sum coin in Chammur; silver equals twenty copper *davs*; gold *cham* equals twenty silver *chams*

Chammur Newtown — section of the city built on the open ground between the heights and the Qarwan River, colonized first by the wealthy, then the middle class

Chammur Oldtown — most ancient part of the city, the apartments and buildings in and on the heights, slum dwellings now except for the *amir*'s palace and Fortress Rock

dav — copper is smallest coin in Chammur; silver *dav* equals three copper *davs*

THE CIRCLE OPENS

doa — daughter of (noble house only)

doen — son of (noble house only)

eknub — foreigner

hammam — bathhouse

hedax — rank similar to lieutenant

Lailan — Chammuran goddess of water, mercy, healing

Mohun — Chammuran god of silence, stone, dark and secret places

Mohunite — completely veiled follower of Mohun (both sexes)

mutabir — head of law enforcement and courts in Chammur

pahan — teacher, mage

Shaihun — Chammuran god of desert, winds, sandstorms, serious mischief and destruction

shakkan — miniature tree form like an elongated S pointing to right of viewer

souk — market

takamer (m), *takameri* (f) — rich person

tesku — leader of a street gang

thukdak — Chammuran slang for street rat

zernamus — parasite like a tick, one that survives by living off the rich

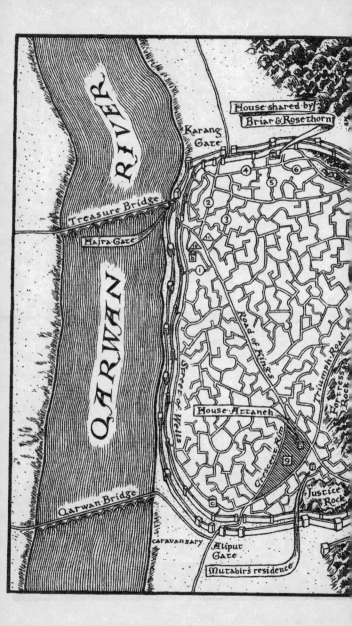

QARWAN RIVER

Karang Gate

House shared by Briar & Rosethorn

Treasure Bridge

Hajra Gate

Road of Kings

Street of Wells

House Attaneh

Triumph Road

Fortress Rock

Crescent Rim

Justice Rock

Qarwan Bridge

caravansary

Alipur Gate

Mutabir's residence

W · E
S

· · · KEY · · ·

1. Oleander·Way
2. Karang·Road
3. Street·of·Tent·Makers
4. Street·of·Hares
5. Cedar·Lane
6. Street·of·Wrens
7. Ibex·Walk
8. Palace·Road

9. Jeweled·Crescent

△ Golden·House
△ Grand·Bazaar
△ The·Market·of·the·Lost

🛆 Earth·Temple
🛆 Water·Temple
🛆 Fire·Temple
🛆 Air·Temple
🛆 Shaihun's·Temple
🛆 Mohun's·Temple

© MM·IAN·SCHOENHERR·MM ©

Princes·
Heights
Evvy's·
Squat
Street·of·Victories
Well·diggers·Island
Heartbeat·
Heights
Eagles·
Gate

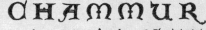

CHAMMUR
on·the·eastern·border·of·SOTAT

Start at the beginning,
and see how the magic unfolds...

The Circle Opens Quartet

Fresh New Look!

The Circle of Magic Quartet

Available wherever you buy books, or use this order form.

■ SCHOLASTIC